HUSBAND AND WIFE

K.L. SLATER

Published by Bookouture in 2023

An imprint of Storyfire Ltd.
Carmelite House
50 Victoria Embankment
London EC4Y 0DZ

www.bookouture.com

ISBN: 978-1-83790-782-3
eBook ISBN: 978-1-83790-781-6

HUSBAND AND WIFE

BOOKS BY K.L. SLATER

Safe With Me

Blink

Liar

The Mistake

The Visitor

The Secret

Closer

Finding Grace

The Silent Ones

Single

Little Whispers

The Girl She Wanted

The Marriage

The Evidence

The Widow

Missing

The Girlfriend

The Narrator

The Bedroom Window

PROLOGUE

SARAH

FIVE WEEKS EARLIER

It had been a strange night out, starting as an online date with a guy that had never turned up. Then, just as Sarah was about to cut her losses and leave, she'd bumped into someone she thought she'd never see again.

The bad blood she thought existed between them was nowhere in existence and they'd had a great night ironing out their differences in the late-night bar... with promises made which she intended to ensure he kept.

When they'd said their goodbyes, Sarah left the bar, staggering past security and out on to an empty street. She'd had far too much to drink and although she felt disappointed the night had come to an end, she knew it was just as well before she made a fool of herself by either falling over or throwing up in the middle of the dance floor.

She found herself now in a small enclave in the trendy Lace Market area of Nottingham. She looked around her, in awe at the tall, red-brick buildings with their Victorian Gothic facades. Tonight the buildings seemed dark and dangerous, bearing

ONE

NICOLA

NOW

At the window, I stand staring out into the near darkness. The weather has been awful today, even by November's bleak standards. We had torrential rain earlier, and now, a blanket of low, grey sky that feels increasingly oppressive.

My husband, Cal, frowns and peers over his newspaper. 'They said they wouldn't be here until four. You might as well sit down, love.'

'They might arrive early and I want to help them in with Barney's stuff.' I perk up as a car turns into our road, but it sails past and all falls quiet again. 'Parker said they won't have time to come in. They'll need to get off right away as the M1 going south is looking super busy.'

'A likely tale,' Cal mutters, rattling his broadsheet.

I twist round to look at him. 'What do you mean?'

He lowers his newspaper and looks at me. 'We both know the real reason they hardly ever come in, Nicola, and it's got nothing to do with the roads. Parker's sparing your feelings because Luna will have already told him she doesn't want to stay.'

I look away, out of the window again, and my worn, anxious face reflects back at me in the dark glass. How did we find ourselves in a situation where our only son, Parker, is a virtual stranger to us and hardly sets foot in the house he grew up in?

Somehow, the years have slipped by so quickly, and now our grandson, Barney, is the same age Parker was when Cal's great-aunt died and left him a good chunk of inheritance money. We didn't have to think twice. We used all the money, topped up with a modest mortgage, to escape our cramped flat with its tiny balcony, and we bought this house with its spacious rooms and large garden bordered by mature trees and flowering bushes. The first thing Cal did was to set up goalposts for Parker on the swathe of smooth, emerald lawn.

'What are you smiling about?' Cal chides me gently.

'Oh, just reminiscing about when we first moved in here; Parker's little face when he saw he had his own football pitch.'

That caring, clever boy is now a grown man, married with his own boy, and we don't see him enough.

Cal smiles affectionately. 'Must've seemed that way to him at seven years of age, having a great big garden to kick the ball around. And now we've got young Barney doing his football drills on there... when he comes, that is.'

Almost every Friday evening, our son and his family travel up to Yorkshire to spend the weekend with Luna's parents. Marie and Joe Barton-James live in a beautiful mansion set in two acres of manicured grounds on the outskirts of picturesque market town Helmsley. With Cal and me both still working during the week, that leaves us no time to see Barney at weekends.

But I feel shackled from speaking up at the perceived injustice, afraid to cause problems because that could well make things worse, not better. Instead, I live in hope things will get easier and we grasp any chance we get to spend precious time with our grandson. Like when Parker rang last week to ask if we could look after Barney overnight.

'I'm up for an award and the company's putting on a swish dinner-dance event at some plush hotel in Leicestershire,' he'd said. 'Be nice if we could go. Especially if I win!'

'Of course you must go,' I'd said, delighted. 'You must have known about it for weeks though, why have you left it until now?'

'We thought Luna's parents might still be jet-lagged from their long-haul flight from Barbados a couple of days ago, so we didn't want to ask them,' he'd said dismissively.

'We'd love to have him,' I'd said quickly.

'Maybe I should try talking to Parker again, man to man,' Cal says from his chair. 'Ask him how they can constantly find the time to visit Luna's parents but can never spare an hour to stop for a cup of tea here.'

'No, don't do that,' I say, turning back to the window. 'I think Luna will come round. She just needs time, needs to get to know us properly, and it's a well-known fact that boys naturally gravitate to their wives' families, particularly when the children are young.'

He puffs out air. 'How on earth is Luna going to get to know us when she hardly sets foot inside this house? They've been married nine years now and the times she's stopped by for a proper visit is barely into double figures. Even less occasions when we've been invited round to theirs.'

I wince as my fingernails dig into the soft pad of flesh below my thumb. 'Cal, don't. Please, not tonight. Don't spoil it.'

'I'm just trying to—'

'You're trying to stop me getting hurt, I know, but I'm fine.' I uncurl my hands and stretch out my fingers. 'I've been looking forward to tonight all week and—'

'Looks like they're here.' He points at the window and I

turn to see my son's sleek new black Mercedes stop outside the gates.

I rush to the front door and fling it open just as Parker gets out and raises his hand cheerily. The streetlight outside our gate lights up his handsome face and I get the full benefit of his genuine smile. 'Hi, Mum!'

'Hello, darling, so lovely to see you.' I stuff my feet into my gardening Crocs and shuffle down the short path to the road, arms folded against the cold as Parker opens the back door, pavement side. Barney springs out, a bundle of vibrant energy.

'Granny!' he calls, barrelling towards me with a foot-long plastic dinosaur tucked under his arm. I grab him in a bear hug and smother him in kisses.

'Here's our big boy!' I relish the weight and warmth of his body. He's getting so tall and sturdy, and I've missed him like crazy. The last time I saw him was a month ago. I picked him up from school and gave him tea when Luna got delayed filming a fashion video and Parker was working up in the North-East and couldn't get back in time.

The sage-green dinosaur appears in front of my face. 'See this, Granny? It changes into a truck in twenty-five moves,' Barney says solemnly.

'Goodness me! You'd better go in and show Gramps; he won't believe his eyes!'

Barney runs into the house at full pelt, and I turn back to the car where Parker is still pulling out bags of toys and clothes and, I presume, Barney's 'special' food. He pauses to give me a hug, folding me into his broad chest, squeezing me with those strong arms. My six-foot-one boy that I used to pick up and shower with kisses like I just did to Barney.

'Love you, son,' I whisper in his ear.

'Love you more, Mum,' he whispers back, before releasing me and going back to the car.

The passenger side door remains closed and I can't see

inside because of the tinted windows. I tap on the window, and slowly, it begins to whirr down.

'Hi, Luna, how are you?'

I peer into the dim interior and her beautiful, surly face appears. Sculpted features, high cheekbones. Her glossy black hair piled on top of her head in curls. And those incredible, amber-flecked eyes of hers that catch the light and seem to spark and shimmer. She smiles and her face transforms and yet I see dark shadows under her eyes and a veil of something that looks like anxiousness.

'Nicola, so nice to see you,' she purrs. 'I'm good, thanks. You?'

She places her hand on the bottom of the window and I lay my own over it and give a brief squeeze. It's then I get a whiff of what smells like alcohol.

'We're fine, thanks, love. Happy now we've got the little man back for a short time. How are your mum and dad keeping?'

'Oh, they're great thanks. They're back from Barbados, but they had a long flight delay so it's taking some getting over. I think Dad fancies buying a place out there, but they hardly get time to use the villa in Portugal because they're away so much!'

'It sounds wonderful and they deserve to treat themselves,' I say warmly. 'Have you got time for a quick cuppa? Be lovely to have a proper catch-up.'

'Sorry, Mum,' Parker calls out over the open boot. 'We've got to get straight off. I've heard there's been an accident on the M1, so...'

'Maybe next time, Nicola,' Luna says and I feel her breath on my face again. I think I can smell mouthwash, not alcohol. 'I'm so sorry, I feel like we're always rushing off.' To give her credit, she does look apologetic.

'Not at all,' I say. 'As long as you know you're always welcome here, that's the important thing. How's work going? I follow your Insta page now, so I can see all the exciting things you get up to.'

'Do you really? I didn't know that. It's so hard to keep track when you have upwards of fifty thousand followers, but next time I'm online, I'll try and remember to give you a follow back.'

'You're obviously doing very well with it all and you always seem to be uploading content. I don't know how you keep up with all the latest fashion trends!'

She gives me a tight smile. 'It's my job, Nicola, not just a matter of posting any old thing. People don't realise how many hours a successful influencer needs to put into their social media. Parker's the first to admit that I work far more hours than he does.'

'True!' Parker calls out and she shoots him a vicious look that takes me back for a moment.

'Well, you're doing a super job by the looks of things. I wish you the best with it all, Luna,' I say a moment later.

'That's sweet of you. Thank you.' She presses her full lips together. 'Now, I've written down Barney's new food triggers.' Her smile fades away and I watch as a raw anxiousness settles around her eyes. 'It's all there, in his food bag. We're trying him on a new vitamin mix that must be sprinkled on all his meals. He hates it, but it's vital you manage to get it down him.'

'Don't worry, I'll make sure he gets what he needs.' My heart sinks. Barney's prohibited food list is already longer than my arm and it never fails to infuriate Cal.

'The woman's bloody paranoid. She's giving him a complex,' he'd raged when, earlier in the year, Luna had sent word with Parker that we weren't to buy Barney an Easter egg on account of a newly discovered dairy intolerance. 'Those two. They always think they know better than everyone else.'

I glance at Parker, who's now loading himself up with bags to take inside.

'I'd better give him a hand,' I say to Luna. 'Have a

wonderful time at the dinner dance. Would you text me a picture of the two of you when you're all dressed up?'

She grins. 'I will. I've been gifted a Miu Miu two-piece to wear. It's sensational, embellished with rhinestones.'

'Sounds marvellous! I'll bring Barney to wave you off before you go.'

'See you soon.' She wiggles her fingers and the window starts to whirr back up.

TWO

.

I catch Parker up on the path and take a bag from him. Before we get to the front door, he turns to look at me. 'What kind of mood is Dad in?'

'He's fine!' I say, as upbeat as I can manage. 'He's a bit disappointed you can't stay for a cuppa, but it can't be helped.'

Parker rolls his eyes. 'He thinks everyone's like him, mending a few leaky taps and dodgy boilers each day and then collapsing down into his chair for the rest of the evening. He's got too much time on his hands, that's the problem.'

'Oh, that's not fair, Parker,' I say as we walk past Cal's work van on the driveway. This is his third van in eighteen years and he still insists on having each one sign-written with *Vance & Son Plumbing and Heating* in fancy black lettering on the side – even though Parker never had the slightest interest in joining his father's small company, even as a child. 'Your dad's well over sixty now and he still works really hard. He feels the workload more since the funding finished and he had to let his apprentice go.'

Over the years, Cal's work has been steady enough, but as Parker has so unkindly pointed out, it's always been fairly small-scale. Cal has never had the raging ambition to expand the business or take on permanent staff. Even so, we'd always managed fine with the business reliably ticking over and with my work as a part-time library assistant, up until my illness, that is. We've never been saddled with a mortgage we can't afford, thanks to sinking Cal's great-aunt's inheritance in this house by way of a larger-than-usual initial deposit. Equally, we've never had the kind of money sitting around to enable us to holiday in Barbados. Never mind buy a house out there.

Just before we step into the hallway, Parker lowers his voice. 'Mum, I need a chat with you.'

I look at him in surprise. We've not had one of our chats since I was ill. Eighteen months ago I got dressed in front of the full-length mirror in the bedroom and noticed some puckering of the skin on my left breast. There was no pain, no discomfort; it just looked odd and I was pretty sure it had appeared recently.

I visited my GP, who referred me to a consultant. The upshot was that the puckering signified a lump underneath. I had it removed and a course of chemotherapy and was given the all-clear. It all sounds very straightforward and clean, but it wasn't either of those things. It was terrifying and awful every step of the way. Not just for me, but for Cal and Parker, too.

I saw more of Parker over that period of time but it wasn't enough to bring him and his dad closer. If anything, there seemed to be more of a gulf than ever between them after my recovery.

'Mum, are you listening? I need to speak to you,' Parker says again, frowning at my vacant look.

'OK, love... go ahead. What do you want to talk about?'

'Not now, but it needs to be soon.' He glances down the drive. 'Thing is, it's a bit tricky as I need to speak to you alone. I don't want Dad or Luna to know anything.'

'Is everything alright, Parker?' A wash of panic reaches my

throat. What's so urgent and secretive that he doesn't want anyone else to know about it?

'Is Dad working in the morning?'

'Yes, he has a job in Linby he's finishing off first thing,' I say quietly. He knows Cal sometimes works on Saturdays, but it's not every week. 'He's leaving the house early so he can be back to watch the footie at lunchtime.'

'Perfect. We should be back no later than ten in the morning as Luna is hosting an online fashion event, so I'll drop her off at home and come straight here. Barney can watch TV or something while we talk in the kitchen.'

I consider his pinched features, his furrowed brow. Is he going to tell me he's having an affair? Or does he suspect *she's* having an affair and wants some advice on what to do? Could he have money problems? 'Can you just give me a clue what—'

He shakes his head. 'I need time to explain everything properly to you, Mum. From the beginning.' He looks down at all the bags he's carrying. 'What do you want me to do with these?'

'Just leave them here, I'll sort them out when you've gone.' He drops everything at the bottom of the stairs and before he can scoot out of the door again, I push him gently towards the living room where I can hear Cal and Barney chuckling together about how best to disassemble the dinosaur. 'Have a quick word with your dad before you get off.'

He opens his mouth and closes it again, then moves reluctantly to the doorway of the lounge.

'Alright, Dad?'

There's a pause before I hear Cal's voice. 'Hello, Parker. How's things?'

I watch from behind him as my son stands a little taller. 'Great... excellent, actually. I just got a promotion, so I'm Regional Sales Director now. Get a new executive motor thrown in, too. A Mercedes.'

Barney puts down his toy and looks at us both in turn. 'I like coming here. I want to see you and Gramps.'

'Of course you do!' I rush over to embrace him and glare at Cal. 'See what you've done? You've upset him. He shouldn't have to listen to this.'

Cal's voice softens. 'I just don't want you falling to earth with a big bump, Nicola. I wish you'd wake up and see that Parker's not the angel you make him out to be. One day, you're going to find yourself on the receiving end of that cold, hard side he tries to keep hidden.'

THREE

PARKER

As he drove off, Luna sullen and silent beside him, Parker's thoughts began to wander. It fascinated him how utterly naïve some people could be. How naïve *most* people could be, in fact.

Being a little deviant did not mean you were a bad person through and through. Take him: he was your regular nice guy. If your elderly great-aunt broke down on the side of the road, and a bunch of people were passing by and going about their business, Parker would be the one to stop. He'd check she was OK. Call the rescue services and even stay with her until the recovery vehicle arrived. He would not think twice.

Parker worked hard, he paid his taxes. He donated monthly to the RSPCA and Cancer Research. During lockdown he volunteered to transport groceries and prescription medication to vulnerable people living in the village.

Parker loved his wife and his son. He loved his mother and felt guilty he didn't see enough of her.

But like most people, Parker had a darker side, too... especially when he had a problem. And right now, he had a very big problem that was getting worse, that he'd been finding increasingly difficult to control. It was a problem he tried not to think about, but that was not going away.

And right now, he hadn't got a clue what to do about it.

From the instant he'd set eyes on Luna Barton-James all those years ago at a church fete, she'd been quiet and shy. Yet Parker had sensed something latent and blooming in her.

Luna had been born into privilege, hadn't wanted for a thing – materially speaking, at least. But that didn't mean she was happy. She'd been cossetted by her father and locked in a gilded cage by her mother. During their first chat at a scruffy little out-of-town pub, he'd felt the waves of discontent rolling off her. A desperation to unfurl her wings and fly before the years rolled by. He understood that sentiment.

If she regretted getting involved with him, if she now wished she hadn't chosen to marry him, then that was a shame. As he sometimes reminded her: Parker had broken her out of the veritable prison she'd been trapped in when he'd met her. He'd helped her to do that.

But now, married with a son they both adored, they were in a mess. A big mess. It would take all of Parker's imagination and determination to wriggle out of this one. But he'd manage it. He would.

He looked at his wife now, fast asleep, her face pressed against the passenger window. She hadn't slept properly for days. He'd heard her padding around the house in the middle of the night.

Parker knew he had let Luna down. He'd steered them both down a dangerously rocky path they'd now found they were unable to veer from. Parker's usually crystal-clear thought processes had turned cloudy. He simply could not decide what the best course of action was and he had no one to ask. No one who could help.

Their lives were in danger, their family unit in jeopardy.

And the only certainty – the one detail Parker could be certain of – was this: it was all his fault.

colleague was taking better care of himself although she wondered how long it would be until he tired of it.

'This area of the city is buzzing with people much of the time,' Brewster remarked as a group of students passed them, laughing and shouting to each other. 'I find it hard to believe nobody stumbled on her before now.'

'Apparently, the body had been concealed in a long alleyway behind some garbage bins,' Helena explained as they turned into Stoney Street. 'There are some building supplies stored there, waiting for a nearby flat renovation to start, and whoever murdered Sarah Grayson decided to take advantage of that.'

Brewster frowned. 'Still, the police search was supposed to be comprehensive. I'd hate to think some officers haven't been as thorough as they might have done.'

'I've already raised this but officers logged a request to contact the building company to move the supplies. That action led to Sarah's body being discovered, albeit far later than we'd have wanted.'

As they neared the police cordon, a growing group of members of the public were spilling off the pavement on to the road opposite the alleyway where officers stood. Men and women of all ages, and even, Helena noted distastefully, a couple of babes in arms.

She flashed her badge and the officer at the mouth of the alleyway moved aside. 'The pathologist is already back there, ma'am,' he said solemnly as she and Brewster moved smoothly past him.

Another officer at the entrance handed them shoe coverings. The detectives leaned against the wall and hooked the protective wear on awkwardly. Helena's nostrils were instantly assailed by the smell of mould and damp and something else highly unpleasant and familiar, as they entered the enclosed space.

'What a grim place for her to end up,' Brewster said quietly.

As they moved further inside, Helena could identify a sweet, cloying odour that caught in the back of her throat. The alleyway was narrow, flanked by very tall buildings that prevented any fresh air from permeating. It was dark and dank, exactly as she'd expected. Temporary lighting had been erected around the walls to enable the team to do their work efficiently.

'Ahh, Helena. Good to see you!' Rolly McAfee, the pathologist, straightened up to greet her, one hand supporting the bottom of his back. 'DS Brewster,' he said, a tad less enthusiastically.

He was a twitchy little man with a rodent-like quickness about him that Brewster had told her he found unnerving. That and the rumours circulating the station that he practised taxidermy in his spare time. 'Found anything interesting, Rolly?' Helena said.

'Tut tut, you detectives are all the same. Only interested in the hard evidence, never the pleasantries.'

McAfee stepped aside and the smirk instantly slid from Helena's face.

'Jeez,' Brewster murmured, holding up a handkerchief to his nose and mouth.

There was little evidence remaining of the young woman who used to be Sarah Grayson. Just a badly decomposed corpse, still fully dressed in the outfit her mother had described in detail to detectives: the short black dress, the silver high heels and a metallic, fashionably quilted handbag on the floor beside her. The powerful lights revealed a tangle of matted red hair that framed a once pretty face before the decay had taken hold. Helena noted the white powder smeared across her face, in her hair and on her clothing.

'Mortar mix from the building supplies,' she murmured to Brewster.

'The condition of the body is consistent with the time frame of the victim disappearing,' McAfee said. 'Fortunately, the cooler temperatures have slowed the rate of decomposition or we might have had even less to work with here.'

'Any idea of cause of death?' Brewster said, his words emerging low and muffled behind the hanky.

'My guess is that ultimately, she was strangled. That's consistent with the marks around her neck, but as you can see there are injuries to the head to consider, too.' McAfee pulled a regretful face. 'At this point I can't say for sure whether there was a sexual motive, but bearing in mind her clothing seems intact, if pressed, my initial reaction would be to doubt this.'

Helena nodded, squinting against rapid camera flashes as the forensic photographer snapped directly in front of her. 'For what it's worth, her appearance is exactly as described by her mother. Same clothes and accessories. She must have been pulled down the alleyway as she walked past.' She hesitated before saying cautiously, 'Any surprises so far, Rolly? Anything you've spotted that's of particular note?'

McAfee dipped his chin and gave her a look. 'Sadly, I can't conjure up information, no matter how hard you push, Helena. Even for you.' He looked over the victim. 'So far, there's nothing of note, but I can't do much here the way things stand with the condition of the body. We'll need to get her back to HQ pronto.'

Once clear of the alleyway, Brewster removed the handkerchief from his face and took in big gulps of frosty air.

'Uh-oh, looks like someone tipped off the local press,' Helena murmured. Two people, a man and a woman, raced by, one of them clutching a long-lens camera.

'Have you found Sarah Grayson?' the woman called out, holding up what looked like a voice recorder. 'Did you find a body?'

Helena looked away. They had a job to do, but often in the rush to beat rivals to available information, the lack of empathy of the press could be staggering. Less than ten miles from here was a four-year-old girl, Millie Grayson, whose mummy had failed to come home from a night out just over a week ago. They knew from Julie Grayson's statement that Sarah had kissed Millie goodbye, her hair curled and smelling fresh, promising her daughter a trip to the park her new bedroom overlooked the next morning. Sarah's widowed mother was in her late fifties and still working two part-time cleaning jobs. She would never get over the loss of her only daughter and would now be raising her grandaughter alone in spite of her devastating grief.

There was a terrible human cost to crime that, in Helena's experience, many journalists simply overlooked or chose not to recognise in favour of getting the juiciest story.

They walked up Stoney Street, the reporters falling back to document the scene, when Brewster suddenly stopped walking as if he'd frozen on the spot.

'Yes!' He gave a short punch with his fist. 'That's *it*. I knew there was something.'

'Something about what?'

'Sarah's appearance.' He turned to her. 'As you said, boss, her clothing and accessories were identical to the description her mother gave us.'

Helena waited. 'And?'

'Well, it was identical, all apart from one detail. The silk scarf.'

Helena's mouth dropped open. 'Oh my God, you're right, Brewster!'

The night she'd gone out, Sarah had worn a distinctive silk scarf her parents had bought as a gift for her birthday only a few weeks earlier. 'Course, I couldn't afford proper Versace, but the modern black and gold pattern was close enough to look like the real thing,' Mrs Grayson had told the detectives, her eyes shining with sadness. 'Sarah's always loved designer stuff and she wore it every chance she got.'

Helena turned on her heel and started walking back towards the baying crowd.

'We're going back?' Brewster caught up.

'We need to take a good look around the surrounding area for that scarf and check her handbag. If Rolly is right and she was strangled, we'll need the media's help in getting images of it out there again to the public and the search will change focus.'

FIVE

NICOLA

By some miracle, despite the cutting words and tension following Parker's exchange with Cal, the three of us eventually settle down.

'I'm hungry,' Barney announces fifteen minutes after his parents have left.

'That's good,' I say, 'because I've got a little surprise for you... we're having pizza for tea!'

He smiles with delight until his expression suddenly dulls. He picks up his cool bag and hands it to me glumly. 'Mum says I have to eat this lentil salad. Bleugh!'

I unzip the bag and open the square plastic container. To be fair, it looks quite nice. Green lentils, chopped up fresh veg and what looks like a homemade bread roll in clingfilm. Luna has also packed the cool bag with snacks for our movie: celery and carrot sticks, homemade hummus. It all looks very nutritious and healthy but it's not the sort of food that any seven-year-old I've ever met would get excited about.

I close the bag and smile at my grandson. 'Like I said, we're having pizza and it sticks to all your mum's dietary rules. And what's more, we're going to make it ourselves. Then if you like it, you can make it at home.'

'Cool... thanks, Granny!' His face lights up and we go into the kitchen where Cal is already surveying the ingredients I've laid out on the worktop. His eyes settle suspiciously on the packet of gluten-free flour and the myriad of colourful vegetables I've chosen for the topping.

'What's all this?' he asks, grimacing.

'We're making our very own gluten-free, vegan pizza for tea, Grandad,' Barney calls out while washing his hands.

'Don't worry, Cal, I've bought you a readymade pepperoni pizza,' I add, grinning at his alarmed expression. 'It's in the freezer.'

He smiles in relief. I'd hoped we might all enjoy the same meal to show support to Barney and his strict regime, but that's clearly a pipe dream on my part. God help Cal if he must eat something meat-free for once.

Barney is in his element, weighing out ingredients, pummelling and rolling the dough with gusto. We spread tomato puree on the cooked base, prepare and pile the vegetables on top and finally, with my help, Barney slides the circular baking tray carefully into the preheated oven.

When I've closed the oven door, he punches his arm in the air like Superman and yells: 'This is going to be the tastiest pizza in the univerrrse!'

The pizza is indeed a great success. I lightly sprinkle some of Barney's vitamin powder on his half as per Luna's instructions and I'm relieved when he doesn't make a fuss. The food is crisp, fresh and bursting with flavour. Barney and I sit on the sofa side by side with our food on trays, complimenting ourselves on our efforts while a quieter Cal sits in his armchair, stuffing his face with pepperoni.

I pour the two of us a couple of glasses of Malbec and mix

up Barney a glass of his spirulina. Once Cal has purchased and downloaded *Jurassic World Dominion*, we turn down the lights and start the movie.

As the room fills with ominous music and men on horseback chase a herd of dinosaurs across frozen wastelands, I turn to watch my grandson. He is completely rapt, absorbed in the action on screen. His eyes are wide, his mouth slightly open in anticipation. His profile looks identical to Parker's at the same age. Barney's hair is finer and a little lighter in colour, but his nose and perfect rose-bud lips are just like his daddy's. My heart swells with pride and love.

'See, Granny, humans and dinosaurs live together on earth now after the volcanic eruption,' he says without taking his eyes off the screen. 'The rangers are trying to round up the stray dinosaurs and take them somewhere safe.'

'Ahh, I see,' I murmur. Cal glances over and winks at me.

I feel so grateful we're in Barney's life, even if we don't see him as much as we'd like. There's a woman I used to work with – a colleague at the library – who's estranged from her own daughter and son-in-law after a family disagreement where things were said that apparently cannot be taken back. She has a four-year-old grandaughter she hasn't seen since her first birthday. I find that so very, very sad.

It's true Parker and Luna have different ideas to our own about how best to raise Barney, but one thing is certain: they both adore their son. Everything they do, I believe it's with the utter love and belief that it's what's best for him.

Hopefully, my chat with Parker tomorrow – whatever it might be about – will help us to feel a bit closer again. I'm surprised and honoured he trusts me above anyone to confide in.

I pick up my wine and take a sip, relishing the fruity hints of blackberry and plum. If I can get Parker more on side, the next step would be to work towards a better understanding of what makes Luna tick and to try to find some things we have in common.

I think tonight has been a real success and I'm hoping this one is the first of many Barney sleepovers to come.

My phone lights up and I see I have a text from Luna. I open it and gasp in admiration when a shot of the two of them loads, ready for the dinner dance. Parker looks so handsome in his tuxedo and bow tie, his crisp white dress shirt perfectly setting off his olive complexion, dark hair, and strong jawline. I'd noticed his hair needed a cut earlier and yet here it somehow looks immaculate. Luna looks nothing short of sensational in a shimmering ivory two-piece dress that shows an inch of perfectly toned midriff. In the car, her black curls had been casually piled up on top of her head but in the photograph, her shoulder-length hair is blow-dried smooth and shiny. Even Cal looks impressed when I show him and Barney.

After the film, Barney goes up to bed without any trouble. Cal reads him a couple of chapters from Jeff Kinney's *Diary of a Wimpy Kid* and when he comes back down, he pours himself another glass of wine and makes me a cup of tea. We sit in companionable silence, watching a nature programme.

'I'll leave the alarm off downstairs in case Barney comes down in the morning before we're awake,' Cal says when we go up to bed. I often nudge him in the night if he's snoring badly and he gets up without a word and slopes into the spare room. But we always start the night together.

He checks the doors are locked and I set the dishwasher going and rinse our wine glasses. Makes me smile how we fall back on our little routines without thinking. Perhaps it's a sign of getting older, but the organisation works and give us a certain satisfaction. We generally live a quiet, ordered life where everything gets done in a timely fashion and unpredictability is kept at bay.

At least that's the case until a few hours later when, just

before 2 a.m., Cal shakes me awake. My heart immediately starts racing when I see our bedroom is full of a flashing blue light.

'What is it?' I whisper, propping myself up on my elbows and squinting at the curtains. 'What's happening?'

Cal slips out of bed and moves quickly over to the window to peer out of the curtains. When he turns back to me, his face is pale and concerned.

'It's the police,' he says hoarsely.

SIX

'The police... at this time?' I croak, rubbing my eyes. 'They're not coming here, are they?'

I slip my legs out of bed and move next to him.

Outside, the silent blue light stops flashing at last and two police officers get out of the squad car. One talks briefly into a radio, and they stand on the pavement looking at our house and the one next door.

'Oh, hell,' Cal gasps as the officers start to move. 'They're coming to the gate.'

'What can they want?' I shiver and wrap my arms around myself. Standing there in my thin cotton nightie, I feel suddenly vulnerable. 'It can't be to do with Parker and Luna because they're staying overnight at the venue.'

'They're heading up the path,' Cal says urgently, grabbing his dressing gown off the chair. 'I'll go down. You stay up here in case Barney wakes up.'

He disappears out of the bedroom and I pull on my own dressing gown. I hear Cal's bare feet thudding softly downstairs and then the doorbell rings. Shrill and deafening in the silent house. Loud enough to wake the dead.

I pad across the landing as Cal opens the front door. I feel cool air channel upstairs, carrying with it the sound of muted, concerned voices. Panic stirs in the pit of my stomach. I peek through Barney's open bedroom door and see that, miraculously, he's still asleep despite the disturbance. I softly pull it shut before heading downstairs.

When I reach the bottom step, Cal has already closed the door and is ushering two uniformed police officers – a man, and a woman – into the lounge. He snaps on the light. 'Please, sit down,' he tells them and then sees me appear in the doorway. 'This is my wife, Nicola,' he says and both officers nod my way. I look at Cal, take in his grey complexion. 'They're saying there's been an accident, love.'

'Who? What's happened?' I hear myself say against the deafening thud of my own heartbeat. They look so young, these two officers. The woman must be in her late twenties, her colleague no more than early thirties. I wonder how long they've been in the job, whether they might be inexperienced and have perhaps made an error. They did seem unsure initially, like they might be heading to next door instead.

'There's been a serious road traffic accident on the A60 just after the Nottingham Knight Island,' the young woman says. 'I'm afraid your son, Parker Vance, and his wife, Luna Vance, were involved in this accident and both have suffered serious injuries as a result. They were—'

'That can't be right.' I interrupt, feeling a tidal wave of dread rearing up inside me. 'They weren't travelling home tonight. They had a room booked at a hotel in Leicestershire. There was a dinner dance...'

The male officer, short and stocky with a crewcut and piercing blue eyes, checks his notepad. 'Parker and Luna Vance, madam.' He looks back up. 'There has been a positive identification by officers at the scene. They were driving a black, C-Class Mercedes, registration ending PCV.'

Parker Callum Vance. The private numberplate on his shiny new black Mercedes. The beacon of success from his recent promotion.

The beautiful photograph Luna sent last night flashes into my mind and a small noise escapes my lips.

'Are they... they're alive?' Cal manages, his voice breaking.

'Yes, but both have suffered serious injuries, sir, and have been taken to the Queen's Medical Centre in Nottingham.'

'What do you mean by serious?' Cal says gravely. 'Are we talking life-threatening, or—'

'I'm sorry, that's all the detail I have right now. Paramedics attended the scene, so you can be sure your son and daughter-in-law received the best care prior to being taken to hospital.'

'We have our grandson here,' I whisper, staring at the female officer. 'Barney. He's upstairs. We were looking after him while they were out. Have Luna's parents been told?'

The young man glances at his notepad again. 'I believe that's in hand as we speak,' he says.

'So, what happened?' Cal says, sitting up straighter and addressing the male officer. 'Did someone hit them? A drunk driver?'

'Or perhaps someone driving under the influence of drugs?' I say faintly, recalling a news article about the growing number of cases I'd read only last week.

'I'm so sorry, sir, madam, we don't have many details at this stage. Our job tonight is to let you know so you are fully aware of the situation.'

'Rest assured Road Traffic Investigation officers are already at the scene and have begun a thorough investigation of exactly how the accident happened. As soon as further details become clear, you'll be the first to know.'

'I can't understand why they decided to come home after all.' I look at Cal, hopelessly. 'They were so looking forward to the evening and being able to have a drink and relax.'

'One of them might've been ill, Nicola. Who knows. We'll find out soon enough.' Cal looks back at the officers. 'Can we go to the hospital?'

The woman nods and they both stand up. 'Of course, although be aware you may not be able to see your relative, depending on their condition.'

'We must go there. It's the only way we're going to get more information,' I say, staring at the wall. The framed photograph on there of the three of us was taken at Parker's graduation at the University of Nottingham over ten years ago.

Cal is walking the officers to the door, seeing them out. I follow and stop dead in my tracks when a movement on the stairs catches my attention.

'Barney?' I whisper, moving to the bottom step. He looks so small and vulnerable standing there in his SpongeBob pyjamas and bare feet. His eyes are dark and wide, his pale face half-shielded by shadow. He could be Parker at the same age. He went through a stage of coming back downstairs for a glass of milk or a slice of toast... anything to delay going to bed. My hand drifts up to my throat. 'Come on, darling. Let's get you back into bed.'

Cal shuts the door and stands there, looking at the floor before turning around. His face looks grey and lined. 'Oh God,' he whispers. 'Do you think they're—'

I cough and he sees Barney on the stairs.

'Hello there, soldier. What're you doing up?'

'What's happened?' Barney descends another couple of steps. 'Why did the police come here?'

I look at Cal pointedly. 'They were... they had to ask us questions, sweetie. About something that's happened.'

'What's happened?'

I hold out my hand and he takes it, walking down the last few steps. 'There's been an accident and they wanted us to know.'

'Are my mum and dad OK?'

'Sure they are.' Cal crouches down in front of him and ruffles his hair. 'How about a glass of warm oat milk, eh? And, if you don't tell Granny, maybe a small biscuit?'

Barney grins and follows Cal into the lounge. I hear the television go on and then Cal comes back out, his expression grave. 'What are we going to do?'

'There's only one thing we can do. You stay here with Barney, and I'll get dressed and drive to the hospital,' I say, glancing at my watch. 'It's two-twenty now, I can be at the QMC in about thirty minutes, once I'm ready.'

'Are you sure?' Cal says, biting his lip. 'I hate the thought of you going there alone.' He's probably thinking about the many visits we made together when I was having treatment, but now's not the time to dwell on that.

'It's fine. Someone needs to look after Barney and I'm better to get to the bottom of what's happened.'

Cal doesn't argue because we both know he's a bit of an introvert. It makes sense I'm the one who must go because I've always done the 'communication' tasks in our lives. Ringing to get important information, calling to complain, making appointments, booking holidays. The list goes on. I know Cal will feel like a duck out of water having to liaise with nurses, doctors and possibly police officers. His strengths lie elsewhere.

Barney is staring trancelike at some impossibly bright and colourful cartoon Cal's put on for him. 'Be back soon,' I whisper and I kiss him on the top of his head, but he barely registers I'm there.

I run back upstairs and dress quickly in jeans, a T-shirt and a warm jacket. I pull on socks and flat ankle boots at the door. Cal comes back through with Barney's warm milk and makes a detour to kiss me on the cheek.

'Text or call me soon as you find out how they're both doing,' he says in a low voice. 'Let me know if there's anything I need to do. I can get Barney dressed and we can come to the hospital if—' I look at him quizzically and he adds, 'You know… if the worst happens. If it looks like—'

I look away from him and open the door. 'Everything's going to be fine, Cal,' I say stoically. 'I know it is.'

I head out to my small Fiat, parked on the road, and slide into the driving seat. I take a deep breath and squeeze my eyes closed for a few seconds. I wish I felt as confident as I'd just sounded. Soon, I'll find out the extent of Parker and Luna's injuries. Then I'll know whether everything is going to be fine.

Or whether – in a mere few hours – all our lives will change forever.

SEVEN

I programme my journey into Google Maps and connect it to the car's small dashboard screen, even though I know this route well enough to find my way blindfolded. The software informs me that traffic conditions are good and the journey will take thirty-two minutes.

Closing my eyes again, I take a few long breaths, in and out. It's going to be OK. I can do this. I desperately wish Cal could come with me, but regrettably, we don't have that choice. Looking after Barney is top of both our lists, and I shudder at the sort of conversations we might need to have when I think about what may lie ahead. The police officers said 'serious injuries' so I know it's going to be bad, but the question is, how bad? I can't get the words out of my mind, but at the same time, I know the only chance I have of trying to navigate a way through this nightmare is to stay focused and push all thoughts of worst-case scenarios from my mind.

The car is cold and unwelcoming. It's ten years old now and, like its owner, needs a bit more time to warm up and get going. I set off, glancing at the house as I leave. The glow of the lamp illuminates the front window and I picture my grandson sitting on the sofa, confused and half-asleep with his warm milk.

The streets are deserted, as I knew they would be. Still, it's a strange experience being out at two-thirty in the morning when the dread of what you might be heading for is pumping through your veins like poison. Streetlights illuminate the smooth black asphalt in front of me but even with the benefit of powerful headlights, the thick black night seems to engulf the car, suffocating any chink of hope.

I pass a row of shops that I often use during busy weekdays when I haven't the time to get into town or to the big supermarket in Daybrook. There's a grocer, a butcher and a small hairdressing salon I visit every month without fail for a trim and root colour. It's usually a bustling area where you'll struggle to find a parking space during peak times, but now the shops all have security shutters pulled down, and a single orange sodium streetlight at the edge of the pavement gives the place an eerie, unfriendly glow.

I drive blankly for a while before glancing at the screen: 6.2 miles. Nineteen minutes.

Cal drove me to this hospital three times a week for four weeks for a course of chemotherapy treatment. I didn't clock watch on our journeys back then. I'd just stare out of the window noticing things that usually passed me by during everyday life. Poppies sprouting in the hedgerows, a striking cloud formation or maybe the pattern of raindrops on the glass. Tiny miracles that made themselves known to me and helped me to get through.

I turn on the radio by force of habit and immediately switch it off again when the car fills with music. I crave silence so I can properly think everything through. I can't seem to stop my mind presenting the worst outcomes. I'm desperate for Parker and Luna to be OK – for their injuries to turn out to be minor after all and easily recovered from – but I know that's unlikely. One of them, Parker or Luna, will probably have come off worse than the other in the accident.

Parker would have almost definitely been driving. Luna has her own little sports car but, when they're out together, I've noticed Parker nearly always drives. He'd driven to our house to drop off Barney and he'd been driving when we waved them off to their exciting evening away. As a rule, do drivers come off the worst in car accidents? There's the benefit of the airbag but that would all depend on exactly what happened and whether other vehicles were involved. My heart drops another inch in my chest as I realise there's so much we don't know. So much that has yet to be confirmed.

I'm aware I'm going round in circles, but I can't control my runaway thoughts. Terrible thoughts I'm ashamed of. The silent praying that Parker's injuries are the less serious. Wicked scenarios presenting themselves complete with solutions: if Luna had an extended stay in the hospital, Cal and I would, of course, instantly step up to enfold Parker and Barney. We'd become a family again. I would be back to doing the school run like when Parker was young and Cal would take over Barney's football practice to enable Parker to focus on his career.

All this detail flashes in and out of my mind in a matter of seconds before I can dispel it. I must be an awful person to even conjure up such dreadful possibilities. I open the window an inch, allow the freezing cold air to blast the thoughts away.

Just 4.1 miles now and 10 minutes' journey time until I reach the hospital.

Luna is a hard person to get to know. From the first time Parker brought her back to the house to meet us – 'This girl I've been dating for a while and really like' – her otherness shone through like an intrusive beacon in our small, ordinary world.

I watched when her long lashes fluttered as her eyes took in our surroundings, how she wordlessly scanned and logged just how little we had. I knew then, before she even told us about her father's property empire, about their family home – a converted farmstead set in acres of land that also incorporated her mother's successful equestrian business – that the two of them had been raised in completely different worlds.

'Luna's parents are wealthy but she's not in the least bit impressed by money,' Parker had declared confidently before her visit. 'She doesn't judge a person on how well off they are.'

'I beg to differ,' I told Cal later when we sat on our own watching *Newsnight* with a glass of wine. 'It's easy to think money isn't important when it's always been there.'

Cal raised an eyebrow. 'And lots of it.'

Up ahead, the brightly lit campus of the main hospital building looms out of the darkness from the ring road. It looks other-worldly, like a vast space centre on a barren, dark landscape. I turn into the main entrance and follow signs on the circular road around the facility's perimeter to a large car park from where I head on foot to the main reception area, about a five-minute walk away.

I text Cal on the move.

Just got parked and heading to reception. Is Barney OK?

He responds immediately with a thumbs-up icon and a short reply.

Barney fine and sleeping again. Keep me in loop.

I breathe a sigh of relief. Our grandson is such a bright little button, I felt fearful he'd somehow guess the awfulness of what had happened. But he seems to have accepted our vague explanations of why the police had turned up in the middle of the night.

My boots scuff the pavement as I walk, my breath puffing and visible in front of my face. I pull the zip on my puffer jacket up as far as it will go and silently berate myself for not grabbing my scarf and gloves before I left home. As I get closer to the building, there are other people approaching and leaving. The odd car passes me, heading for the parking area, each driver staring ahead. I recognise myself in their hollowed-out faces and dark eyes. Unless you work here, there's never going to be a joyful reason in trying to find a parking space on a major hospital campus at three in the morning.

I walk into the main reception where the explosion of stark fluorescent lights and ringing telephones swallows me up in its chaos, instantly expelling the dark silence of the outside world. At the desk, I explain what's happened and give Parker's name and I'm given instructions to head for the major trauma wards, which have their own information desk.

I head for the lifts, passing a Costa Coffee outlet where we'd often grab a hot drink to get us through long hours of waiting and a small general store, both deserted and closed for business until 7 a.m. Once I move out of the main entrance area, the footfall is greatly reduced and, apart from passing the odd porter or medic in the seemingly endless corridors, I am completely alone.

My stomach is churning, and I feel so thirsty. I've seen the odd drinks machine, but I can't afford to delay by even a second or two. I must get up there as quickly as possible, locate my son first and find out exactly what's happened. Soon I will know the extent of his injuries, Luna's too, and that thought only serves to make me feel even worse.

Entering the major trauma unit feels like I'm passing through one portal into another dimension altogether. The pace is frantic here, all the staff engaged and busy. As far as I can see from my vantage point, there are no windows, and it would be difficult to judge whether it's morning or night if you were stuck in here for any length of time. There are quite a few visitors in the seating area, including weeping relatives. Some people are chatting in low, confidential voices while others sit alone and silent with thousand-yard stares.

At the reception desk, I wait behind a young couple and, when it's my turn, I identify myself and give Parker and Luna's details to the calm, efficient reception clerk.

'You're Parker Vance's mother?'

'Yes, and Luna Vance is my daughter-in-law.'

'OK, let's see.' She taps a keyboard and watches a monitor. 'Your son is currently here in our critical care unit receiving treatment.' My fingers flutter to my throat. 'You won't be able to see him at this time, but if you'd like to take a seat, I can get someone to come out and speak to you.'

'Is he... is he going to be OK?'

'I'm afraid we don't hold individual patient data here at the desk, Mrs Vance, but the doctor should be able to answer all your questions.'

'Thank you... and what about his wife, Luna? How's she doing?'

She hesitates as if she's not sure whether to tell me.

'It's just, we have their young son at home. Our grandson. We were babysitting when we got the news, so it's important I get an update for him on both his parents.'

'I understand,' she says sympathetically, tapping again at the keyboard. 'So Luna Vance is still under observation and she's also unable to take visitors at this time.'

'Is Luna in critical care, too?'

'No. She's in the acute assessment unit while her injuries are being evaluated.'

I thank her and sit down on one of the red, plastic seats as far away from anyone else as I can manage. I knew it. I just knew Parker's condition would be worse.

I take out my phone and send Cal a quick text.

'He's just waking up from surgery. He sustained serious internal injuries in the car accident and so we had to perform a procedure to stem severe gastrointestinal bleeding. That seems to have been a success, but there are other problems that we'll need to address without delay once he's recovered.'

'Oh, that's incredible. Thank you. Thank you so much.' The operation has been a success and I have to stop myself from hugging him. 'Can I... can I see him? Just for a few minutes?'

I anticipate having to plead harder, but the doctor smiles and nods. 'Only for a few minutes though. He's extremely tired and needs to rest before we start further tests and investigations. Wait here and I'll ask someone to take you through.'

He turns to leave just as a beeping sound starts. I call out. 'Dr Rehman, I still don't know exactly how the accident happened.'

'Sorry, you'll need to speak to the police to get that information.'

'What about Luna? Luna Vance, my daughter-in-law, is in the assessment unit. Is she—'

'Best to ask at the front desk. She'll have a different team looking after her.'

I thank him and he rushes off, snatching his beeping pager from his waistband. A few moments after he's gone, a middle-aged nurse with a friendly face and ruddy cheeks appears and asks me to come with her.

I follow her past the reception desk and down a corridor. Once we're in a wider corridor, she drops back to walk beside me.

'It's aways a terrible shock when something like this happens,' she says in a soft, North-East accent. 'But you can rest assured your son is in the right place and he'll be receiving the very best care. Do you know how the accident happened yet?'

I shake my head. 'The doctor doesn't know. I've got to try and find out from the police. We were babysitting our grandson because my son and his wife were supposed to be staying overnight at the hotel. For the life of me, I can't understand why they were driving home.'

'It's very frustrating until you can put all the pieces together. But you'll get there, I'm sure.'

We turn the corner and a large black and white sign catches my eye: Adult Critical Care Unit. An arrow points in the direction we're headed.

A high buzzing noise begins in my ears. I start to feel a bit disoriented and stumble slightly.

She slows down and eyes me with concern. 'Are you OK?'

'Yes, it's just... It sounds silly, but I'm scared he'll look worse than I've imagined.'

'Doesn't sound silly at all; his appearance may well be a shock.' She touches the top of my arm. 'You can expect extensive swelling and severe bruising following even a minor road accident, but from what we can tell from your son's injuries, this was a serious one. The medical equipment around him might seem quite intimidating, but the thing to remember is that it's all there to help and it's allowing us to do our job. Here we are.' She stops walking in the front of some double doors. 'Do you feel up to going in, or would you like to take a minute or two first?'

'No, no, I want to see him,' I say firmly. 'I'd like to go through now.'

The nurse punches in a number and the double doors click open. After the silence of the corridors we've travelled through, I'm not prepared for this noisy, echoing space with its harsh lighting and shiny, hard floor. I follow her, past a nurses' station where doctors hold X-rays aloft and staff confer with serious, concerned faces.

Soon, the bustle is behind us and we enter an area filled with beds, most screened by privacy curtains. Occasionally, we pass a still, silent patient lying prostrate, their pale arms and heads surrounded by snakelike tubes and oxygen masks that conceal their features.

My lips are sticking to my gums. With every step, I feel less and less capable of dealing with what I'm about to be confronted with: the moment I see my son and learn the extent of his injuries.

'This is Parker's bed,' the nurse says, her hand hovering at the edge of the pale-green curtain. 'Remember what I said: try to see past the immediate obstacles if you can.'

She pulls the stiff fabric back and time seems to slow, the sounds around me magnified. The soft clink of the curtain rings against the metal rail, the hum of voices filling my ears. The smell of antiseptic and something else... something dark and unidentifiable that turns my stomach.

Then reality snaps back and I'm staring at a person, a shape in a bed that the nurse is assuring me is Parker.

It can't be him. It can't be him.

I'm repeating it again and again. Only in my head – I think – but then maybe I speak it out loud too because she glances at me, concerned, and says something I don't hear.

I shuffle closer until I'm next to the bed. I touch his cool, pale hand and my eyes travel up his arm, a mass of black and blood-red bruising with cuts. His upper arms are bandaged and his face – what I can see of it – is not Parker's face. At least not the one I know every feature of as well as my own. His entire head is grotesquely swollen. One cheek bears a thick pad of gauze and tape. His shiny, puffed-up eyelids are closed, his usually sleek hair is plastered back from his forehead, glistening red visible on his scalp.

'Dear God,' I whisper before I can stop myself. 'Oh no. No.'

Just as a deluge of emotion threatens to swamp me, I feel a steady hand on my shoulder and the scrape of a chair behind me. 'Sit down, pet,' the nurse says in her soft, comforting tones. 'You're wobbling. It's a shock to see him like this, I know.'

Obediently, I sit down heavily and stare at my broken boy. I squeeze his hand and lean forward so I can press my face a little closer to his. 'Parker? It's me... Mum. I'm here with you, my darling. I love you so much.' I turn to the nurse. 'Do you think he can hear me?'

'He might well be able to; he's starting to wake up from the operation,' she says.

Encouraged, I carry on. 'You're not to worry about a thing. Me and Dad are looking after Barney and he's fine. We'll keep him safe until we can bring him to see you. All you have to do right now is concentrate on getting well.'

I rub my cheek and realise my face is wet through. Tears are rolling, blurring what I can see of him.

'OK there, Mrs Vance?' the nurse says gently. 'Probably we should let him rest now.'

'We've got our grandson at home,' I tell her, glancing at Parker. 'I think we'll be keeping him a while, so I'll need to get him some clothes.'

'Right,' she says, puzzled.

'What I mean is, I haven't got a key to his house. Luna, his wife, is in the assessment unit and... well, I wondered if I could have Parker's keys if you have them.'

'Of course. There's a bag with his clothes in here and another containing his valuables at the desk. As you're his next of kin, there should be no problem in you taking them. I'll just go and check with the ward manager and explain about your grandson.'

She walks away, her soft shoes squeaking faintly on the hard floor.

I look back at Parker and, at that moment, his eyelids flicker.

'Parker... can you hear me? It's me, Mum.' I jump to my feet and bend forward so my face is directly in front of his. I take his hand again and he squeezes it faintly – so lightly I wonder if I've imagined it. His eyes are closed but there's another flicker and another and then, incredibly, his poor, swollen eyes slowly open and he's looking right at me.

'Oh, son, you're awake! You're going to be OK, darling. I love you so much.' Tears are streaming down my face and it's a battle to speak.

Then I hear the nurse's voice again from behind me.

'Yes, that's fine, Mrs Vance. You can pick his belongings up from the desk when you go and... oh my! Hello there, Parker.' She checks the machine that he's wired up to and then picks up the clipboard hanging from the unit. A faint scowl shadows her face.

'This is a good sign, isn't it? That he's awake, I mean?' I hear the desperation in my own voice, but Parker waking up like this must be a positive sign. It has to be.

'It's a good sign, yes. I need to get the doctor here, Mrs Vance, so I'm afraid you'll need to leave now.'

I turn back to Parker. 'I have to go now, son, but I'll be back tomorrow and you mustn't worry about Barney. I'll go to the house now and pick him up some clothes.'

Parker's swollen eyes widen a little further and his lips part. There's a small hiss, an exhalation of air.

'What's that, love? What are you trying to say?'

'Mrs Vance, he needs to relax,' the nurse says, firmly now. 'Best he doesn't strain to speak.'

I press my ear closer and Parker squeezes my hand a little harder. Then, just as I begin to move my head away, I'm sure I hear the faintest whisper. I freeze and press my ear closer to his mouth. So, so faint, but his words are crystal clear.

'Don't... go... there.'

NINE

PARKER

SIX WEEKS EARLIER

His eyes sprang open and he knew instinctively, without checking the clock, it would be around 3 a.m. It happened virtually every night unless he'd had too much to drink and was mercifully knocked out as soon as his head hit the pillow.

Hatred was so powerful and it could last for the longest time. Only someone infected with it could understand how pervasive it was. How it resisted any cure, any type of reasoning. How it trickled almost unnoticed into the bloodstream, soaking the bones through, drop by toxic drop. How it corroded the brain until every thought, every waking moment, was filled with pure, undiluted hate.

Parker sat up in bed. The room was pitch dark and silent, but he thought he could just hear the whisper of Luna's breathing in the other room. It sounded deep and measured.

Did the thoughts haunt her, too? Or was she better at pushing stuff away? He didn't think so.

He was trapped. They both were, like two rats in a cage.

Both had the capability to destroy each other, but there was a catch.

If they revealed each other's secrets... they'd end up destroying themselves, too.

TEN

NICOLA

Before I leave the critical care unit, I sign for Parker's belongings and, when I ask if I can see Luna, the ward manager, a stern-looking woman with a severe grey bun and fleshy, freckled hands, kindly calls the trauma ward to enquire.

'She's comfortable but sleeping,' she tells me matter-of-factly when she finishes the call. 'She has a broken pelvis and they're concerned about her high blood pressure, but she's stable for now. They said her parents are on their way in and, as they are her next of kin, they're the only people currently allowed access.'

'I see,' I say, disappointed. I would have liked to be able to tell Barney I've seen both his parents and to have held Luna's hand. I know the Barton-Jameses' flight was delayed and they got home late last night, so I'd imagine it might take them a little longer to get here. Luna's broken pelvis sounds extremely painful and will probably be a lengthy heal. But at least she won't have to worry about Barney's care while she's incapacitated. Cal and I can take that worry from her mind, at least, being the only people who can keep his weekdays undisturbed in terms of school and the various extra-curricular clubs he regularly attends. Cal will have to continue working, but I can manage fine.

The ward manager slides over a small piece of paper with a telephone number written on it. 'You can ring here in the morning to check on your son. We do ask that just one person is nominated to call each day rather than us having to deal with numerous enquiries.'

I thank her and leave. It's obvious to me now that Parker has come off far worse in the accident. The nurse seemed to be quite concerned when he woke up from his op and I pray there was nothing to that. Hopefully, after a good night's rest, he'll be feeling much more himself tomorrow. I wonder, for the umpteenth time, why they were headed home instead of staying over as originally planned. Could it have had something to do with what Parker had asked to talk to me about? I decide to call the hotel in the morning before I travel back here to visit him, to see if anyone can shed any light on why they checked out in the middle of the night. With any luck, I'll be able to ask Parker himself tomorrow.

After the bright lights and bustle of the critical care unit, the route back to the car park seems more deserted than ever. It's started to drizzle and coming out of the warmth so quickly, I feel the sudden drop in temperature even in my padded jacket as if the cold is seeping into my very bones. I walk quickly, keen to get back to the car where I'll text Cal and let him know I'm on my way home.

I wonder what time Joe and Marie, Luna's parents, will get here. Helmsley is about twenty-odd miles north of York on the River Rye. It's quite a journey – well over a hundred miles from here – and, I'd guess, about a two-and-a-half-hour drive even with no traffic on the roads.

Cal and I have visited their impressive home just twice in our son's nine-year marriage. We were invited for Parker and Luna's engagement party, and then again two years later, for the wedding. They had a stunning marquee erected in their vast grounds: all folds of pale-pink satin and tiny white fairy lights. With circular tables set with crisp linen and top-notch tableware, the event was worthy of a *Homes & Gardens* feature.

Cal and I were amongst a very small number of privileged guests who'd been allocated a bedroom in the manor house and invited to stay for breakfast with the bride and groom the following morning.

Back in our room after a memorable day, Cal, worse for wear after drinking for the entire event, began larking around in the en suite bathroom. I'd also enjoyed a good few glasses of champagne and I couldn't help laughing as he danced wildly with flailing arms in his attempt to demonstrate to me how Joe, the father of the bride, had thrown some shapes to 'Stayin' Alive' on the dance floor. The smile was wiped off my face when Cal inadvertently knocked off a shallow glass shelf over the sink and it had crashed down in pieces, chipping a couple of expensive Italian porcelain floor tiles in the process.

The next morning, Marie had waved away our apologies, insisting it didn't matter but I couldn't quite believe her. I saw the way her nostrils flared just a touch and her smile didn't quite reach her eyes. Parker had been embarrassed after finding out that Joe had been unable to source the matching tiles and had been forced to replace the whole floor. Suffice to say, we've never received another invitation to visit the manor house after that.

Back at the car park, I send Cal a text.

On my way home. Tell you everything when I'm back.

His characteristic thumbs-up reply boomerangs back while I pay for parking. Back in the car I start the engine and switch on the heated seats, but I don't drive away immediately. The window wipers are hypnotic, sweeping the drizzle from the glass in a wide arc as I stare blindly out across the mostly empty car park towards the blurred lights of the hospital.

The only thing I can see in my mind's eye is Parker's face in the hospital bed. Swollen and bruised, his handsome features were distorted beyond recognition. It's driving me crazy that I don't know the details of the accident yet, but I accept I'm not going to get the answers I need at this hour. I'm so tired, I could close my eyes and sleep right here in the car park but my son's words... his request for me to stay away from the house... niggle at me. Urges me to go in what might be a narrow window of time before I'm challenged by Luna, or Parker when he recovers.

I get back home just before 4 a.m. and, as I park outside on the road, I see our house is the only one with a light burning in the front window and hall. Cal opens the door before I'm even at the gate. His face looks washed out and drawn, his features pinched with concern.

I step inside and he says nothing, simply embraces me. I press my cool cheek to his warm chest, sinking into his solid reliability. Within seconds, his dressing gown has a damp patch from my silent tears.

'How's Barney?' I say at last, my voice thick and muffled.

'Barney's fine. He's fast asleep.' He gives me a squeeze and lifts my chin with a gentle touch. 'Come on, let's get you inside.'

I slip off my coat and shoes and Cal disappears into the kitchen to make me a cup of tea. I drag my heavy body into the lounge and sink into the sofa, finding relief in the soft cushions. I lean my head back and close my eyes, but I can't shake the image of my broken son and his swollen, pleading eyes.

A minute or so later, Cal reappears with a mug of tea. He places it carefully on a coaster on the arm of the sofa next to me and then he clears his throat.

'Tell me now,' he says simply. 'Tell me everything.'

'He woke up, Cal. While I was there. I was able to tell him how much we love him and that he's not to worry about Barney.'

Cal looks surprised. 'Well, that's a brilliant development. Him being awake, I mean.'

'He looked so ill though, not like him at all. He was covered in tubes and... the bruises, the swelling on his face... it was shocking.' I wipe away a tear. 'He looks so ill. Not like Parker at all.'

'And he knew you were there, do you think?'

'At first I didn't think he could hear me, but then he woke up and he did speak to me at the end. He was hard to hear, it was just a whisper and he wasn't making much sense, but the nurse said it was a very positive development.'

'What did he say?'

I shrug. 'I was talking about getting Barney some stuff from the house. He must've been confused because he said: *Don't go there.*'

'He said not to go there?' Cal looks concerned. 'Maybe he doesn't want you in the house, Nicola. We've never been a given a key.'

'That might be so, but as his next of kin the hospital staff thought it important I had a key when I explained about Barney. We've got to keep life as close to normal as we can for him.'

Cal nods his agreement. 'So, what's this operation he's had?'

'When I got there, the doctor told me they'd had to operate because he was bleeding internally. Something gastric.' I sip my tea and sigh. 'I couldn't find out anything about the accident and how it happened. Or whether there was any other vehicle involved. It seems that only the police can give us that information; I honestly don't think the hospital know.'

I tell Cal about the other medical investigations and issues the nurse mentioned that will need to be addressed once Parker has recovered from the accident. 'She didn't clarify exactly what those issues might be. I couldn't get to see Luna, but the ward manager was good enough to ring the assessment unit for a progress report and, apparently, she has a broken pelvis and high blood pressure.'

'But she's not bad enough to be admitted to critical care or need an operation,' Cal remarks. 'At least that's something to reassure Barney.'

'True. And Luna's parents are on their way to the hospital. No doubt fighting their jet lag.'

Cal looks at me then and I register for the first time how grey his skin is, how washed out and exhausted.

I stand up and hold out my hand. 'Come on. Let's go to bed, see if we can get a couple of hours' sleep. We're going to need all the strength we can get tomorrow.'

Cal doesn't reach for my hand. He doesn't move.

'Sit down, Nicola.'

I look at him questioningly. 'What is it?'

'I wasn't going to tell you this until the morning because I know full well it will play on your mind, but just in case they come here—'

'Who?'

'Luna's parents. I know they're on their way to the hospital because Marie rang me about twenty minutes ago.'

I sit down again. 'To see if we'd been told about the accident?'

'Not exactly. She said they were on their way to the hospital. I told her you were already there and she said they wanted to do a detour here afterwards to pick up Barney.'

I feel my face crumple in disbelief. 'They wanted to take Barney to the *hospital*?'

'No, no. She meant call here on the way back, after they'd left the hospital,' Cal says forlornly. 'She said as Luna and

Parker were badly injured, they'd need to take Barney back to Yorkshire with them.'

'Rubbish!' I feel my face inflame with indignation. 'His routine needs to be kept as normal as possible. He can hardly go to school in bloody Helmsley!'

Cal raises his hands. 'Calm down, Nicola. I told her it wouldn't be possible tonight. I said Barney was fast asleep and it wasn't fair to wake him, but—'

'It won't be possible *any* night!' I fume. 'Honestly. Who do those two think they are? He's our grandson too and until Parker tells us they're taking him, he'll be staying here. With us.'

Something about the way Cal falls silent, bows his head and looks at his hands stops me ranting. We'll have been married thirty-five years in January. During that stretch of time you learn a thing or two about your partner and that gesture Cal just did with his hands gives me the shivers. It tells me there's something he's not saying. Something he's trying hard to bury, but that he just can't keep to himself.

'What else, Cal?' I say quietly. 'Whatever it is, I want to know.'

He shakes his head and laces his fingers together. 'Marie said there had been some sort of measure put in place after Barney was born.'

'Measure?' I scowl.

'That's what she called it. Some legal paperwork exists that dictates, in the event of anything like this happening, that Marie and Joe will become Barney's official guardians by default.'

ELEVEN

NOTTINGHAMSHIRE POLICE

ONE WEEK EARLIER

Superintendent Della Grey looks up sharply as Helena taps on the door of her office and walks in.

'Hello, Helena. Let's take a seat.' Grey stands up and walks over to the comfy chairs clustered around a low coffee table. When they're both sitting comfortably, Grey unbuttons the jacket of her tailored plum trouser suit and leans forward. 'Tell me where we're at.'

'As you know, ma'am, three weeks ago, Sarah Grayson's body was found in an alleyway in the middle of the city and the distinctive scarf around her neck – thought to have been used to strangle her – was missing,' Helena says carefully, feeling the burn of her superior's eyes on her. 'We conducted a thorough search of the area again and organised a far-reaching media campaign with pictures of the scarf and pleas for information from the general public.'

Grey nods. 'What results have we had from that?'

'Sadly, nothing solid. We had a few calls come in at the beginning, people claiming to have found a similar scarf or bought one just like it in a charity shop, that kind of thing. But, ultimately, it led to nothing.'

'And in terms of the overall murder investigation?'

Helena clears her throat, hears her own voice emerge a little too high. She outlines their efforts so far. The search operation, the online reconstruction.

'There was an early witness description of a silver Audi seen around the area at about the time Sarah left the bar. Our initial CCTV sweep proved inconclusive, but the witness managed to get the year of registration. We accessed the DVLA database to identify vehicles matching the description provided.'

'You narrowed that search down to the Nottinghamshire region?'

'Yes. We compiled a list of potential matches, contacting the owners of the vehicles and checking out alibis. All were satisfactory.'

Helena explains that Sarah Grayson didn't have many friends, was devoted to her young daughter, Millie. 'A night out was unusual, but she'd told her mother she'd been asked out on a date. Someone she met online.'

'What do we know about this date?'

'He came forward right away. He owns an independent film company and never actually made it to the agreed meeting place that night. He had an accident on set. He spent several hours in A&E before he managed to text Sarah. His story checks out.'

'There's some ambiguity about her work, I understand?'

'Yes, ma'am. We're calling her a social media influencer in all our press communications, but we have reason to believe she sold sexual photographs and videos for an online platform. Our digital forensic team are looking into that, but as you know, it's not easy to get online companies to hand over their data. Also, her mother is completely unaware of her daughter's source of

TWELVE

LUNA

Luna Barton-James never spoke about her childhood to anyone. If she was asked about it in the various online interviews she took part in regularly, she had several well-rehearsed replies. All skimped over the facts and quickly focused on little anecdotes about days at the seaside, riding a favourite horse at the local stables, or memories of her mother's delectable homemade puddings after Sunday lunch that Luna would look forward to all week – real enough but made by the housekeeper the day before and which her mother had warmed up.

Luna didn't want to talk about any of it. Not her teenage years, or even beyond that, because her life up until her mid-twenties had been dominated by her mother.

Luna loved her mother deeply. She did. At the same time, she'd never felt quite good enough for her. As Luna got older, Marie's warm, comforting protection had turned into a veritable stranglehold that she'd worried she'd never escape from unless she took off abroad somewhere and never came back. She was critical of everything: Luna's looks, any achievements and, particularly, her relationship with her dad. She'd heard about some mothers becoming jealous of their daughters as they grew older and blossomed, but Luna could not bear to think this was the case. Instead, she internalised her blame and turned on herself. If only she could do better then she felt sure her mother would be proud.

Over time, and as the realisation had dawned that Luna would not be following the path her mother had mapped out for her, Marie's grip had tightened until Luna had begun to feel suffocated. The more she'd tried to pull away, the more she couldn't seem to breathe.

Life had felt endlessly flat and disappointing. The doctor had prescribed a course of anxiety medication. When Luna had felt the pressure increasing, and like she might implode, she'd used a clean dermaplane blade to press down into the soft, thin flesh near her shoulder. Release had come with the sharp, quick fix of pain and the neat beads of claret that had patterned her tissues. Small nicks of instant release that had been easily hidden by choosing tops with good coverage.

It had been a way of holding it all in. A way of trying to continue the exhausting quest to be what her mother had wanted her to be, even though Luna had never been quite sure what that was.

Then Luna had met Parker Vance and, for the first time, her mother's grip had begun to loosen.

Luna had been at a mind-numbingly boring garden fayre in the grounds of the big church near home. Someone had dropped out due to illness and left the church ladies in a tizzy, so, on her mother's insistence, Luna had spent the morning selling what looked like unappetising little blobs of lard with coloured icing and sprinkles on. *Fairy cakes*, the large lady selling artisan bread on the next stall had informed her.

'I'll take a half-dozen of your little cakes, so long as they're low calorie.'

Luna's head had jerked up at the deep voice and she'd

looked straight into the mesmerising brown eyes of Parker Vance.

'It was a joke,' he'd said when she hadn't responded. 'No offence. Did you bake them?'

'God, no.' She'd pulled a face. 'Six balls of fat coming up.'

She'd felt his eyes on her as she'd picked each cake up with tongs and popped it in a white paper bag. She'd dropped one twice and he'd laughed as her face had burned.

They'd chatted a little. He'd told her he'd just finished uni and started a new job. She'd said something about working on a new project. She hadn't said she'd left her uni course but not sorted anything else out yet. 'I soon found out Business and Finance wasn't for me. No matter how desperate Mum was for me to work with Dad in the family property and landscaping business.'

'Well, you're working hard now.' Parker had grinned. 'I'm sure your mum would be proud.'

'Lucky I finish at one o'clock before they fire me,' she'd said, handing the cakes over.

'That *is* lucky because I'm free at that time too. Fancy a drink? I can pick you up outside.'

Someone else had taken over the stall at one o'clock and Parker was waiting outside the church as he'd promised. He'd driven her in his little Fiat – his mum's car, he'd told her sheepishly – to a small pub at the end of a country lane. An old man's pub, she'd have called it, but she hadn't minded. Not when it had meant she could be with him a bit longer. She'd turned off her phone and tucked it into the pocket of her skinny jeans.

Inside, it had been a typical old-fashioned pub. Then and now pictures on the walls, a patterned carpet underfoot and scratched, oak tables with mismatched chairs. She'd sat on a cushioned pew that had run the whole length of the back wall, and had imagined her mother's face if she could see where Luna was. And with a boy who drove a battered little Fiat, too!

'What are you smiling at?' He'd grinned and slid his arm around her shoulder and a little shiver had vibrated down her spine.

'It's just funny how I was in a church twenty minutes ago and now I'm here with you.'

He'd chuckled and pressed his face closer to hers. His stubble had touched the softness of her cheek, grazing her just for a moment and her scalp had tingled.

Parker had gone to the bar and she'd watched his tall, broad frame walk away. He wasn't one of those spoilt, cossetted boys of her mum's friends. Driving round in full designer gear and brand-new sports cars leased by their parents. The boys Marie had always tried to hook her up with.

Parker was four years older than Luna. He'd had a 'so what?' confidence about him that had given her the shivers. She'd imagined him walking in one of those stripped-down brasseries her peers frequented and Luna hated. The sort that sold trendy small plates alongside an eye-wateringly expensive wine list. 'So *what* if I drive a crappy car? So *what* if I'm wearing cheap jeans?' he might say. 'I still look better than all of you.'

It was only when Parker had come walking back carrying a bottle of red wine and two glasses that she'd realised he hadn't asked her what she'd like to drink. Somehow, she'd found she didn't mind at all. In fact, she'd found his decisiveness quite attractive.

They'd chatted for an hour. He'd seemed quite happy to listen to what she loved, disliked and what she wanted for her future. The way he'd just let her be, accepted her as she was, had reminded her of her dad, Joe. She'd felt emancipated from Marie's control. Parker had loved the thought of travelling around Asia, he'd adored the same music, preferred eating meat to fish and, incredibly, he too had been single and looking for a relationship.

He'd given her permission to be herself. He'd given her no

advice, hadn't tried to change her opinion on things. He'd just listened and accepted her, and for the first time in her life, she'd felt she had finally found a place where she could be content.

When they'd left the pub, her whole body had buzzed pleasantly. She'd climbed into the passenger seat of the Fiat and, as she'd buckled up, he'd leaned forward and kissed her.

Luna had been on fire and she'd known right there, right then; she hadn't cared what her mother would say or how she might disapprove.

Parker was her soulmate and she wasn't going to let anyone take him away from her. Ever.

THIRTEEN

NICOLA

'Nicola! Calm down. Don't do anything rash,' I hear Cal pleading as I clamber into the understairs cupboard and haul out the large suitcase. 'Legal paperwork or not, nobody will stop us from seeing Barney.'

'I'm not doing anything silly,' I say as I back out of the cluttered space. 'I'm just going to speed up my plan to get what Barney needs from the house.'

Who knows how long I'll have a key? I don't want Marie and Joe beating me to it and taking all Barney's clothes and belongings in one fell swoop when they've been to the hospital. That would only help their cause of insisting Barney should go back with them. Cal is more naïve than I thought if he truly believes the Barton-Jameses will consider us in any arrangements they make. They've been getting their own way in life for far too long.

'But it's 5 a.m.!' Cal tries to reason. 'Your time would be better spent getting some rest and going over there first thing in the morning.'

'It *will* be morning in an hour's time. I'm wide awake now, so I might as well make it count. I can't sleep a wink in this state anyway.'

He lets out an exasperated sigh. 'Fine, but you look exhausted, love. If you're hell-bent on getting his stuff right now then at least let me go and do it. You stay here with Barney and snooze while I zip over and—'

'I should go,' I say firmly. Cal hasn't got a clue what to bring. Barney will probably end up with all of his favourite toys and games and hardly anything to wear. 'I know exactly what he'll need for the next few days.'

'Fair enough,' Cal says irritably, blowing out air. It's clear he thinks I'm over-reacting. Being unreasonable.

I crouch down and unzip the suitcase to check it's completely empty before looking up at him. 'That nasty little legal agreement they've managed to sort out for themselves? It sounds serious to me, Cal. It means – God forbid – if the worst happens to Parker and Luna, we'd have no rights to see our grandson.'

'You're scooting ahead to one hell of a worst-case scenario there.' He pinches the bridge of his nose. 'I know Parker isn't out of the woods yet, but he's awake from his operation and it sounds like Luna's broken some bones. Neither one is at death's door, thank God.'

'You didn't see Parker,' I say, my voice cracking as the image of our injured son rushes in again. 'He's in the critical care unit, Cal. They don't take up a bed in there unless you're seriously ill.'

He swallows. 'I know,' he says softly. 'I'm just trying to put things into perspective, Nicola. I know we're not the best of chums with Marie and Joe, but I'd like to think they'd never stoop as low as to cut us off from seeing Barney.'

A small, derogatory noise escapes my throat. 'I'm not so sure.'

Cal frowns. 'Put it this way, we've enough to worry about without you foreseeing more doom and devastation ahead.'

I'm not going to get into an argument about how bad things might get. I pick up the empty suitcase and head for the door. 'I'll be as quick as I can,' I say.

Cal follows me. 'I'll see you out,' he says, planting a kiss on my cheek. 'Just collect what Barney needs and then come back home to get some rest. And drive safe.'

I walk down the path and see a light on upstairs in one of the houses across the road. A couple in their forties moved in there last year. Another neighbour told me she's a restaurant manager and works shifts. I don't know their names, but we've waved hello a couple of times when we've gone out to the car at the same time. When Parker was growing up, we knew most of our neighbours but now everyone seems to have moved on. These people, virtual strangers, waking up and getting on with their lives around us. Just another tedious day for them while our world is wobbling on its axis.

I wave to Cal and he closes the front door. I put the suitcase in the boot and get in the driver's seat, opening my mouth to try and breathe. I feel like something is sucking the air from my lungs and I can't get enough back in there. I can't put a name to it yet, but I can feel tendrils of dread creeping up my spine, icy and foreboding.

This is a very bad situation but like a faint rumble from afar or a dimming of light, I'm sensing there's worse to come.

Parker's family home is in Ravenshead, about a ten-minute drive from our own village. It's a detached four-bed property in a small cluster of relatively new executive homes in a quiet cul-de-sac. As I head there, I think about how delighted I'd been when he and Luna had announced they'd be living fairly close by. I'd let my imagination run away with me.

'I'll be able to cook a couple of extra meals for their freezer,' I'd told Cal, enjoying the warm feeling I'd got when I'd thought about the ways I could help out. 'It's hard when you're both working and, who knows, in time they might have children, and then I'll really have to pull the stops out.'

'I wouldn't go overboard. We had to manage.' Cal had sniffed. 'We had nobody to help out. My parents lived too far away and your mum was in agony with her arthritis, so...'

'Times change, Cal,' I'd said lightly, unwilling to let him dampen my mood. 'Parents help out their grown-up kids a lot these days, and Luna's parents are too far away to do much. If they do have children, they'll probably rely on us quite a bit.'

'Give them a chance, they're not even married yet!'

It had been a waste of time trying to get him on board so I just let it go.

Their garden isn't huge, but when they'd first moved into the new house, I'd offered to keep it tidy. 'Don't waste money on a gardener or anything like that. I can pop over on my day off and mow the grass when you're out at work.'

Parker and Luna had glanced at each other.

'Up to you, but it's no trouble at all.'

'Thanks, Mum. But Luna works mainly from home anyway.'

I'd glanced at her long nails and perfect clothes. I couldn't imagine Luna getting her hands dirty at all.

'Thanks, Nicola, but my dad has people working all over the country,' Luna had said, squeezing Parker's hand. 'He's going to get someone to pave it all so it's minimum fuss.'

'Oh, that seems a shame. It's a lovely lawn and you'll get far more birds and wildlife if you have—'

'Thanks, Mum,' Parker had interrupted. 'We'll bear that in mind.'

It had just got worse from there. Everything I'd offered help with – from moving-in day to inviting them to Sunday lunch most weeks so they didn't have to cook – was turned down instantly.

'We'll go and see my parents most weekends, and Mum is a mean cook. Parker's in love with her Sunday roasts, right, darling?'

At least Parker had had the decency to look sheepish when he'd mumbled his agreement.

Turns out they didn't just go up to Helmsley on a Sunday; they were gone Saturday morning and sometimes, even on Friday night. At that point, Parker was still popping over for a cuppa and a chat after work during the week. Even though he'd had his own flat for years, he'd still kept stuff in his old bedroom so he'd wanted to sort through all that. It was during these times we'd got to know all about his weekend life.

'Joe took me clay pigeon shooting and we had a fantastic time. They're a great group of guys and we all went to the pub afterwards. Next month he's taking me to his private country club. You have to be invited to be a member.'

'He'll be dressed in tweed knickerbockers with a feather in his cap when we see him next,' Cal had quipped when I'd told him. 'Sounds like he's in training to become a proper country gentleman.'

I'd made light of it, but secretly I'd worried they'd go to live in Yorkshire permanently. And what if they had kids? I'd probably never see them. I'd figured we were probably safe for now; I knew Parker's commute would be crazy while he was based in Nottingham for work, but who knew what the future might bring?

'Don't go fretting about things that haven't happened yet.' Cal had eyed me suspiciously as I'd fallen quiet. 'I'm only joking.'

I'd known he was. But at that point, neither of us could have foreseen how bad things were going to get.

· · ·

I drive into Ravenshead and take a sharp left turn, approaching the gated development. There are two fobs on Parker's keyring and one of them is clearly a house alarm fob. I lower my window and point the other fob at the gate sensor. A small red light illuminates, and the ornate metal gates start to swing open. The cluster of executive houses were built about ten years ago and are all very smart, but their house looks brand new because Luna wanted it done up so it stood out from the other properties. It's very modern-looking now with white plaster walls and dark-grey windows. Within eighteen months of buying the house, they'd put a two-storey extension on the back and had a new kitchen fitted.

Cal and I haven't been invited over for a very long time now. So long, I'd rather not think about the exact length of time. I had pushed to see the new extension when it was finished and we'd gone over one Saturday morning.

'It'll have to be early, Mum,' Parker had told me, 'because we'll need to get on the road to head up to Yorkshire by ten at the latest.'

We'd arrived at nine and Parker had immediately shown us the beautiful new rooms. Out of the kitchen window I'd seen a modern spread of cream ceramic tiles and grey decking. There were flowers, all contained in pots but not a blade of grass or free-growing bushes to be found. I could see it looked very stylish in its own way, like something you might see in a posh magazine, but it had made me sad that five-year-old Barney had nowhere to kick a ball around. They'd made us a drink and Barney had insisted he wanted to show us his bedroom and then it was made very clear, through various means like watch-checking and long puffs of air, that they were waiting to get off.

The development is well lit. There are six houses arranged in a crescent shape and all the windows are dark, although most have outside lights. I head for the middle section and, as I push away the denial and realise what it is I'm seeing, I slow the car even more. Outside number 4, Orchid Close, I stop the vehicle completely and stare ahead in disbelief.

There's a for-sale sign up outside my son's property.

They're moving house and he hasn't said a thing.

FOURTEEN

MARIE

Marie Barton-James stands at the hospital bedside and looks down on her sleeping daughter's bruised and battered face. She clenches her jaw in an effort to control her emotions. Yet the tears that prickle at the back of her eyes are not born of sadness, but of fury.

Fury at what her girl might have been if only it wasn't for Parker Vance.

Twelve years ago, eighteen-year-old Luna had carefully lowered her cutlery at the dinner table and announced, 'Mum, Dad? I met a boy I like.' Joe had been sucked in, asking all sorts of questions about Parker, who, it seemed, had ambitions to secure a corporate position in sales. As Joe had continued to probe into Parker's background, Marie had stayed quiet and listened closely. It hadn't taken long for alarm bells to start to ring.

'His dad has had his own successful business for years,' Luna had gushed, warming to Joe's interest. 'It's something to do with plumbing and heating.'

It hadn't taken long for Joe to establish that Cal *was* the business. He was little more than a self-employed plumber, taking on the odd apprentice.

'Parker's really looking forward to meeting you both,' Luna had said, her cheeks flushed pink.

She'd had a couple of short-lived relationships, but Luna always started out keen and then gradually lost interest as the prospective partners failed to make the grade.

But Parker was different and as soon as Marie had met him, she'd known this threat was for real. Tall, dark and handsome, she'd recognised immediately why Luna had fallen for him. Within a matter of seconds her eyes had taken in the strong, square jaw and full lips, the wide, powerful shoulders with a toned physique... and she'd seen all of her plans for Luna fall away.

Infuriatingly, after they were married a couple of years later, Joe had suddenly taken to Parker and, since then, he'd become the son Joe never had. Marie had wanted another child after Luna. But having suffered three miscarriages in quick succession before Luna, and another two after they'd been blessed with her, she'd had to give up and accept the reality to save her health and mental wellbeing.

She looks down at her daughter, wishing she would wake up. Marie has confusing emotions about Luna; sometimes she is a hard woman to love. But now, all Marie wants to do is to tell her how much she needs her.

'Are you OK there, Mrs Barton-James?' Marie looks around to see the nurse who initially brought her through. 'It's a terrible shock to see your daughter like this, I know. Is there anything I can do for you?'

'No, thank you,' Marie says stiffly. 'I'm just waiting for my husband to join me.'

Joe is currently speaking to the doctor to find out how soon Luna can be moved from this god-awful unit and into a private hospital that's close to their home in Helmsley. When she'd first entered the ward, Marie had looked around in horror at the close proximity of the patients to each other, the visitors who watched each other with interest, neither possessing the sense nor the decency to look away at displays of emotion as people were confronted by their loved ones in sick and injured states.

She can't wait to whisk Luna away somewhere more comfortable, under the care of doctors who don't look sleep-deprived and constantly flummoxed.

At least Luna isn't in the critical care unit like Parker. He'd been the one driving and the one who'd put her daughter in a hospital bed with catastrophic injuries she might never fully recover from.

Everyone seems to find Parker so congenial, a generally nice man. But Marie has never been fooled. He is arrogant and strong-willed, forcing his young family to live in a sub-standard house instead of accepting Marie and Joe's generous offer to gift them a hefty deposit towards a far better property. Preferably in Yorkshire.

Luna claims to be happy, but Marie knows better. Her daughter used to have big ambitions. She was raised in the comfort of a high life and she's been forced to savagely cut her expectations since marrying Parker because, essentially, he wants to do it all himself. He set out to control Luna and, although it pains Marie to admit it, he's succeeded.

'I admire him,' Joe had countered when Marie complained. 'Most young guys would snatch our hands off, but Parker has a sense of achievement and pride in going after his own goals.'

Marie had sneered. 'Misplaced working-class pride, that's all it is. The kind of attitude that keeps people stuck.' It was important to her that Luna had her own career, that she wasn't just a wife and parent, as her own mother and gran had been. Men might say they wanted to support you and there was no need to work, but in reality, the ones they always chased seemed to be career women who knew their own mind and paid their own way.

There has always been something about Parker that Marie can't quite trust. Yet when Barney came along, she'd been shocked how quickly her heart had melted from the moment she set eyes on her grandson. It had been so easy to set aside the knowledge that the child had half of Parker's genes. When Marie looks at her grandson, she only sees Luna's pert nose and she recognises Joe's high forehead and good bone structure. And that makes her heart ache in a different way.

She bends forward now and kisses her daughter's face. Although she could have never foreseen this tragedy, somehow, deep down inside, Marie had known that Luna marrying Parker would all end in tears.

But she loves her grandson in a way she wouldn't have thought possible. And if anything good can come of this whole heartbreaking event, it will be that Barney can come back to Helmsley to live with them and, once again, Luna will again be back in the family fold.

And, more importantly, then Marie can finally lay her own shameful secret to rest.

FIFTEEN

NICOLA

With my heart pumping hard against my chest wall, I grab my handbag and get out of the car. The slam of the driver's door seems like a thunderclap in this small, sleepy cul-de-sac, but that's the least of my worries.

I walk up to the for-sale sign, stop to glare at it illuminated in the well-lit front garden. If I had the strength, I'd wrench it out of the ground right now. I feel angry and hurt. As Parker's mother and Barney's gran, I have a right to be told about major decisions.

And then... I realise. This must have been what he wanted to speak to me about when he came to pick Barney up in the morning. This morning.

Yet something still feels off about that because Parker had stated quite clearly that he didn't want Luna or Cal to know about our conversation...

I turn my back on the sale board and walk up to the front door. I pull out Parker's keys and open up. A short, staccato beep starts up and I swipe the second fob over the alarm pad before snapping on the hall light. Finally, I lock the door behind me.

It's so long since I've been here. Perhaps it's even two years. We've seen Parker when he's dropped off Barney, or picked him up. Snatches of conversation and mostly refusal of our invitations to stay for a cup of tea and a chat. Way back when Parker and Luna announced their engagement, I remember taking pleasure in imagining how we'd enjoy long, lazy Sundays together and perhaps a little walk around the local woodland Cal and Parker used to spend hours building dens in when he was a boy. I fantasised about taking our future grandchildren to the seaside and enjoying garden picnics together in the warmer months.

But we got rather a different deal. I stand in my son's unfamiliar clinical white hallway with its glossy white floor tiles and spotless ivory stairs carpet and try to work out how it got to be this way. How hardly seeing Parker and feeling grateful for the scraps of time we spend with our Barney became our new normal.

It's deathly quiet in here and I find myself creeping down towards the lounge door so as not to make a sound. There's really no need for that as I'm alone but I feel such a stranger... an imposter.

I peer into the lounge. A Nordic blonde wooden floor, oversized Natuzzi white leather sofas and a TV wall bearing a space-age electric fire and the biggest television I've ever seen. Not a thing out of place and certainly no sign of a child living here. It's a similar story in the other rooms; Luna's office is impossibly neat with the numerous clothing samples and accessories she receives in return for a review hung neatly on a rail in the corner. The dining room – with its reclaimed wood table and ten chairs, which has fully dressed place settings with crockery, cutlery and glass – looks like it's never been used. There's the enormous glossy white dining kitchen with its wall of glass leading to the large, manicured garden. This room features quite a bit on Luna's social media channels when she'll post a reel from the breakfast bar to discuss the latest fashion trends. There are other rooms down here I don't bother going in. The important thing is to get Barney everything he needs to last him for the next week or so and then... who knows what our role might be in our grandson's life. I stop and take a breath. I'm getting ahead of myself. One day at a time. That's what my motto should be.

I slip my boots off and start to climb the stairs. The carpet's expensive weave feels firm beneath my feet. A long, spiral crystal light cascades down from the floor above, illuminating the framed photographs on the stairs wall. Professional portraits of Parker, Luna and Barney as a family. A photograph of each of Barney's birthdays as he's about to blow out candles. As I near the top, a large formal portrait of Barney with Luna's parents – obviously at some grand event – faces me on the dog-leg part of the stairs. Barney stands at the front looking smart in long trousers, a white shirt and dicky-bow, smiling weakly at the camera while Joe and Marie stand behind him, dressed up to the nines with her hands placed on his narrow shoulders.

I think about the photo we had taken with Barney at Alton Towers earlier this year. His school had had a staff training day, on a Monday. They'd just returned from their weekend in Yorkshire. Marie had several Zoom meetings and Parker had to leave early for a day in Newcastle, so I'd jumped at the chance to volunteer to have Barney for the day. Cal had taken a rare day off and we'd headed to the theme park just over an hour's drive from us. From the moment we arrived to the moment we left, the three of us never stopped laughing. The log flume photo we bought is just joyous. All of our faces animated with hysterical laughter. Our copy has pride of place in the lounge and I hope, if I was to search, I'd find Barney's copy displayed here in the house somewhere, too.

Upstairs, I head straight for his bedroom. I turn on the light and look around, gratified to see a bit less suffocating order in here. Toys out, PlayStation wires snaking over the floor and a crumbed plate and empty glass on his bedside table. The room is themed in Spider-Man colours; even the carpet is blue with the odd flash of red web. Any seven-year-old boy would love it.

I open his wardrobe and take out an assortment of clothes. His school uniform with a couple of shirts, a jumper. I make a note to look for his school shoes downstairs. I spot his reading folder tossed carelessly on to the bed and add that to the pile. I find underwear, some tracky bottoms and T-shirts for him to change into after school. He has his trainers and a coat at our house.

I pick up a few of the comics from the side of his bed and a couple of Nintendo Switch games as I'd noticed the console in one of the bags Parker carried in. I stand back and appraise the heap of stuff. It should be enough for now. It's certainly the bulk of what he needs for the next few days and, if there is anything else crucial, well, I have the house key now and I'll need to be surgically separated from it to give it up if Marie Barton-James kicks off.

I leave Barney's room to go and get the case out of the car. I'd left it there in case I had any problems getting in because of the alarm. Before I go back downstairs, I pop my head around the door of the master bedroom. It's big and white with a faux four-poster bed taking up a good deal of floor space. The bedding is white too, and there must be more than a dozen white, lacy cushions beautifully arranged on there. Imagine having to take them off every night and rearrange them each morning... I can't imagine Parker doing that! There's an en suite bathroom and a dressing room attached, which I remember from when we were lucky enough to be shown around when they'd first bought the house.

I know I shouldn't, but I walk over to the dressing room and its wall of wardrobes to take a sneak peek at Luna's incredible clothes collection. I open the first two doors and it's packed with evening gowns, sequins and crystals flashing as the light pours inside. The other doors contain equally fabulous designer outfits, most of the expensive dresses zipped into garment bags designed to let the clothes breathe.

I get to the end of the wardrobes and frown. Turning around I briefly open each drawer in a tall set. Exquisite sets of lingerie in some, more practical everyday underwear in others. Scarves, belts, hats... it's a treasure trove most women would kill for. But one thing strikes me as very odd: there's not a single item of Parker's in here.

I walk back into the bedroom. Fluffy slippers on one side of the bed and a White Company robe hung on the door. No slippers the other side and although I know Parker likes a light silky dressing gown to relax in, there's not one to be found here.

I take a quick peek in the bedside drawers. One has a women's fiction paperback in there, tissues, lip salve, paracetamol. And, tucked right at the back, a couple of empty vodka miniatures. I pause for thought a moment, the fleeting memory of Luna's 'mouthwash' breath returning. Over on Parker's side, the other bedside drawer is completely empty, as if someone has just swept the contents into a bag.

I check the other bedrooms as I move down the hallway. The first one is clearly unused but the room next door to that, opposite Barney's own bedroom, is filled with Parker's stuff. It's a decent size and there's a short run of fitted wardrobes. One of the doors is ajar and it's full of my son's clothes. There are shoes and worn T-shirts and underwear strewn around the floor. He's always been a scruffy beggar like that. On reflection, I suppose Cal was right. I molly-coddled him too much.

The bed is unmade and the bedside drawer, which has been left open, contains one of Parker's watches from his extensive collection, a hankie, a couple of letters and a tube of prescription steroid cream, I presume, for the eczema he's suffered with on and off since childhood. A 'World's Best Dad' mug sits by the lamp, half-full of skinned cold coffee.

It's painfully clear what's happening here. Parker and Luna are sleeping in separate rooms. Now I feel certain this is what Parker wanted to discuss with me.

He was going to tell me their marriage is in big trouble, and I think he was going to tell me why.

SIXTEEN

After popping back out to the car, I head back inside to pack Barney's stuff into the case, all the time thinking about the chat Parker and I were due to have later this morning. The house is up for sale, they're sleeping apart... it doesn't take a genius to work out their relationship is breaking down. Maybe it's worse than that... maybe they've agreed to divorce. I can't bear to think about what that might mean in terms of us seeing Barney.

I activate the alarm, turn off the lights and lock up. As I'm pushing the packed suitcase out to the car, I notice all the bins of the other houses are out. Parker must have forgotten to put theirs out before they left last night. I put the suitcase in the car boot and walk around to the side of the house to their bin store. The area instantly floods with a powerful movement-sensor external light. I pull the black bin, which is for general rubbish, and when it's out of the brick housing, I see there's a tied bin bag behind it. When I check inside the bin, it's only half full, so I heave the bin bag – which is heavier than I thought – out of the store. I'm just about to lift it again to dump into the bin when I notice the sharp corner of something poking out where it's torn the plastic. I look at it in disbelief and pull open the top of the bag.

Feeling a mixture of anger and sadness, I lift out the framed photo of Cal and me with Barney at Alton Towers. I push it back inside and peer at the other items. There's some clothing in here and what looks like a brand-new bottle of bubble bath and an unopened, shrink-wrapped cosmetics box. I know Luna receives a lot of gifted products as part of her influencer work, but it seems a crime to throw stuff like this away.

I roll the bin down and tuck it slightly into the drive as the other residents have done. Then I go back to the bin bag and half pull, half carry it down to the car. I can just say I put it in the wheelie bin and they'll be none the wiser.

I drive home zombie-like, staring ahead at the wet road, the windscreen wipers breaking up the bleak view with an intermittent swipe of the blades. If only they had the power to break up the constant churn of thoughts running through my head.

A brief visit to the house has answered some of the questions I had about the chat Parker had requested. In doing so, new queries have now been raised. Why would they go to a dinner dance together if they were about to split up? They had looked so happy in the photo Luna had sent me. Was he really planning to move out of the family home? My mind buzzes with scenarios. Maybe he was finding a way to ask if he could move back in with us for a short time to give them some space from each other. Bearing in mind how we've drifted apart as a family and the antagonism between Parker and Cal, it would explain Parker wanting to keep our initial talk quiet, without the knowledge of his wife or his dad.

Now, my boy is lying in a hospital bed recovering from his operation with a whole host of tests and investigations waiting, according to the doctor I spoke to earlier this morning. If he and

Luna are on the verge of splitting up then it's a reasonable assumption that Barney would stay with his mum. Marie's phone call to Cal earlier about them taking Barney back to their house in Yorkshire suggests to me Luna's parents perhaps know about the rift. With Luna in hospital, they're moving in strategically to try and take control of our grandson.

The journey home passes in a blur and, before I know it, I'm turning into our street. I almost expect to see Marie and Joe's big S-Class Mercedes sitting outside the house and I breathe a sigh of relief when the space is clear.

The sky is getting lighter by the minute. A blackbird provides a beautiful tune to lift my heavy heart. I open the boot and lug out the suitcase full of Barney's things and wrestle up to the front door with it. I open up as quietly as I can, managing to lift it over the doorstep. I leave it in the hall and listen. The house is quiet, but the living room light is still on. I take off my shoes and pad in there, expecting to see Cal asleep on the sofa but he isn't around.

Upstairs, I check on Barney. He's fast asleep, breathing softly but deeply. I cover his arm with the quilt and leave. A quick check in our bedroom reveals Cal, snoring heavily beneath the sheets.

I close the door and return downstairs to put the kettle on. I'm far too wired to sleep, but hopefully a drink will help to relax me and I'll grab a couple of hours' shut-eye if I can. I'm going to need some strength for going back to the hospital and possibly facing Marie and Joe, too.

I suddenly remember the bin bag on the back seat of the car. While the kettle is boiling, I quietly open the front door and go out to get it. I put it by the sofa and make a cup of tea. Finally, I sit down, savouring the hot drink and closing my eyes for a few moments, trying to find an elusive sense of peace.

After a short time, I open the bin bag and start emptying it of items. There's no rubbish in here, no mess. The first thing I remove is the Alton Towers photograph of us with Barney. It saddens me to think it was destined for the refuse collectors. Why not just put it in a cupboard somewhere? It's got to be Luna who's cast it aside. I don't feel as close to Parker as I used to do, but there's no way he'd do that. After all, we're still his parents, whatever happens. Nothing is ever going to change that.

Next, I lift out the shrink-wrapped box of make-up, a couple of brand-new hardback books and pull out the clothing. There's a wrap dress, size 8, still with labels attached, a pair of skinny jeans and a pussy bow blouse in a neon-green colour that, if I'm honest, would be hard to blend into anyone's wardrobe.

The bottom of the bag contains mainly small items like belts, screwed-up paper, empty packaging and one more thing. A small bag. I pull it out and look inside only to find another bag containing something soft.

I peer into that bag before taking it out and holding it in front of me. A square of coloured silk that perfumes the air when I shake the creases out.

I frown and stare at it a moment. I've seen this scarf somewhere before but I can't think where. Maybe Luna's worn it and the distinctive black and gold geometric design has stuck in my mind. Thinking for a moment, I look at the wall and my eyes lower to Cal's newspaper folded over on the arm of his chair. The headline jumps out at me.

POLICE NO FURTHER FORWARD IN LOCAL MURDER CASE

The words stare back at me in bold, black print. The young woman, Sarah… her body had been found about four weeks ago in the city's Lace Market area. When she went missing, police went to great lengths to publicise the outfit she was wearing that night, including a distinctive patterned neck scarf. All the newspapers, both local and national, had included colour photographs of a similar scarf in their articles.

I reach for the paper.

Police have launched a fresh appeal in their search for a piece of vital evidence in the investigation of the murder of local woman, Sarah Grayson, 25.

Ms Grayson's body was discovered in the Lace Market area of the city following an extensive search. A post-mortem examination confirmed the cause of death as strangulation. Detectives are now searching for a missing scarf.

Detective Inspector Helena Price of Nottinghamshire Police told the North Notts Post, *'Ms Grayson wore a distinctive black and gold patterned silk scarf in the hours before her death. It is clearly visible on CCTV footage as she left the nightclub but was missing when officers discovered her body.'*

Police immediately launched a comprehensive search but a week later have yet to discover its whereabouts.

'It's vital we recover this essential piece of evidence to assist us in apprehending whoever murdered this vibrant, innocent young mother and bring some closure to her distraught family.'

My eyes fall on the photograph at the bottom of the article. A woman of around my age, pale with dark circles under her tear-filled eyes. She has her arm around a small, sweet girl with pale-red hair, who looks about four years old. A notation under the photo reads:

Sarah Grayson's daughter, Millie, and her mother, Julie Grayson

The sister of a friend I see periodically lives near Julie

Grayson. She told my friend one day that her sister knew a woman whose daughter had just gone missing.

Now, I stare at the woman's haunted, wretched face, the little girl's bewildered expression. Suddenly it all seems a lot closer than it did before. My chest tightens and I think about Barney. How we're going to have to explain his mum and dad are in hospital. But little Millie... she had to be told her mummy had gone to heaven.

I fold the newspaper up and put it face down on the sofa.

Parker was questioned in relation to Sarah Grayson's disappearance. Questioned and cleared of any wrongdoing. A silver car, reportedly a silver Audi, was seen by a witness in the area shortly before Sarah disappeared. Parker still had his silver Audi back then – it was just before he took delivery of his new company car.

Police made it clear they were speaking to him purely as a routine enquiry, acting on matching vehicle data they'd received. That was all there was to it, nothing more. Parker was questioned briefly, was able to give an acceptable alibi immediately, as he'd been attending an overnight sales conference in Newcastle. And that had been the end of it. He'd heard nothing more.

I look down at the black and gold scarf that's fallen into a small, crumpled heap on my knee.

It looks identical to the one the police are still searching for.

SEVENTEEN

PARKER

SIX YEARS EARLIER

When they first met six years ago, Parker didn't think of Luna as being the jealous sort at all.

They fell in love quickly and deeply, both wrapped up in the warm, sensual bubble that excluded everything and anyone else. They couldn't get enough of each other, yearned to be together every minute of every day.

He proposed to Luna a year after meeting her and they were married a year after that. Then Barney came along and their little unit was complete.

Parker soon relaxed into the calmer and less excitable state of marital contentment and fatherhood. Luna put time and effort into creating their comfortable and beautiful home and began to build a presence for herself online as a sort of fashion consultant. Later to be known as a successful influencer.

Parker was focused and ambitious, putting maximum effort into his career, which increasingly meant nights away from home.

As time went on, he began to notice a change in Luna's

behaviour. Firstly, there was the drinking. A glass or two of wine at night turned into the best part of a bottle and, most nights, that was before Parker got home from work.

Marie had let slip one weekend that Luna had drunk heavily in her teens, getting into trouble at school and at home. 'Thanks to their terrible parenting,' Luna had said bitterly when they'd retired to their room. 'The things I had to put up with...'

Parker knew better than to ask for more details. He'd done so once before and Luna had clammed up, gone quiet on him for hours. 'I don't want to talk about it,' she'd said, tears in her eyes. 'I probably never will.' That had been good enough for Parker. He had a problematic relationship with his own father he didn't relish thinking about, never mind talking about.

Parker learned not to press Luna's jealousy buttons and Luna learned to control her drinking. At least when he was home. As he rose up the ranks of the company from Senior Sales Executive to Assistant Regional Sales Manager, Luna's jealousy grew steadily worse.

His new positions came with more travelling and nights away from home. Every trip was preceded by a frosty reception each day he got in from work. Then there was the endless questioning, which both irritated and exhausted him.

What's your room number? How can I reach you in an emergency? Can we FaceTime from your room every night before you go to sleep?

He loved her, but she was crazy. And it was worrying.

But it was just the start of what was to come.

EIGHTEEN

NICOLA

I've put everything back into the black bin bag except for the silk scarf. That, I've wrapped in the two plastic bags again and stuffed at the bottom of my handbag.

I'm not sure how long I've been sitting here, googling and reading press articles about the disappearance and murder of local young mother Sarah Grayson, five weeks ago, but when I look out of the window, I see it's still dark outside. A glance at my watch tells me it's five-thirty in the morning.

It's clear from press photos that the scarf I've found at Parker's house is a match for the one the police have been searching for. Sarah's decomposing body was found and the post-mortem showed the cause of death as strangulation. She was fully clothed and her handbag, containing credit cards, cash and her ID, was next to her. The only thing missing: the accessory that police have been combing the city for since discovering her body. The silk scarf she'd knotted stylishly around her neck before heading out for the evening.

I feel physically sick with fatigue and fear, knowing that what I've found is not just one of Luna's innocent unwanted possessions. There must be hundreds... thousands of these scarves throughout the country but there's only one that poor Sarah's mother gave to her as a gift. Have I found that gift, carefully wrapped up and concealed at the bottom of a bin liner destined for the wheelie bin? The hard, sour knot lodged in my throat gives away my gut feeling, however hard I try to shake it off.

I don't feel I can tell anyone about my discovery yet. Not even Cal. He's the most strait-laced person I know. I swear, if I committed a terrible crime he'd feel a duty to hand me in. It's too early to involve anyone else. The fact that Parker has already been questioned about his car could spark accelerated police interest. They'd then have two reasons to look at him much closer.

Once that happens, the police can't just be called off. They'll be like terriers going after a scent and if the press get wind of it... dear God. No. I have a parental duty to my son to find out the truth before I inadvertently start something that could prove very difficult to stop. The media is full of stories about people who, despite being proved innocent, have nonetheless had their lives ruined.

I won't let that happen to my boy while he lies fighting for his life in a hospital bed. It's true I find it difficult to see much wrong in my son, but Cal is mistaken when he says I believe him to be an angel. I know Parker has a temper, I know he likes his own way. But I know he's far from being a killer.

What if Parker knows nothing about it and Luna is the one who knows the truth?

Think, think, think.

I cover my face with my hands. Oh God, what a terrible, terrible mess... in the middle of a terrible, terrible situation.

Last time I spoke to my son, he could barely get the words out, telling me to stay away from the house. Why did he warn me off? Was it because it was up for sale, or because of something far more sinister?

His request to chat with me before they left for the dinner dance rings in my ears. Did he want to get something off his mind? Or had he discovered that Luna had a secret? Over the years, Parker has made one or two remarks about her being jealous and possessive. He's always clammed up when I question him about it, but it's obviously a feature of her personality he's struggled with. And those miniatures in her bedside drawer, the lingering smell of alcohol on her breath... has Luna got a drink problem he's never told me about? It's the sort of thing that will wear you down in a marriage, the sort of thing you'd probably want to keep to yourself.

A noise at the living room door makes me turn. Cal stands there in his dressing gown, his face haggard and drawn. 'Come to bed, love,' he says. 'Just for an hour or two. You must be exhausted.'

I swallow down my worries and shake my head. 'I can't sleep, Cal. Go back to bed and get some rest. I'll doze on the sofa and give Barney his breakfast when he comes downstairs.' I hesitate. 'I want to get back to the hospital for about eight o'clock. As early as I can. Will you watch Barney? I know you haven't seen Parker yet, but I need to go and see him again. Sorry, I—'

Cal holds his hands up. 'Don't worry, I understand. You and him, you've always had a special bond.' He turns to leave before saying, 'Anything you need, just come and wake me up, OK?'

I nod and listen to his bare feet padding back upstairs.

You and him, you've always had a special bond.

It's true. We have. And that's why I'm currently wrestling with the plethora of emotions threatening to choke me.

'Nicola. Nicola, wake up!'

My eyes spring open and I sit up on the sofa in a rush of

panic, my heart banging in my chest. I was dreaming, in a deep sleep...

Cal stands over me, his hand on my shoulder, shaking firmly.

'The hospital have just called, love.'

'What's wrong... what time is it?'

'It's eight-thirty.'

'Oh no! I need to go to – where's Barney?'

'Barney's fine. He's on his Nintendo in his bedroom. Listen to me, Nicola.' He perches on the seat next to me, his features pinched with concern. 'It's Parker. They say he's taken a turn for the worse.'

'What?' I stand up and feel instantly dizzy. My hand clamps over my mouth. 'What's happened?'

Cal pulls me gently back down to sitting.

'That operation he had, there's been some kind of adverse reaction. He's in a bad way and if things don't improve they're going to put him into an induced coma. They said they'll call us as soon as—'

I jump up again. 'I'm going in.'

'I don't think there's any point, Nicola. You won't be able to see him and—'

'I don't care. I'm going in and I'm going to try my darndest to see him before they put him under.'

Cal's pale cheeks ignite. 'You're being illogical!'

'I don't care!' I yell and then soften when I see the shock on his face. 'You don't understand. I can't explain right now, but I must see him. It's important I speak to Parker.'

NINETEEN

When Cal realises he isn't going to change my mind about going to the hospital, he insists I take a cab.

'You've had virtually no sleep. I don't want another medical emergency on my hands. So if you're going, then you have to take a cab.' I recognise his 'no room for compromise' voice and I book an Uber before running upstairs to see Barney.

He puts down his game as soon as I enter his bedroom.

'What time are Mum and Dad coming to pick me up?' he says, his face pale and questioning. I feel bad. He senses something is wrong, but the adults aren't telling him anything.

I walk over to the bed and sit at the edge. 'I know things seem a little strange here, Barney, and I'm so sorry about that. Thing is, Gramps and I must sort a few things out and get some information together before we can speak to you about what's happening. Do you understand?'

'Not really,' he says forlornly. 'Is it about the police coming in the night?'

'It's partly to do with that, yes.' I sigh. This is hard. So hard. 'You're a big lad now and I promise we will speak to you very soon.'

'Okaay.' His voice is flat and he reaches for his console again.

'I've just got to pop out for a while and when I get back we can have a chat. I won't be too long.'

The game has already pulled him back in. I kiss him on the head and he mumbles a distracted goodbye.

The cab drops me off right at the main entrance and I feel glad I listened to Cal. At least I haven't got to deal with parking and walking before I can get near the place.

I rush straight to the lifts and take the route to the critical care unit. The walk through the echoing corridors seems longer than ever although there are a few more people about – mainly staff – who pass me with a nod of acknowledgement and a smile.

At the critical care reception there's a different person on duty. I give her Parker's name and she asks for mine. 'He's taken a turn for the worse apparently and they might have to put him in a coma. Thing is, I must see him before that happens. It's imperative I speak to my son.'

She asks my name and taps on a keyboard before looking up at me. 'I can get a doctor to come and speak to you, Mrs Vance. If you'd like to take a—'

'No! I don't want to take a seat.' Then something occurs to me. 'Parker isn't... I mean, he's not—' She seems to move out of focus and I hold on to the counter. 'Nothing's happened to him, has it?'

'I'll get someone to speak to you as soon as possible,' she reiterates. 'Are you feeling OK? There's a water station over by the entrance there, if you'd like a—'

'I don't want any bloody water, I just want to see my son!' I slap my hand down on the curved reception desk and she visibly jumps.

'Madam, please do not raise your voice. I've told you I will get a doctor as soon as I can.'

Several staff and visitors turn to stare at me and the raw fury and terror melts away in an instant. Overnight, I've turned into one of those universally despised people who abuse NHS staff. My eyes prickle in shame and helplessness. 'I'm sorry,' I say quietly. 'This is not like me at all. I didn't mean to yell at you.'

'Apology accepted,' she says magnanimously. 'Someone will be through to see you shortly, Mrs Vance.'

Mortified, I sit back down and look at my hands so I don't have to see the expressions of disapproval on the faces of the other people waiting here.

I just need five minutes with Parker. Just five minutes so he can dispel any notion of this scarf being a damning piece of evidence. Five minutes where I can tell him I love him and that everything is going to be fine, that we're looking after Barney and that if he and Luna are splitting up then he can come home for however long he needs to get back on his feet.

It's twenty minutes before the doctor appears in front of me. It's the same guy I saw last time and I feel grateful I haven't fallen asleep again.

I stand up. 'How is my son? Someone rang and said he's taken a turn for the worse?'

The doctor nods. 'Your son suffered some complications earlier this morning and it looks like we might have to operate again on the internal gastric bleed.'

'Is it serious? Is he unconscious?'

'Potentially it could be very serious, but we're hoping to prevent the worst of it by operating. Parker is exhausted, but he is awake. He's heavily medicated and keeps slipping in and out of sleep.'

'Can I see him?'

'I really don't think that's a good idea at this stage, Mrs—'

'Please, doctor. I beg you... just for five minutes. I must speak to him about something incredibly important. I wouldn't ask unless it was so crucial.'

He looks at me and twists his mouth to the side as he considers my request. 'Very well. But five minutes only.'

'Thank you! Thank you so much.'

'He must conserve his strength and energy, so please, no excitement or distressing conversations.'

'I promise,' I say, thinking about the unpleasant subject matter I have to tackle with him. But it's not like I have a choice.

The doctor takes me into the critical care ward and leaves me at Parker's bedside. I swallow down my shock and distress when I see his face looks even more swollen and discoloured than a few hours ago when I saw him last.

His eyes flicker open when I take his hand and press my face close to his. 'It's me, son. Mum. I'm here for you, Parker. I love you so much.'

He squeezes my hand and his bloodshot eyes open wider.

I glance around to make sure nobody is near. 'I went to the house earlier,' I whisper in his ear. 'I – I have to ask you something really important and you have to tell me the truth.' I feel a sense of time running out. Any minute now, a nurse will appear from nowhere and tell me my time is up.

Parker opens his eyes again and stares at me.

'I found a scarf. A woman's scarf by the bins.' The cardiac monitor at the side of the bed starts to beep faster. He doesn't blink, he doesn't say anything. He just stares at me. 'I have it here.' I glance around to make sure the coast is clear and then pull the scarf out of my handbag and unwrap it quickly. I hold it in front of him, standing at an angle so nobody could see it if they walk up behind me. 'Have I got need to worry, Parker? Does this belong to Luna?'

The cardiac monitor beeping speeds up again. Parker's eyes

are wide and frantic. He gasps, 'Get rid of it... you can't keep that...'

I'm spooked. 'Why? Who does it belong to?' A sweet, floral perfume wafts up and I swallow down the sickly taste in my mouth. 'Parker, why? Why can't I keep it? Tell me now... you must tell me!'

I can hear his breathing coming in small raspy bites now as he tries to turn his face away. 'Get rid of it now,' he manages to croak, squeezing his eyes closed. 'Get... rid... of it!'

'Parker, is this the scarf the police are looking for? That belongs to Sarah Grayson?'

The beeping on the cardiac monitor reaches a new level. Parker tries to thrash his head from side to side, but his current incapacity means the movements are small.

A cold, stark fear grips my throat as my worst fears start to take shape. I stuff the scarf back into its bag.

Suddenly I'm aware of movement around me. A nurse rushes up, the one who brought me to see Parker the first time, closely followed by another.

'What happened? His heart rate is through the roof,' the first one says, moving urgently to the beeping cardiac monitor. She looks at me. 'This is just what we're trying to avoid. He needs to rest.'

'He... the machine just started beeping,' I say hopelessly. 'He got a bit upset.'

Parker looks at me then, his eyes red-rimmed and raw. He opens his mouth and I press my ear closer.

'L... Luna... she—'

'Luna what? Speak up, Parker. Tell me.'

'OK, you need to leave him now, Mrs Vance,' the nurse interrupts again but I ignore her.

'Does Luna know about this, Parker?'

'She... she'll try to ruin me. She's the one who—'

He falters and starts to cough.

'You'll have to go now,' the second nurse says firmly. 'We need to stabilise him before the doctor can see him again.'

More medical staff arrive and I'm ushered away. I turn to take one last look at my son's bruised and battered face. His eyes are open and looking at me pleadingly. What is he trying to tell me? That Luna knows about the scarf?

She'll try to ruin me.

I'm not going to sit back and do nothing when my son has basically signalled she knows something. Whatever it takes, I need to speak to her today.

Shame mists my eyes as I walk towards the main reception of the critical care unit. The last thing I wanted was to cause a setback in Parker's recovery, but what could I do? I had to ask him while he's still able to speak to me.

Get rid of it, now, he'd said. *Get... rid... of it!*

Why would he say that? And why would he look so panicked?

There can only be one reason: my worst fears must be true. And yet... I refuse to believe Parker could be involved in such a heinous crime.

As I approach the exit doors, I notice a large rubbish bin to my right. It's already quite full with discarded coffee cups, sweet and crisp wrappers. I glance over my shoulder and see the only people heading for the exit are some way behind me.

Before I can overthink it, I snatch the wrapped scarf out of my handbag and push it down under a few wrappers.

Then I stride out of the hospital, promising myself to put it completely out of my mind.

TWENTY

LUNA

Parker's new assistant was called Shannon O'Rourke. She was twenty-four years old, single and had taken advantage of the company's relocation scheme to travel from her home in Galway, Ireland, on a two-year placement.

'She's confident for her age but she has a lot to learn,' Parker told Luna over dinner, in answer to her many questions one night. 'As you know, I really liked Moira. It's a shame she had to retire.'

'What does she look like, this Shannon?' Luna immediately asked.

'What? Oh you know, just your regular Gen-Z kid. Wild hair, too much make-up,' he said dismissively. She watched as Parker pushed a potato around the plate with his fork. 'Thinks the world owes her a living.'

Parker was thirty-one and ambitious. He wouldn't have much patience with a young person who didn't want to work their socks off, Luna thought, reassured.

A month later, a two-day conference was held at Center

Parcs Sherwood Forest and Luna met her for the first time there at a family fun day organised by Parker's company. Barney was still very young but he'd loved every minute. While the employees spent the mornings taking part in motivational climbing activities and a 'conquering the forest' team-building experience, their families were able to use the facilities, including the swimming dome where there were activities for kids from babies up to bored teens. In the afternoon, the employees were free to join their families, and everyone, including top management, came together for the black-tie evening dinner where they'd provided entertainment, and everything, including the champagne, was on the house.

Luna had been gradually increasing in her confidence to be around other people. There were a small group of mums with kids a similar age to Barney who she'd met before and who she gravitated towards. She sat at the edge of the group listening more than contributing but nobody seemed to mind and it was a relaxed environment. Just what she needed.

On the first morning, a couple of hours in, the women sat by the pool area with coffee and cakes, watching the Center Parcs staff entertain the children.

'Have you seen the hot new addition to their raft of assistants?' one woman said, rolling her eyes. 'My hubby says they've all been fighting over who'll get her. I told him if he's that desperate, just leave me and the kids in the house and take off with her.'

Another woman laughed. 'That would never happen, he's crazy about you, Petra.'

'I saw her the other day.' Another woman speaks. 'She's really pretty. Masses of blonde curls and a perfect size ten. Curvy, young. Yuk. Pass the sick bucket.'

The women laughed.

Luna put down her cup. 'Parker has a new assistant,' she said carefully. 'Her name is Shannon.'

The banter and sniggering stopped and an uneasy silence fell over the group.

'That's... the one I'm talking about,' the woman called Petra said, watching Luna's face. 'We're exaggerating though. Joking about the fighting-over-her bit. I'm sure Parker didn't get a say in it.'

She caught one or two women glancing at each other, shifting in their seats.

'Speak of the devil and she will appear,' someone muttered.

Luna looked up and saw a young woman in micro-shorts and Converse bounce into the tropical dome. Luna followed endless brown legs up to a toned stomach and a fitness crop top. Blonde curls were tied up on top of her head, framing soft, pretty features and a dazzling smile.

'Hi, ladies,' she said brightly in a soft West of Ireland accent. 'I wanted to come and say hi; I'm Shannon O'Rourke, a new sales team assistant.'

'So lovely to meet you, Shannon,' Petra said, all smiles. 'How gorgeous are you!'

'Ahh, stop that now!' She blushed, waving Petra's compliment away.

'Only speaking the truth. Shannon, this is Luna Vance, Parker's wife.'

'It's lovely to meet you, Luna.' She held out a small hand with a natural manicure. Up close, Luna noted her skin was smooth and flawless and she wore barely any make-up at all.

Luna took her hand and stretched her mouth into the semblance of a smile. 'Nice to meet you, Shannon. Parker's told me all about you.'

She stared at the younger woman and kept hold of her hand. Shannon's smile faded as she started to pull away, but Luna held on.

One of the other women coughed and Luna blinked, letting go of Shannon's hand.

'Excuse me,' Luna said tightly, standing up. 'I need the bathroom. Can someone just keep an eye on Barney for me?'

'Sure,' Petra said brightly. 'Take as long as you like.'

Luna walked quickly across the floor of the dome, heading for the loo. Her heart thumped against her chest as something powerful rose up inside her, threatening to blow her head clean off.

Just your regular Gen-Z kid. Wild hair, too much make-up...

She could kill him. The liar.

Inside the bathroom, she checked the cubicles were empty before kicking one open with all the force she could muster. Again and again, she battered the door until the bottom hinge bust and it just hung there, bringing her to her senses.

She ran the cold tap and splashed some water on her face. She couldn't show those bitches out there she was bothered by what had been said.

Walking back across the pool area, Luna saw the women nudge each other and sit up a bit straighter. Shannon had gone now but they'd obviously been gossiping about her; about the fact her husband had netted himself the new hot assistant. She had no option but to calm down and go back there to wait for Barney.

Still, one thing was certain: she'd have this out with Parker later when he returned. One way or another, she'd make sure they weren't working together for much longer.

TWENTY-ONE

NICOLA

Feeling a little dazed after tossing away the scarf, I make my way down to the nurses' station. I'm not a bad person, but I've potentially just done a very bad – and possibly illegal – thing.

My shoes clip on the hard floor, the fluorescent lighting takes me back to long hours spent here sitting in a stark, large space with a drip tube in my arm, amongst other cancer patients.

We were all different people with varied occupations and lives. The one thing that bound us together, the crucial similarity, was that every single one of us wanted to live. We all wanted it above anything else. If there's one thing chronic disease teaches you, it's that life is precious.

Sarah Grayson's life was precious to her. It was also precious to her mother and to her small daughter.

It's easy to sit in moral judgement about the right and wrong thing to do; until you're torn between being a good mother and a responsible citizen. But now I can't help but think: what right did I have to destroy possible evidence that the police may be looking for? Evidence that could help to solve the mystery of who took the life of that poor young woman?

The nurses' station is up ahead and I'm hoping to see the ward manager who'd enquired about Luna's condition for me earlier. As I approach, I see her behind the counter. I hover nearby and, after a few moments, she looks up from signing some paperwork.

'Everything OK?' A small frown plays between her eyes.

'I need your help.' The words burst from my mouth before I can stop them. 'I'm so sorry to have to ask, but could you possibly call the trauma ward and ask if I can have five minutes with my daughter-in-law? Luna Vance.'

She pulls her mouth wide at the sides. 'I don't think I can—'

'Please!' I lean across the desk. 'I'm begging you. I wouldn't ask if... it's literally life or death. I have to see her, to ask her about something that might be life-changing.'

She looks at me but doesn't say anything. Perhaps she thinks I'm a little unstable.

'It won't take more than five minutes. I beg you.' I keep my voice calm and level. 'If I could only explain, you'd understand and—'

'OK, OK.' She puts her hands in the air. 'I'll call the ward manager there but I can't make any promises.'

'I understand. Thank you.' Then I remember something. 'Could you possibly check if Luna's parents are with her? I wouldn't want to intrude if they are.'

'I thought you said it was urgent?' She turns back to her paperwork, freezing me out.

She's fearsome and acts put out, but I can sense underneath she does care about her patients and their families.

I take a few steps to back off a touch. The last thing I want to do is ruffle her feathers any more than I am doing already.

'Sorry. I know I'm not making any sense. The thing is... I need to speak to her about something confidential.' She looks up. 'Something she won't want her parents to know about.'

I take a breath when she reaches for the phone. She turns

her back on me and speaks in low tones so I can't discern anything apart from the odd word.

'... a few minutes... important... favour.'

I force myself to breathe as the seconds pass and feel like full minutes.

She puts down the phone and turns to me, her face unreadable. 'I got you five minutes. Her parents are due to visit this afternoon,' she says. 'I called in a favour out of visiting hours, so don't overstay your welcome.'

'I won't,' I say. 'You don't know what this means. Thank you so much.'

Five minutes later I'm heading down a corridor to the double doors that will take me to Luna. A short walk to the truth I must establish but that I'm terrified to hear.

I buzz at the double doors of the assessment unit, say my name and that the ward manager in the critical care unit has sent me. The doors buzz open and I walk in.

This is a very different environment from critical care. For one thing, there's no reception to speak of, just a small nurses' station.

'Mrs Vance?' A short nurse with dark hair and a regretful expression approaches me. 'I've spoken to Luna and she says she's not really feeling up to having a visitor at the moment.'

'Oh! I... I'll literally just be a couple of minutes. There's something extremely important I need to speak to her about and then I'll be gone.'

The nurse bites her lip. 'Thing is, it's important she rests. She's taken medication and —'

'I totally get it. My son, Luna's husband, is in critical care so I do understand. But we're looking after Luna's son, Barney, and I really need to speak to her.'

'Oh, I see. OK, well...' She looks around but there's no other member of staff close by. 'Just a few minutes then.'

'Thank you,' I say.

I follow her to a regular ward, patients either side. Some are sitting up, some watching us with interest. They all look ill with their tubes and machines, but none look like Parker. None look in that terrible liminal state between life and death.

Luna is lying in a bed towards the end of the ward. She's pale and bruised but, compared to Parker, she's looking good. When she sees me, her nostrils flare.

'I told them I don't feel up to...' Her voice fades out and I can't quite hear.

The nurse says something to her and Luna nods curtly.

'I'll leave you for five minutes, but no more,' she says, walking past me.

'Hello, Luna,' I say, approaching her bed. 'How are you feeling?'

'I'm not feeling well at all, Nicola. I don't really feel up to talking.'

'What happened, Luna? The accident... how did it—'

'I fell asleep in the car. I don't remember any of it,' she says quickly and I'm not convinced. 'I can't talk about it now. The nurse says there's something you need to tell me about Barney.'

I nod and move closer still. 'I'll tell you about Barney in a moment, but first there's something else I need your help with.'

She stares at me but doesn't say anything.

'Thing is... I went to your house.'

'What?'

'I went to your house. I had Parker's keys to get inside.' I hold up a hand as her expression darkens. 'I had to get some things for Barney. But I was shocked to see the house is up for sale.'

'Parker was going to tell you.'

'Oh, really? When was he planning to do that? I checked on Rightmove and it's been up for sale for two weeks.'

She shrugs. 'It was Parker's decision. My parents knew from the off but...'

'But?'

'He was stalling because he said you'd cause a fuss.'

My throat burns with both the injustice, and the inherent truth of it.

She closes down again. Turning from me slightly and staring at the wall.

'But the sale board isn't why I came here. I wondered if... you threw away a scarf recently?'

'A scarf?' she says faintly.

'Yes. I found a rubbish bag behind the bins. It was full of your things and at the bottom, there was a black-and-gold scarf wrapped in a bag. It looked just like this one.'

I hold up my phone where I've already saved a photograph from one of the many articles about the police campaign to find the missing piece of evidence.

Luna's reactions play out as if in slow motion when she sees the image. I watch as her hand flutters to her mouth, her eyes widen, her perfectly groomed eyebrows pull together at the top of her nose.

After a few moments, I ask again, 'Does this scarf belong to you?'

Her face is white. Paler than when I arrived. She whispers, 'Where is it? The scarf?'

'I have it. Is it yours, Luna?'

'You had no right to enter our home without permission. You—'

'Only the police are looking for a scarf just like this. They've been searching for it for weeks,' I say carefully. 'It looks identical to the one that belonged to Sarah Grayson. The girl who was murdered.'

'I've never seen it before,' she says, her expression blank again. 'Maybe it's Parker you should be talking to. He's the one who's already been questioned by the police regarding that case.'

'Well, he wasn't questioned as such. It was a routine enquiry, as you well know.'

She looks at the picture again. 'Whatever. If you've found a scarf, it's got nothing to do with me.'

'Yet it was in a bag full of stuff that belonged to you. A bag that had been put out with the rubbish.'

I see her hand slide to the side of her bed where her fingers deftly press a button.

'I'd like you to leave now, Nicola. Speak to Parker... or go to the police if you're convinced of what you've found. That's my advice.'

I push my phone into my handbag. 'That might be difficult. Parker is in a very bad way. Far worse than yourself, but I'm guessing you know that. The last thing he needs is the police hassling him about this when he's trying to recover.'

I turn and see a nurse walking towards us.

'Oh, I also came to reassure you that Barney is fine. I've got about a week's worth of clothes for him from the house. We're going to speak to him later about what's happened, but —'

'My parents will be picking Barney up when they've visited this afternoon. They're staying in a local B&B. Say nothing to Barney, they'll explain everything to him.'

'What about Barney's school?' My prickliness wilts instantly as she skilfully reminds me of her power. 'Isn't it best to keep his routine as normal as possible under the circumstances?'

'My parents are arranging for me to move to a private hospital near Helmsley,' she says smoothly. 'If not today then definitely on Monday. They're going to apply for a temporary placement at an independent school up there. I want Barney close to me, not down here.'

Every inch of my body feels rigid. The house is up for sale; her and Parker's relationship is in trouble. The Barton-Jameses are taking our grandson away and, on top of everything, Luna seems to be nervously batting all questions about the scarf back to Parker, who can't currently defend himself.

'Everything OK here?' The nurse looks from Luna to me.

'I'm very tired,' Luna says. 'Nicola is just leaving.'

The nurse fusses around her, adjusting her pillows and smoothing her bedding. She picks up the clipboard on the end of the metal-framed bed and checks it.

As I walk towards the exit, I realise Luna has never once asked me how Parker is.

Something is off. I know it. I should never have disposed of the scarf. It might well have nothing at all to do with Parker but everything to do with her.

I double back on myself and walk quickly to the entrance to critical care. I wait until I can see there's nobody close by and approach the bin with a handful of tissues. I move next to the bin and push the tissues into it, at the same time delving down the side and plucking out the bag containing the scarf.

As I push it back into my handbag and walk away, I honestly don't know if I'm doing the right thing. I could swear Luna recognised the scarf when I showed her the picture. That, and the fact she seemed to be trying to implicate Parker in some way.

I came away with the impression it would suit Luna just fine if the scarf didn't exist and that's why I decided to get it back.

TWENTY-TWO

When I leave the critical care unit for the second time, I order an Uber. Then I get a text from Cal.

Barney woke up asking questions. Think we should all chat when you get back.

Of course we need to sit Barney down and talk to him. But there's something else taking up space in my head and burning a hole in the bottom of my bag. *The evidence.* The scarf that might belong to a murder victim... that the police have been searching for these past weeks. That, and the fact my son was questioned about his car.

I rattle off a quick reply to Cal.

Agreed. Just waiting for cab, should be back by 9:30.

I sit in the hospital foyer and wait for the Uber. It's already busy with patients checking in to the main desk and visitors asking for directions. Costa is now open and most tables are taken from what I can see. But I don't want a coffee. My mind is too full of what I should do next. Of how I'm going to tell Cal we have another problem – a very big problem.

I stare at the glass sliding doors: *open, close, open, close.* Never staying still for more than a few moments.

The scarf could be nothing. It could be that Luna just didn't want it.

But she said she'd never seen it before.

If Luna didn't put it at the bottom of a rubbish bag... then who did?

Parker. Parker may have hidden it because it's the evidence that ties him to something terrible.

I cover my face with my hands. How can I even think such things about my own son? Parker is a good man. He loves his family, he works hard. He's our only son and although we don't see much of him these days, I know he'd be there in an instant if we needed him.

But Parker is troubled. His marriage is falling apart and they're selling the house. He wanted to speak to you about something important...

My hands fall away and I see an Uber is outside. I grab my handbag and head for the exit.

The ride home is smooth and there are no delays on the roads. Cal meets me at the front door.

'I've got something to tell you,' I say. He takes my coat as I shrug it off and reaches for my bag but I hug it closer. 'Let's speak to Barney first.'

Cal frowns. 'Everything OK? How are they?'

I force myself to focus on what he's saying.

'Parker's bad, Luna is pretty much herself apart from physical injuries.' The gold and black pattern of the scarf is imprinted in my mind's eye, over-shadowing everything else. 'But let's get this over with first, Cal. Let's speak to Barney.'

He nods. 'Fine. He's in the lounge watching TV.'

We walk in there together. 'Morning, sunshine.' I kiss Barney on top of his head. 'How are you?'

He looks up, instantly suspicious when Cal turns off the television.

'We need a little chat with you, Barney.' I sit next to him on the sofa and Cal sits in the armchair opposite.

'Is it about Mum and Dad?'

'It is, love, yes.'

Panic shadows his face. 'When are they coming to pick me up?'

I lay a hand on his arm to calm him and Cal clears his throat.

'Remember when the police came to the door in the middle of the night?' I say and Barney nods. 'Well, they came to tell us that your mum and dad were involved in a car accident when they left the hotel.'

'But they're both OK, lad,' Cal says quickly. 'They're in hospital and getting really good treatment from the doctors and nurses.'

'Are they coming home today?' Barney says, his bottom lip trembling.

I want to scoop him up in my arms and tell him not to worry and that everything is going to be fine, but more than that, I want to be as truthful and as honest as I can be.

'No, they'll have to stay in hospital a little while longer,' I say gently. 'Your mum has some broken bones that need to be mended and your dad...' My voice wobbles and I'm grateful to Cal when he continues.

'Your dad is a bit more poorly than your mum. He sends all his love to you, but he's had to have an operation.'

'Why?' Barney frowns.

'Well, your dad was driving,' Cal explains. 'So he came off a bit worse. When you take a big hard blow here—' Cal pats his abdomen '—it can cause bleeding inside. That's what happened to your dad and they've operated to put it right.'

'The doctors have got to do lots of other checks and it might be he has to have another operation. That's why he can't come home yet,' I say, recalling what I've been told at the hospital.

I can't get Parker's bruised and battered face out of my head. The thoughts about what's in my bag and how it might have the power to destroy my son. Destroy all our lives. Maybe I should have left it in that bin. So many emotions are at play, I can't think straight anymore.

'Can I go and see them?' Barney's eyes are shining with tears and I slide my arm around his narrow shoulders.

'Of course you can,' I say. 'Just as soon as the doctors say it's OK.'

'Alright, champ?' Cal ruffles his hair and Barney gives a little nod.

'Where will I go?' Barney asks. 'If Mum and Dad are in hospital?'

'That's all being sorted out now. Your grandma and grandad are down from Yorkshire and it'll be up to your mum where you go.' I give Cal a meaningful glance. He doesn't know about my exchange with Luna. He doesn't know a lot of things yet. 'There's no need to worry yourself about all that because, for the time being, you're staying here with us.'

'Good, because until Mum and Dad come home, I want to stay here with you and Gramps,' Barney says emphatically.

TWENTY-THREE

PARKER

THREE YEARS EARLIER

Parker had put it off as long as he possibly could. But the time had come when he had no choice but to tell Luna he must attend a national sales conference in York just three weeks before Christmas.

'It's not something I can just opt out of,' he told her when he explained the details. 'I hate the thought of leaving you and Barney so close to Christmas, but it's crucial I attend.'

Luna's reaction was unusually calm. She didn't rant and rave as he'd expected. She didn't say much apart from, 'Will your new assistant be going?'

His heart sank. They'd had a god-awful argument when she'd briefly met Shannon at the Center Parcs meeting a month ago. To put it mildly, she was *not* impressed. She'd had too much wine and had turned nasty. She'd accused him of having a torrid affair and disrespecting her. She'd demanded he fire Shannon or ask for her to be moved to another team.

He'd tried to explain he couldn't do that because it would cause eyebrows to be raised by senior management and bring him the wrong sort of attention. She'd clammed up after muttering tightly, 'We'll see.'

It was anyone's guess what she meant; he didn't hang around to ask. Mercifully she hadn't mentioned Shannon since then, but now he'd had no choice but to raise the subject of him having a few nights away.

'It's a whole company thing,' he said carefully. 'Everyone is expected to attend.'

She looked annoyed, sniffed and made some excuse about making dinner. He couldn't believe his luck; maybe he should have taken this forceful attitude a long time ago instead of treading on eggshells every time he had something unpalatable to tell her.

'Which hotel will you be staying in when you go to York?' Luna asked when they sat down to dinner.

'The conference is at The Grand in the centre of York, so I'm guessing it'll be there.' He poured them each a small glass of chilled white Rioja. 'Be nice to enjoy a bit of luxury for a change and the hotel is really close to the centre.'

'Why does that matter? Being close to the centre, I mean?'

'Well, when we're not stuck in boring sales talks, we'll get some downtime. There's so much to do in York, as you know.'

Luna brightened a little and took a big gulp of her wine. 'Here's an idea. Why don't I drop Barney off at my parents' and come and stay with you at The Grand? You can attend your conference and we can enjoy York together in your "down-time"... what do you think?'

Parker laughed, the fresh citrus flavours of the wine popping pleasantly on his tongue. 'Much as I'd love that, it's not going to work!'

Her smile dissolved. 'Why not?'

'It's a national sales conference, honey. There are people coming over from all over the UK and even from Europe.'

'You said you'd have plenty of downtime.'

'Yes, but we're expected to socialise and network in between the formal sessions. I'm not just free to do my own thing.'

He watched as Luna drained her glass before giving him a hard stare. 'Are there going to be women at this conference?'

Before he could stop himself, he laughed again at her ludicrous question. 'That's a yes. Some of our best sales people are women.'

'So you'll be taking *them* out to the pubs and clubs?' She refilled her glass.

'Not me personally. We'll be networking, talking shop.' He glanced at his own glass, still over half full. 'That's just how it works, Luna. If I want to make it into top management, I must be seen to be doing what's expected. I have to play the game.'

'That's an interesting choice of words,' Luna said quietly. '*Play the game*. As long as that doesn't include *playing away*.'

Parker put down his cutlery.

'Hey, what's brought this on? You know I'm sometimes expected to spend time away from home.'

'But not for three days before! You're taking me for an idiot!' She slammed the thin-stemmed glass down so hard, it broke in her hand. Parker jumped up from his seat as drops of blood spilled from Luna's fingers.

'Christ! What's got into you?' He rushed for a cloth to wrap around her hand.

Later, Luna apologised. Cried into his chest as he held her.

'I love you so much, Parker. I don't know what Barney and I would do without you.'

'But you'll never be without me. I love you both more than life. You know that, right?' He lifted her chin gently so she was forced to look at him.

She nodded morosely. 'I just... I know what some women can be like. Single, ambitious, driven to sleep their way to the top if they have to.'

'God, Luna! That's a bit of a harsh critique. The women I

work with are nothing like that. And anyway—' he kissed her nose '—I have the best woman in the world at home, so why would I even notice them?'

She smiled and kissed him softly on the lips.

Fool that he was, he thought that was the end of it.

It seemed as if the York trip was cursed from the beginning.

Firstly, the admin and hospitality team totally screwed up because they managed to somehow cancel Shannon's room. Fortunately, two of Parker's younger guys, both sales execs trying to make an impression, offered to share a room.

Then, on the second morning, Parker was confronted by a crying Shannon at breakfast.

'Hey, sit down. What's wrong?' He was alarmed to see her hair mussed and dark, smudged eyes when she usually looked so immaculate.

'Reception put a call through in the early hours.' She choked back tears, her face bloated. 'It was a nurse ringing to tell me my father had suffered a major heart attack and I should go back home as it might be my last chance to see him.'

'Oh Jeez, I'm so sorry, Shannon.' Parker touched her arm supportively. 'We can sort your travel home out, no problem. Your dad sounds in a bad way and—'

'That's just it, Parker,' she cried. 'My dad hasn't had a heart attack!'

Parker noted her scowling face, the tight line of her mouth. She didn't look relieved. 'Oh! Well, that's great news... isn't it?'

'It was a hoax. Whoever rang, the woman, she wasn't a nurse from the hospital at all.' She dabbed her eyes with a tissue.

'What?'

'Soon as the call ended I rang my ma, woke her up. She

didn't know what the heck I was talking about. I was near-hysterical so she put my dad on the phone. He'd been asleep right next to her and he's fine.'

'Shit! I mean, thank God he's OK but what the hell?'

'Who'd do that, Parker? Who'd do such a cruel thing, and why me?' She sniffed.

The back of Parker's neck prickled. 'I can't imagine, Shannon. Really, I can't. It's a terrible thing to do to someone.'

'Thing is, though, I can't stay here. Not now. What's happened, it's frightened me. I just need to see my parents with my own eyes, make sure they're OK, you know?'

'Course, course. I totally understand,' Parker said, silently running through all the extra stuff he'd need to sort out for his sales talk this morning if Shannon left now. 'You get yourself off, take some time with your family. I'm so sorry you had to go through this.'

She sniffed and nodded. 'Thanks for understanding, Parker. I just... knowing there's a psycho out there who's targeted me for no reason, I'm a nervous wreck.'

'Don't think about that. Just focus on getting home.'

When Shannon left the breakfast room to pack her suitcase, Parker pushed away his full English breakfast. For some reason he didn't feel remotely hungry now.

TWENTY-FOUR

NICOLA

Barney seems as OK as he can be after our chat. He asks if he can have some time on his Nintendo Switch, which Luna has long dictated is not allowed in the morning.

I agree immediately much to Cal's surprise. 'It'll help him process what's happened and it'll give us time to sit and have a chat.'

Cal takes Barney upstairs while I make tea and force half a slice of buttered toast down me. I have to keep going. Somehow, I must find the strength to get everything sorted out.

When Cal comes back down, he says, 'He's bright as a button, that lad. He's just asked me how the accident happened and why they didn't stay at the hotel. He said, "Did Mum and Dad have another argument?"'

'Oh God. What did you say?'

'I told him there were still lots of things we were trying to find out and as soon as we have answers, we'll share them with him.'

I nod. Parker and Luna have been careful about covering up their relationship problems but poor Barney has been in the thick of it without us knowing. Goodness knows what he's witnessed and what he's made of his dad sleeping in the spare room.

But there's worse to tell Cal.

First I break the news about them selling up.

'Huh?' His eyes widen. 'You're sure the sign wasn't for the house next door?'

'No, it was in their front garden. But that's not the worst of it.'

I tell him about putting out the bin and finding the tied-up bin bag out there.

'It caught my eye because remember that framed photo we gave them of Alton Towers? It was in there and had ripped the bag open.'

'Charming!' Cal rolls his eyes.

'I had a rifle through the bag to see what else was in there and... well, I found this.'

Carefully, I remove the scarf from its wrapping.

Cal sits back in his seat and squints at it. 'What is it, a scarf?'

I nod and hold it in the air. 'Does it look familiar?'

He purses his lips and studies it for a moment. 'Can't say I've seen it before. Whose is it?'

I reach for his newspaper on the arm of the chair and show him the front page.

'You can't be serious... the dead girl?'

'The *murdered* girl. It was all over the news, the online media, Cal. The police have been searching for weeks for a scarf exactly like this one.

Cal stares at the colour photograph in the newspaper and shakes his head. Like me, he's now wrestling with the horror of the possibilities.

'It can't be *that* scarf... I mean, what the hell would it be doing in their bin bag?' I look at him and there are a few moments of silence as I watch it sink in. 'Surely you don't think that Parker is... the police spoke to him, but he had an alibi and that was the end of it!'

'I know all that, Cal. But here it is.'

He thinks for a moment, rubbing his chin. 'So what do you think we should do?'

'That's what I'm struggling with. I've spoken to them both about it. Parker was practically out of it, he just said I should get rid of it. It's understandable he'd say that; he's already had to deal with police officers questioning him.' Cal's expression changes. 'What's that look for?'

Cal pinches his chin. 'You won't like it, but... I've often thought that maybe there was more to it than Parker said at the time.'

I put down the newspaper. 'What do you mean?'

'They seemed to accept his alibi without question, but...'

'Go on.'

'Look, Nicola, I can't believe I'm saying this, but... would they have checked with his employer that he was at the conference? It's a terrible thing to say as a parent, but I've often thought, what did it prove, really?'

'That he was telling the truth?'

'Yes, but how long was he at the conference... did they check that? He could've come home very late that night and easily been in the city around the time the girl left the club. In fact, he could've even made it back to Newcastle in time for breakfast, if he'd wanted to.'

I shake my head slowly. 'With a parent like you, Parker doesn't need enemies!'

'I'm not saying I believe he did it!'

'The police did all the checks behind the scenes, I'm sure. They would have come back in a jiffy if they were the least bit unsure or had any further questions.'

I swallow my anger. The last thing I want is a full-blown

argument with Cal while Barney is upstairs and Parker is still in hospital. But he's not finished yet.

'What did Luna say when you showed her the scarf?'

'She claims never to have seen it before and yet it was double-wrapped at the bottom of a bin bag filled with all her things.'

Cal frowns. '*Her* things. Maybe Luna knows a lot more than she's owning up to here.'

I nod. 'I've got a really bad feeling about this, Cal. It's scaring me because if there's even a chance it belonged to that poor girl... I've even thought about throwing it away. Getting rid of it like Parker told me to.' I fall short of telling him I *did* for a time.

Cal stares at me. 'Why are you torturing yourself like this? It's a no-brainer; just get rid of it. Give it to me and I'll do it!' When I don't answer, he sighs and touches my arm. 'I know what it looks like, love, but come on. Just think about it logically. You know Parker and Luna can't be involved in a murder... they just can't!' He runs his fingers through his thinning hair. 'Despite what I've said, Parker did have an alibi and they hardly ever go out in Nottingham, do they? They're up in Yorkshire nearly every weekend.'

What he's is saying is true but... 'My conscience won't let me ignore the fact that the scarf exists,' I say quietly. 'Double-wrapped and hidden in the bottom of a bag heading for the bin. I don't like it, Cal. I can't get it out of my head.'

Cal makes a noise of exasperation. 'Sounds like nothing I say will make any difference.'

'So what then? You expect me to throw the scarf away and just forget about it?'

'No. But I do think you should hold fire until Parker is on the road to recovery at least. You shouldn't have even told them you've found it.' He fixes me with a stare. 'If you go to the police and your suspicions turn out wrong then you've got to accept the consequences. Parker and Luna will more than likely cut all contact with us and we'll probably never see Barney again.'

I rub at my forehead with the back of my hand and he sighs. 'Think about it, love. You honestly think Parker or Luna could kill a young woman and just continue to act normally, live their lives? If you hadn't gone for Barney's things you'd have been none the wiser.'

'But I *did* go and I did find it.' I know he's right, though. Once the police are involved, there'll be no going back. And Parker, as someone they've already spoken to, albeit routinely, will no doubt be first in the firing line.

Then something else occurs to me. 'What if someone else planted the scarf there? Someone who wants to frame Parker. You do hear of it happening.'

Cal groans. 'Nicola, we can't let this get out of hand. We've enough on our plate as it is. Hopefully Parker will improve in a couple of days or so and he'll able to dispel all your worries. We owe him that before unleashing Nottinghamshire Police to his bedside.'

He's right. I know he is. But inside, I'm tying myself in knots. 'It's just... that poor girl... her family are grieving. Life is so precious and it feels wrong to ignore this, Cal. Even for a short while.'

He turns away, a faint look of disgust on his face.

'I've said what I think and now it's up to you,' he says shortly. 'But I'm telling you now, Nicola: if it all goes horribly wrong and you lose our son and grandson over this, then on your head be it.'

TWENTY-FIVE

MARIE

When the shrill ring tone of Marie's phone sounds in the sitting room of the quirky little boutique hotel they found near the hospital, she puts down her iPad and stares in surprise at the name displayed on the screen. She snatches up the call.

'Luna, darling? Is everything alright?'

'Mrs Barton-James? It's Nurse Fletcher here at the Queen's Medical Centre. Your daughter has asked me to call you on her phone.'

'What's wrong?' Marie sits down on the purple velvet couch. 'Is she OK?'

'I'm afraid she's rather distressed. She wants to speak to you so I'm going to put her on the phone now. The doctor has asked if you can keep the conversation short as she should be resting. She's had quite enough excitement for one day.'

Marie frowns. 'Yes. Yes, of course.'

The nurse drops her voice. 'We still have concerns about her blood pressure, so if you could help put her mind at rest from whatever is troubling her that would really help.'

'Put her on.'

There's a short silence, a few muffled words and then Luna's trembling, high-pitched voice says, 'Mum? Can you come?' She sounds stuffy, as if she has a bad cold.

'What is it, darling? What's wrong?'

'Nicola's been here.' She's speaking quickly and fighting an intermittent sob. 'I told the nurses I didn't want to see her, but she came anyway.'

'What?' Marie feels heat rush into her face. She's already stressed to the staff that nobody was permitted to visit Luna but herself and Joe.

'She used Parker's keys to get in the house and she says she's found a silk scarf there that might belong to that murdered girl the police questioned Parker about.' She pushes the words out in one long breath.

'Luna, it's a little difficult to understand you. Slow down, take a big deep breath. Nicola's been in your house without permission, you say?'

'Yes. She said she needed to get stuff for Barney.'

'And what's all this about a silk scarf?'

Marie's eyes scan her open Twitter feed on the iPad, searching out a post that had caught her attention just before her phone rang.

NottsLiveNews @nottslivenews

Notts Police appeal for info on missing evidence. A scarf worn by murder victim Sarah Grayson...

'She showed it to me. A black and gold scarf she said was in our yard. She says it belongs to that murdered girl... Sarah Grayson. The police found her body and they've been searching all this time for her missing scarf.' More stifled sobs. 'I... I don't know what to do, Mum. I—'

'You do absolutely nothing. Your father and I will deal with Nicola. All you have to do is focus on getting well and we'll take care of everything else. Do you hear me?'

'Yes,' Luna says in a small voice.

'Your dad is working hard to get you into the new hospital. God willing, you won't still be at that awful place after tomorrow.'

'I hope not.'

'Now, I want you to calm down. I'll leave now and come over there.'

'There's no need, Mum; you must be so tired from driving down in the early hours. I just had to speak to you... to let you know.'

'You did exactly the right thing. But I want to make sure you're OK and see you with my own eyes.'

After reassuring Luna she'll be at the hospital very soon, Marie emerges from the lounge area, her chest tight, her head buzzing. How dare Nicola Vance barge to Luna's bedside to accuse her of having something to do with a murder case?

At the same time, she's intrigued. She knew there was more to the police contacting Parker than it first seemed. They spoke to him about his whereabouts on a Friday morning a few weeks ago and he and Luna had travelled up to Helmsley that night with Barney. Parker was fidgety and awkward as Luna told them the police had called at the house. He kept reiterating it was only a routine enquiry because he'd had a similar vehicle to one the police were seeking.

Marie walks into the large bedroom now, past the four-poster bed where she starts to get changed.

Nicola Vance had no right to let herself into Luna's home and no right to intrude at the hospital, distressing her like that. The audacity of her, inferring Luna might know something about that young woman's death!

Marie brushes her hair and grabs her car keys, a small smile playing over her lips.

She's always hoped that, one day, Parker Vance and his mother would disappear out of their lives for good. With any luck, that day may be dawning soon.

TWENTY-SIX

LUNA

TWO MONTHS EARLIER

She'd suspected for a while he was playing around again. Parker was a flirt, always had been. But she'd loved it when they first met and it was her who was on the receiving end of his attentions.

Luna had lost count of the number of times they'd been out with friends and he'd got a bit fresh with someone's wife, or had a young waitress slip a scrap of notepaper with her number scrawled on it at the end of the night.

Parker always handed the notes straight to her in full view of their table and sometimes, toe-curlingly, while the waitress in question still attended their group.

'You have a laugh with someone, act friendly, and they take it the wrong way. I like a bit of banter but I'm a very happily married man.' He'd hold up his hand and show his wedding ring around their crowd.

The men would laugh knowingly, the women smiled sympathetically at Luna. And Luna would accept a kiss on the cheek from Parker and try to change the subject just to stop everyone staring at her like they were trying to read her thoughts.

Then there had been that young assistant of his, Shannon O'Rourke, who was now happily history. That was a long time ago and, when she wasn't drinking, she could almost start to believe her husband did love her after all. That maybe it was true what he told her; that he was happy in their little family unit.

And then, just a few months ago she started to notice some things about Parker. Things she hadn't noticed before. She'd opened a notebook and written a list:

- *He's often out of the house twelve hours a day*
- *His phone is turned off for hours on end during the day*
- *Access code and password changed on his phone and iPad*
- *Sometimes his shirts and jackets were dry-cleaned before appearing back in wardrobe*
- *Found several big cash withdrawals on the bank statement I was unable to identify*

Luna read the list back and sat for a few moments, thinking. She remembered a few more anomalies:

- *He hardly looks at me anymore when he eventually gets home from work*
- *Whenever I've remarked that he seems quiet and pre-occupied, he tells me I'm imagining it*

One day, late morning, she got a call from the school office manager.

'I'm afraid Barney is unwell,' the secretary told her. 'He's been sick and looks very pale. I shouldn't think it's anything to worry about; a few children have come down with it this week.'

Barney had complained of a stomach ache this morning, but mindful of a busy day online, Luna had chivvied him along. 'You'll be fine,' she'd said. 'Once you see your friends your tummy ache will disappear.' Now though, she felt racked with guilt.

She rushed over to the school and brought Barney back home. She called Parker and got his voicemail. She left a harried message.

'Barney's sick. I had to collect him early and he's got a temperature so can you get some Calpol on your way home? Call me when you get this.'

She heard nothing back from Parker and, at 2 p.m., Luna rang his office. 'Mr Vance is out for lunch and has left instructions not to be disturbed.'

This, from Parker who had specifically told her he was in the office all day.

Luna didn't mention she was his wife. 'Ahh yes, I've been asked to check that our representative arrived on time for their lunch meeting. Her name is... where is that note I made. Her name is...'

'I don't seem to have her name,' the clerk said apologetically.

'Her? He's with a woman?'

'Sorry... who did you say you were again?'

Later, Luna said nothing to Parker about calling the office. She'd given Barney some Calpol she found in the cupboard and he slept for a couple hours and then picked up during the afternoon.

'How was your day?' she asked when he got home that night.

He took a beer out of the fridge and taken a swig before glancing briefly at her. 'Been OK. Thanks. How about you?'

'Apart from picking Barney up from school, fine. I called your phone but it was off.'

'Yeah, sorry about that. I've been holed up in a conference room with the team all day trying to get the latest big sales drive sorted. Bloody nightmare.'

'Gosh, you've been stuck in there *all* day, no breaks?'

Parker drank more beer, looked away and yawned. 'Yep. Got a sandwich lunch sent in and just got stuck in.'

Luna walked over to the fridge and opened it. 'Why don't you take a shower and I'll cook you something nice for dinner?'

'I...' He put down the beer. 'You know, I'm not really hungry. I'll take a shower and just grab a snack later.'

'You need a proper meal if you've only had a few sand-wiches, Parker.'

'I'm fine.' His voice hovered on snappy and he put up a hand. 'Sorry. Sorry, it's just been problems all day, that's all. I'll go and take a shower and then I'll spend some time with Barney, give you a break.'

When she heard him climb the stairs, her eyes gravitated to his work jacket hooked over the bar stool. She waited until his footsteps reached the landing above her head and then moved over to the jacket.

Her fingers slid down into each of the tacked pockets and then the inside pocket where she pulled out a cloakroom ticket embossed with the letters: GSK. It was stamped with today's date.

Granary Street Kitchen. An upmarket eatery she knew well. It was where Parker had taken her in their first months together. It was a place they'd visited after their engagement party, their wedding. It was the place Luna told him she was pregnant with Barney.

It was their special, special place. And today, Parker had been there with another woman.

TWENTY-SEVEN

PARKER

TWO MONTHS EARLIER

Parker parked up across the road and waited, watching the never-ending throng of parents, grandparents and carers walking their kids into the big open gates that led into the sprawling playground of the primary school.

About five minutes before the bell went, he spotted her. She looked very different in the flesh. There are so many clever filters available online, he hadn't known quite what to expect, but it turned out she was a genuine looker. Enticingly girl-next-door, but with an edge that he imagined would appeal to a certain sort of man.

She held her daughter's hand as they walked together and she didn't look at any of the other adults bustling around her. The girl glanced up at her and smiled, and she ruffled her hair and said something before they disappeared inside the school grounds.

Parker waited until a few minutes later when she emerged with her phone in hand.

Parker knew her real name. He knew plenty about her.

She was petite with neat breasts and pale, almost translucent skin with light-red hair. Strawberry blonde, he'd heard it called. Not his usual type. She looked vulnerable and sort of innocent at the same time, although by this time, he knew enough about her to realise that couldn't possibly be the case.

Oblivious to his eyes pinned to her, she texted as she walked, glancing up every few seconds to avoid walking into the late stragglers heading towards the school gates. She pushed the phone into her pocket and neared the corner of the street where she'd either have to cross a busy road or turn on to a quieter road. Parker got out of the car, pulled up the lapels of his jacket against the cold breeze and began walking towards her.

Her shoulders were narrow and clad in a leaf-green short mac, a loose ponytail swinging softly as she strode along.

She turned instead of crossing and Parker cursed under his breath, knowing it meant he'd have to hang back even further. Still, there were a few people around and he waited until a group of three women turned in behind her before he too began walking along the road.

In trainers, she was quick on her feet unlike the three dawdling, chattering women. When they slowed their pace even further, Parker took his chance and overtook them. Now there was nobody else between them but he was still a good way back. If she did turn around, he wouldn't, he hoped, raise any suspicion.

A few minutes later, she turned right again and then took a left on to a quiet residential street. He knew the park to be behind here. A couple of years ago, it had been refurbished with a wooden adventure play area for older kids and he'd brought Barney here a few times at the weekends.

She slowed halfway down the road and turned into a low block of new flats. Parker recalled seeing a mesh of scaffolding from the park for a period of time last year as the flats were constructed across two large plots. He raised an eyebrow. These weren't top-end luxury residences but they were smart and well-built and would certainly cost more to buy or rent than the older terraced properties that made up the rest of the street. She must be doing quite well for herself, he thought cynically.

Her phone rang as she reached the gate to the small front garden of the flats. Her back facing him, she answered, hunching her shoulders and speaking into the phone. Thirty seconds later she walked up the short path and reached to punch in a code on the entrance door's security keypad.

'Sarah?' Parker said pleasantly as he jumped over the low fence and approached her from behind the CCTV camera that pointed at the entrance door.

Her eyes widened and she craned her neck to look up and down the street. There was nobody else around.

'I need to speak to you,' he said, keeping his voice calm and reasonable. 'But not here. Let's go for a walk in the park.'

'I'm not going anywhere with you,' she said, her voice surprisingly bold.

'Why's that? I feel like I know you very well.' He smiled tightly and jumped back over the fence to the road. 'It wasn't an invitation. I need to speak to you whether you like it or not. That is, unless you want details of your grubby little life to reach your mother and everyone at your daughter's school?'

Something in her eyes dulled and she walked out of the gate and stood before him. 'I haven't got much time, I have to be online in an hour.'

He took a step back and allowed his eyes to travel down her body and back up again. 'Well, that depends on you being able to give me what I need, Sarah.'

NOW

Luna Vance is sitting up in bed when the nurse takes the detectives through to her room. Her face is pale and angular and her haunted eyes hint at pain and discomfort. Even so, Helena can see she's a beautiful woman.

Brewster makes the introductions and Luna indicates for them to sit.

'Thank you for agreeing to speak with us, Mrs Vance,' Helena says, taking one of the seats next to the bed. 'We'll try to keep it as concise as we can.'

'Call me Luna.' She gives a weak smile. 'I'm dosed up to the back teeth with painkillers so I'm comfortable enough for now.'

'We're here because you contacted our campaign hotline regarding some missing evidence in the Sarah Grayson murder investigation,' Brewster says, taking out a notepad and pen as he sits down next to Helena. 'Just to confirm: you did make that call?'

Luna nods. 'Well, strictly speaking, my mother did. She suggested I contact the police and so I asked her to do it.'

Helena looks at the door. 'Is your mother still around?'

'No. My parents had to leave to deal with another matter. But they're aware of what's happening if you need to speak with them.'

'Not at this stage, but thank you,' Brewster says. 'Luna, we've got quite a few questions as you can imagine. It may be, in your current condition, we'll need to do that in chunks of time so you don't get too overwhelmed. The nurse was very clear that we're not to tire you out.'

Luna gives a watery smile. 'Her bark's worse than her bite. I'll tell you if I get too tired to continue.'

'Thank you,' Brewster says. 'Firstly, and most importantly, do you have the scarf in question in your possession?'

Luna shakes her head. 'Nicola – that's my mother-in-law – she didn't actually show me the scarf. Just a picture of it on her phone.'

'Just to clarify, this is Nicola Vance, mother of Parker Vance?' Brewster makes a mark with his pencil when Luna agrees. 'Could you tell us exactly what happened?'

Luna reaches for a glass of water from the side and Helena sees numerous angry black and blue bruises patterning her fore-arms. Her pale-blue gown gapes a little wider at the neck revealing strips of white medical tape covering her right clavi-cle. Luna takes a sip of water before placing her glass down again.

'I hadn't seen Nicola since yesterday when we dropped off our son. Parker's parents had agreed to babysit him overnight. The nurses told me they'd had a couple of telephone enquiries from her to see how I was doing. But later on, they came and said she'd made a special request to come in and talk to me about something important concerning Barney.'

'Did she say what the urgent matter was?' Brewster asks.

'No. The hospital staff said it had been mentioned that Barney was fine and I knew my parents were going to pick him up shortly anyway so I wasn't worried about him. I was feeling a bit out of it, so I told the nurses I didn't really feel up to seeing Nicola.' She glances at Helena. 'Let's just say she can be a bit... overwhelming.'

'Overwhelming in what sense?' Helena pushes.

'She doesn't like us being so close to my family. The three of us go to my parents' home in Yorkshire most weekends and I suspect she's become rather bitter about it.'

'So you said no to her visiting,' Brewster prompts.

'Yes. Mum had just left – she'd been here most of the day – when Nicola came rushing in. I was a bit taken aback and the nurses were apologetic but apparently she'd just turned up distressed and told them that there was an incredibly urgent issue she needed to talk to me about that concerned Barney.' Luna shakes her head. 'Typical Nicola, I thought. Drama queen. But once I saw her face, I saw the panic was real. I knew it must be something big.'

'So who was in the room at this point?' Helena says.

'Just me and Nicola. The staff left when I said it was OK for her to stay for a few minutes.'

'What happened next?'

'Nicola seemed a bit unhinged. She told me she'd got hold of Parker's keys and let herself into our home without permission to supposedly get Barney some clothes and toys. We've never given her a key. Even Parker admits she's a bit of a snooper.' Luna looks at her hands before continuing. 'She was angry because she'd seen that the house is up for sale and... the fact that Parker and I are sleeping apart at the moment.'

'You and Parker are having marriage problems?' Helena asks carefully.

'You could say that.' Luna folds her arms. 'But it was none of her business. Anyway, she told me she'd found a black and gold scarf at the bottom of a bag full of my things. She showed me a photo. Said something like, "Is this your scarf?" And I told her I'd never seen it before.'

'So you didn't recognise the scarf at all?' Brewster says.

'No, I didn't. Then Nicola said the police were looking for a scarf just like it and started talking about that poor murdered girl.'

'Sarah Grayson. What exactly did Nicola say about her?'

'Just general stuff. She said it looked just like Sarah's scarf and that she'd been murdered and she kept asking if I knew anything about it because she'd found it amongst some rubbish I'd put out by the bins.' Luna shakes her head. 'I told her again I hadn't seen it before and that maybe she should be talking to Parker about it because he was the one who'd been questioned by the police in relation to the case. She didn't like that suggestion.'

'Did she mention anything specifically about Parker and the scarf?'

'Just that he was in a bad way and she was worried about the police hassling him if they found out what she'd found. Then she started talking about Barney, how they were going to keep him and take him to school and... she was clearly mad. I told her I'd be moving to a private hospital and my parents would be taking care of Barney. And of course, she didn't like that, either.'

'Going back to the scarf for a moment,' Brewster says. 'What were your thoughts? Were you shocked?'

'Not at first. I thought it was just Nicola catastrophising. But when she told me it smelt of perfume, it made me feel sick that it could belong to a murder victim.'

'We believe the scarf we're looking for was used to strangle Sarah Grayson.' Brewster frowns.

'Oh... oh that's truly awful,' Luna whispers, touching her fingertips to her lips.

'Did you advise Nicola to contact the police?' Helena says.

'Yes, I did and I also told her to talk to Parker. I mean, if it had been earlier, I would've done but I wasn't thinking straight. But my mum was adamant I had a responsibility to contact the police. She said if there was a chance it could be the missing scarf, then you needed to know about it. So we did what we hope was the right thing.'

'You absolutely did the right thing,' Helena confirms. 'How do you think the scarf came to be at your house, Luna?'

She lets out a long sigh. 'I've given this a lot of thought and, honestly, I don't know. But I've never seen it before.'

'Is there a possibility your husband could know?'

Luna presses her lips together and looks towards the window. 'I thought I knew Parker inside out, but the last few months he's been acting strange. He hasn't been himself.'

'Can you give us an example of what you mean by *acting strange*?' Brewster says.

'He's been going out more, his phone is off a lot, telling me he's one place while I know he's somewhere else entirely. Doesn't sound like much but he's been hiding something from me. I know it.'

'Have you ever considered Parker may have been unfaithful to you, Luna?' Helena says softly. 'The things you've described resemble the behaviours people often see in that situation.'

'Oh, I've thought about it a lot.' Luna gives a bitter laugh. 'When someone is a master gaslighter – sly and determined enough to look you in the eye, tell you it's all in your mind and to lie through their teeth – it's pretty hard to get to the truth.'

'You're saying that's what Parker does?'

Luna hesitates before speaking. 'He had a new assistant who turned down his advances a few years ago. The things he did to that girl to get revenge... you wouldn't believe it. He thinks he has a God-given right to take what he wants, but everyone who knows him thinks he's wonderful.'

'What was this assistant's name?'

'Shannon O'Rourke. He drove her out of the company.'

Brewster writes down the name before looking up again. 'Luna, is there any part of you that believes that your husband had anything to do with the murder of Sarah Grayson?'

'He's already been questioned in relation to the investigation. He told everyone it was just routine, but privately, I saw how stressed he was about it. He scoured every article, every newspaper he could get his hands on. In answer to your question, it would be devastating to find out he was involved in her death. But truthfully...' Luna looks at her hands, 'truthfully, part of me wouldn't be surprised.'

'You didn't think to contact the police with your doubts?'

Luna looks surprised. 'I had no evidence. What would you have said if I'd come to you with suspicions or gut-feelings?'

Brewster says gravely, 'Is there anything significant, anything you can think of now with the benefit of hindsight that could point to your husband hiding that evidence at your home?'

Luna looks back at the detectives. 'I know Parker. I know what he's capable of. But I think you should ask him yourself.'

TWENTY-NINE

SARAH

On the first day of her new job working from home, Sarah felt incredibly nervous. It was understandable, she supposed. Most people's nerves jangle in brand-new situations and she was no different.

But Sarah was nothing if not determined, and by the end of the first week she'd gathered more confidence. She hadn't really known what to expect but everyone had been so nice and respectful. There was a zero-tolerance policy in place regarding the customers and Sarah felt reassured by the fact that if anyone stepped out of line, it was in her power to reject them. No questions asked.

Still, she'd remained cautious, wondering if she'd made the right choice in her career path. Until the cash started rolling in. After the second week, she'd earned more money than the whole of the previous month working all the hours God sent in two waitressing jobs. By the end of the first month, her earnings had almost tripled. Getting out of her mum's spare room and putting down a good deposit on a flat overlooking the park for herself and little Millie had seemed a pipe-dream, but now it was going to become a reality.

Halfway through her second month and she was really getting into her stride. That saying about how life could change in an instant was so true, and Sarah was living proof of it.

She'd always been a quick learner and this job had been no different. She'd swiftly grasped the most popular products and services and incorporated them into her business. She made a point of chatting to other people who'd done the job for far longer and she'd picked up and implemented their tips. She was doing well financially, she'd started to imagine the future in technicolour and could see light at the end of the tunnel for the first time in years.

Sarah glanced at the clock. Millie was at school and her mum was out shopping and wouldn't be back until lunchtime. Time to get to work for that sunny future that would be free of worries. She was working hard for both herself and her daughter: that's how she liked to think about it. She logged into the laptop, turned on her music playlist and – the most important detail – ensured the red blinking camera was pointing at the exact right angle.

Sarah took a sip of the single glass of wine she allowed herself to relax and then she reclined on the pretty pink bedding with the new matching sparkly cushions. She smiled at the tiny red flashing light and, slowly, began to peel off her top.

THIRTY

NICOLA

SUNDAY 11 A.M.

Cal has just left the house to attend a plumbing emergency on a bathroom he recently fitted in the next town.

'I'll call them and explain I can't get there until next week now,' he'd told me when I walked into the kitchen to find him with his head in his hands. 'I can't think straight while I'm worrying if Parker's going to pull through. I'd never forgive myself if I couldn't get back if... if the worst happened.'

After years of Parker and Cal being at odds, I'm touched by his concern. But I really need some space to think about what I'm going to do about the scarf. My mind is in pieces; I'm constantly pushing away the raw fear that Parker may not pull through. I feel like I'm losing track of everything. Last night I couldn't bear to keep it in the house and I left it in my car boot. I understand Cal's position on it but there's the victim's grieving family to think about in this, too. I spent half the night considering every scenario I could conjure up, no matter how unlikely. I pondered whether someone else could have hidden the scarf at the house... the real perpetrator. Someone wanting to frame Parker and possibly Luna.

When I finally dragged myself out of bed this morning, tired and worn out, there was one feeling I had above the guilt and concern. Rightly or wrongly, I wish I'd never set eyes on it.

'I'll call you if there's any news and you could come back. They told me to ring after lunch,' I reassured Cal. 'God willing, he'll start to improve.'

But he still looked unsure. 'I can hardly disappear and leave you to it here, love.'

'You might as well go and finish the job,' I said. 'There's nothing we can do at the moment until Parker's had his second operation. It's best you don't have an unfinished job hanging over you just in case things don't go the way we want them to. Then you'll be free to go to the hospital.'

'Only if you're sure. Family comes first and work can wait.'

'Honestly, go and get it done, Cal. I've plenty to do and I'd like to spend a bit of time with Barney instead of him being stuck on his Switch all morning.'

'Well, if you're sure. I can get the job finished, invoice them and be back by lunchtime.'

Free of guilt now, I see relief soften his face as he kisses me on the cheek and heads out to his van. Despite what he said, work has generally come first with Cal for more years than I can count. I've rarely felt resentful because anyone who's ever been self-employed understands how tricky it can be to find that elusive balance.

I glance my watch. 11:21. Not long now and I can call the hospital to see how Parker's second operation has gone.

My phone rings, the screen displaying a withheld number. I snatch it up in case it's the hospital with news. 'Hello? Nicola Vance speaking.'

'Mrs Vance, it's DS Kane Brewster here, Nottinghamshire Police.'

'Oh, hello,' I say, deflated.

'I wanted to update you on information we've had regarding the car accident your son and daughter-in-law were involved in.'

'Yes?' I perk up, listening attentively now. New information could help us piece together the mystery of why Parker and Luna left the hotel in the early hours. 'Is there a witness?'

'I'm afraid not. After their initial enquiries, our Road Traffic Investigation team have reported that evidence shows there was no other vehicle involved in the accident your son was involved in. Your daughter-in-law was knocked unconscious for a short time upon impact.'

'But how do they know about other vehicles if there are no witnesses?'

The team use a variety of methods including the measurement of skid marks, vehicle damage and also, on newer cars like the one your son was driving, vehicle data which can provide information on the vehicle's speed, brake application and other pertinent information prior to the crash.'

'I see.' Parker was driving, no one else was involved... I don't like the way this is developing.

DS Brewster coughs. 'They're concluding that whatever caused the accident was contained in the vehicle. Perhaps an altercation or the driver's reaction if an animal dashed in front of the car and he lost control.'

'You mean whatever caused the crash was Parker's fault?'

'No, I didn't mean to infer that. But until we can conduct a proper conversation with your son, we're not at liberty to make any judgements, Mrs Vance.'

After a few more platitudes and non-committal responses from the detective, we end the call. They're gearing up to blame Parker for the accident. I can feel it.

I stand up just as a gleaming black limousine-type vehicle pulls up outside the gates. I hover, waiting to see where the occupants are going and my heart leaps into my mouth when

Marie Barton-James unfolds her tall, slim frame out of the passenger seat.

This is all I need! I scramble to pick up my phone to call Cal, but Marie, with her short red hair and full face of make-up, is already opening the gate. Her haughty expression and tightly pinched mouth leave me in no doubt this is not a social call and it occurs to me that the last thing we need in the middle of all this upset is a disagreement amongst adults that will be witnessed by Barney.

I place my phone back down on the coffee table. Cal, when pushed, does not mince his words and under the circumstances, it's perhaps better I'm alone. But I'm sure she'll have something to say about me seeing Luna yesterday and also to lay down the law about taking Barney.

I get to the front door before Marie can ring the bell.

'Hello, Marie,' I say pleasantly. 'I didn't realise you were calling here this morning.'

'Really?' she says, turning to watch as Joe follows her up the path when he stops to take a phone call. She turns her incisive green eyes on me again. 'I know Luna wasn't expecting you to turn up unannounced at the hospital. What were you thinking, Nicola?'

'I needed to speak to her about something very important,' I say as confidently as I can but inside I'm already wilting in the face of her belligerent manner.

'Yes, I heard about the silk scarf. But I'm not sure Luna is the one you need to be speaking to.'

'What do you mean?'

She looks at Joe and laughs. 'Are you going to tell her, or am I?'

'Marie,' Joe says in a warning voice.

I glance over the road and see one of the neighbours craning his neck.

'You'd better come in,' I say, closing the door behind them.

Marie enters and pauses at the bottom of the stairs. 'Is Barney upstairs?'

'Yes, he is. And I'd prefer him to stay there for now rather than witness anything we might be discussing.'

I lead them through to the lounge where Marie's eyes sweep over the room, reminding me of the first time Luna came here.

'What did you mean with that comment about who I need to be talking to?' I say, unwilling to let her open disrespect go.

Marie sits down without being asked and looks up at me. 'Nicola. I suggest Parker is the one you need to be questioning about the scarf, not Luna.'

'And why's that? I found it at the bottom of a bag full of Luna's things. A bag she'd put out for the bin.'

'Parker has already been questioned by the police in relation to the murder of Sarah Grayson,' Joe says gravely, bouncing lightly on the balls of his feet and clasping his hands behind his back. 'Whether you like it or not, that link already exists.'

'It was just a routine enquiry; the police said so themselves. A coincidence that Parker owned the same car a witness claimed they saw,' I say, feeling wounded. At the time, Parker told us that Marie and Joe had been dismissive of the incident and reassured him it meant nothing. Privately, they clearly thought otherwise.

'But now you appear to have found a vital piece of evidence that police are actively searching for,' Marie says. 'So the "coincidences"—' she hooks her fingers in the air '— are stacking up. I assume you've already contacted the police?'

'What?' I feel myself jolt a little and I sit down. The last thing I need are other people weighing into the police debate, particularly if their sympathies have changed. 'No, I haven't contacted them yet. I want to speak to Parker again and that's impossible at the moment. It's highly unlikely it's the missing evidence they're looking for.'

'Yet you thought it urgent enough to bother our daughter with when she's in hospital.'

'I... I panicked, I suppose. The fact is, we all know neither Luna nor Parker are cold-blooded murderers.'

Marie raises an eyebrow. 'They've not been happy for months. Did you know that?'

'I know they're sleeping apart and the house is up for sale.' I feel a sense of satisfaction at her obvious surprise.

She brushes a tiny fleck from her jacket sleeve. 'Parker was adamant he didn't want either of you to know.'

The truth of her comment stings but I don't let it show. 'Their marriage is their own business. Hopefully they'll get closer after their ordeal. These sorts of challenges make you realise what's important in life.'

'But this isn't a new thing, Nicola. Parker has been making my daughter's life a misery for some time now.'

'That seems a very subjective view.' I'm not going to ask her what she means, give her the opportunity to tell me about my own son's marriage. Particularly as she clearly thinks their problems are all down to him. 'Did you know Parker is having a second operation this morning? Neither you nor Luna have asked me how he is.'

Marie's face is blank. 'I called Cal earlier to say we'd be picking Barney up at some point and here we are.'

I won't let them take Barney. Not now he's told me he wants to stay here while his parents are in hospital and while Parker has indicated he also wants him to stay here.

'I think it's best he stays here with us until Luna or Parker are in a position to care for him.'

'Joe's got Luna booked into an excellent hospital close to Helmsley and she'll be moving there in the morning. It should only be a matter of days before she's out of hospital and recovering at our home.'

'What about Barney's school and his friends?' I say shortly.

'Not to mention the various clubs he attends like football and bushcraft.'

Marie gives me a patronising smile. 'I'm sure there'll be plenty of opportunity for all that and more at his new school. It's rated as Outstanding by OFSTED, unlike his current place.'

'I don't want to go to a new school!' Barney's distressed voice cuts through the room. We all turn to the doorway where he stands. His body is stiff and his fists are balled.

'Here he is!' Joe says in a jolly manner. 'Come and give Grandad a hug.'

Barney ignores Joe's outstretched arms. 'I want to stay here with Gran and Gramps until Mum and Dad come out of hospital.'

'Don't you want to see your mum?' Marie says. 'We can take you to see her this afternoon. She's been asking about you.'

Barney's face brightens. 'Yes, I want to see her. And Dad, too.'

'We'll see Mum first and then you'll come back with us,' Joe says.

Marie says through a forced smile, 'It's been agreed with Mummy that you'll come home with us.'

'Well, his dad has said he's to stop here,' I say carefully. 'I've got enough clothes and things for him to stop comfortably for another week.'

'Ahh yes, Luna mentioned you'd taken the liberty of entering the house without her permission.'

'It's Parker's house too, and his keys I used.'

'From what I hear, Parker is in no fit state to say what he wants.'

I glance at my grandson, who's taking in every word of the verbal battle that's heating up. It's time to defuse it.

'I'm sorry, Marie, Joe, but you've had a wasted visit because Barney is staying here for now. I'll be taking him to school tomorrow morning to maintain as much normality as possible.'

Barney stomps across the room towards me then, shouting, 'I'm staying here! I don't want to go to Helmsley; it's boring. I've got no friends there.'

When he's halfway across the room, Joe catches hold of his arm.

'That's quite enough, young man!'

Joe is using a firm grip and Barney twists and turns, trying to escape.

'Joe, I think you're hurting him,' I say.

His face like thunder, he lets go and Barney runs over to me, rubbing his arm. He buries his face in my side and I hug him close. Marie can hardly contain her fury.

'This is ridiculous!' she snaps. 'Nicola, you need to understand, Barney coming home with us is not something that's up for negotiation.'

'I agree,' I say calmly. 'I'm hoping to take him to the hospital to see his dad in the next couple of days after he's had his second operation. So I suggest you stop this nonsense right now.'

'You want to do this the hard way? Fine.' Marie looks at her husband and back at me. 'Show her the papers.'

In one smooth movement, Joe reaches into his inside jacket pocket and pulls out two folded sheets of paper, which he offers me. 'This is a legal, binding agreement that gives us guardianship of Barney in the event both his parents are incapacitated. Which I think you'll agree they both currently are.'

I don't look at the papers and I don't say anything.

Barney starts to cry and Marie moves in front of me.

'I suggest you put your efforts into finding out what sort of lies your son has been telling you,' she says in a low hiss. 'Because that's the only thing the police are going to be interested in, the second he's able to speak to them.'

THIRTY-ONE

I feel so angry with myself for letting Marie and Joe get away with pulling this stunt, but what could I do? I'm no lawyer but even I could see the document Joe handed me was real. And my son's signature was on there.

I take two headache tablets with a swig from my water bottle and think about what Marie meant by that cryptic comment about the police speaking to Parker about his lies. DS Brewster didn't mention anything in his phone call about the accident investigation.

Surely they won't take it upon themselves to tell the police about the scarf! Marie obviously can't stand my son and blames him for everything, but Parker is Barney's father. Any kind of scandal or gossip linking him to Sarah Grayson's death would have negative connotations for the whole family, including their daughter and grandson.

I now wish I'd just not answered the door to Marie and Joe. They would've been forced to come back later. At which point Cal would have been home. But it's too late for regrets. My sobbing grandson has been forced to go with them and I feel utterly impotent and useless in the face of those couple of sheets of paper covered in legal speak.

I'd rushed around, pulling together all the stuff I'd collected from the house yesterday. After reassuring him he could stay with us until his mum and dad got out of hospital, I now feel like I've let him down.

The house feels impossibly quiet without Cal and Barney. I feel frantic with worry about having the scarf here at home. I get a mad urge to just get it from the car and burn it. Deny I'd ever had it, say Luna must be confused...

I glance at my watch and see it's just turned midday. I snatch up my phone and call the hospital. It rings and rings and then, finally, just as I decide to go over there, my call is answered.

'It's Nicola Vance here, mother of Parker Vance. I'm ringing for an update on his operation this morning.'

'Bear with me a moment, Mrs Vance.' Tinny Muzak starts playing in my ear and I squeeze my eyes closed, willing her to come back and give me good news.

'Mrs Vance? Sorry for keeping you waiting. Your son is out of theatre now and the operation appears to have gone as expected.'

'Oh, thank God.' I feel relief wash over me. He's going to be OK. The operation went well.

'He's still in recovery and—'

'Can I visit him? I wouldn't stay very long, I—'

'His condition will be reviewed this afternoon when he recovers and it will be up to the doctor whether visiting will be possible today.'

I make a frustrated sound in my throat. 'I need to see him, need to make sure he's OK.'

'I understand. If you can call back after four-thirty then...' Her voice fades out. She's fobbing me off. They're not going to let me see him today, I know it. '... still in a serious condition and it could be another forty-eight hours before we can allow visits.'

'If I call at four-thirty can I get a full update on my son's condition?'

'Of course. We should know far more then.'

I thank her and end the call. It sounds like it might be a couple of days at the earliest until I get to see him. I'm so worried he's not going to pull through and this scarf business is just making things so much worse. I must have been mad to even mention finding it to anyone else, to Luna or her parents... what was I thinking? Now I'm reliant on others keeping quiet. People who seem to have a waning loyalty to Parker.

The house is echoing with emptiness. I turn on the television to dispel the awful silence and the deafening thoughts competing in my head. It's midday and the local news headlines are on. Not wanting to hear more doom and gloom, I pick up the remote again to turn it off when Sarah Grayson's smiling face fills the screen. A second photo is overlaid, showing Sarah cuddling a pretty little girl of around three or four with pale-red curls and dimpled cheeks. I gasp and drop the remote as the voiceover says:

'The grieving mother of a local woman murdered after a night out has made an emotional appeal for the public's help in finding a vital piece of evidence in their daughter's case.'

The photo of Sarah disappears and viewers are shown a weeping woman with black hair and hunched shoulders in her late fifties or early sixties. She's being comforted by a female officer. She dabs her eyes before speaking into a fixed microphone in front of her.

'It's been a month since my Sarah's body was found, five weeks since she went missing. Whoever did this is a free man, walking around living his life. What am I supposed to tell her little girl? Millie keeps asking me all the time when her mummy's coming home.' She looks directly at the camera, her eyes red-rimmed and sore. 'Somebody must know who did this. Somebody has suspicions.' She wipes her eyes again. 'Please, please come forward. I know you might be telling yourself this person can't possibly be a murderer, but if you have your doubts, you must tell the police. If they are innocent, they can be ruled out.'

The camera switches to another woman in her late thirties with a brown bob and a serious face. 'DI Helena Price, Nottinghamshire Police.' She introduces herself. 'There's a vital piece of evidence out there that could help us find the killer of Sarah. We're appealing to the public to help us trace this item. It's a silk scarf with a distinctive black and gold pattern, worn around the neck. We're showing an identical scarf now.'

The screen fills with a scarf that looks exactly like the one in my car and then switches back to the detective.

'Sarah was wearing this scarf when she left the nightclub and it was the only item missing from her person when Sarah's body was found.'

Mrs Grayson wails. A terrible sound of loneliness and pure suffering. 'Please,' she cries out, as the police officer next to her tries to calm her. 'Please, someone must know something. If you suspect your partner, your son, your work colleague... if you knew this pain, this hopelessness, you would help us!'

The news presenter appears on screen again, her face sombre and concerned.

'That was Julie Grayson, mother of murdered local mother Sarah Grayson. If you have any information that might help the police, you can contact them anonymously on...' The screen fills with a phone number and various other methods of contact.

I pick up the remote and turn off the TV. The silence is waiting for me again but this time I welcome it. The suffering in Mrs Grayson's voice... the fading hope, the desperate plea for someone, anyone, to help her. Her words echo again in my head.

I know you might be telling yourself this person can't possibly be a murderer, but if you have your doubts, you must tell the police. If they are innocent, they can be ruled out.

I am utterly certain my son is not a murderer. In my very bones I know he isn't. He couldn't possibly do a thing like that. He just couldn't.

Parker is selfish and one of these days you're going to wake up to that fact.

Cal's words hit hard every time I think about them. He's often alluded to something similar over time and I've always regarded it as jealousy.

Mummy's boy. That's how Cal has regarded Parker ever since childhood when it became clear he liked spending time with me rather than to be out fishing or gardening with his father. Gentle teasing turned into a more resentful observations when Parker became a teenager and made it crystal clear he had no interest in ever joining the family business.

'You can be my apprentice.' Cal beamed. 'I'll even pay you a fair hourly rate if you can grasp the basics.'

'I don't care.' Parker would scowl. 'Plumbing and heating is the most boring thing in the world. I'm staying here with Mum.'

'What lad would turn down coming out with me in the van in favour of baking with his mother?' Cal would say unkindly, but even back then I could sense that underneath he was hurting.

It was true Parker was the opposite to his father in many ways. He's always been quiet and thoughtful where Cal could often be brusque. He was creative and enjoyed reading as opposed to sitting in front of the television and watching football or cricket.

I admit, up until he married, I've always felt assured I had a special bond with my boy. A closeness and understanding that

Cal not only hasn't experienced, but now, I see, has been actively excluded from.

I've blamed Luna for Parker distancing himself from us. Blamed her for putting pressure on him to spend most weekends up in Yorkshire. Yet Parker is an adult man who holds down a responsible job. He's a father, a husband and a son, and he has made decisions in those areas.

He decided not to tell us they've put the house up for sale. He signed a document completely cutting us out of a legal right to see our grandson should the worst happen.

I've had a wake-up call, a lightbulb moment, on the kind of man my son really is. I've been proven gullible and naïve and, right now, it hurts like a sucker punch to the guts.

Can I really say with utter certainty that he knew nothing about that scarf?

The doorbell rings and I glance at my watch before jumping up. I've sat here staring into space for ages and, now at last, Cal's home. He often rings the bell if he's got his hands full of tools that he doesn't want to leave in the van.

I rush into the hall, full of everything that's going to spill out about the Barton-Jameses' visit. The one thing I can be sure of is that Cal's first thought will be to take me into his arms and tell me everything is going to be alright. Even though I'm fully aware it's far from that, I need to hear him say it.

I unlatch the door and open it, ready to take one of his lighter tool bags. 'You'll never guess who's just... oh!'

A broad, weighty man with short red hair and a beard stands on the doorstep. Next to him is the woman I've just seen on the TV news.

'Good afternoon. Are you Nicola Vance?' The man holds up a warrant card. 'I'm Detective Sergeant Kane Brewster and this is Detective Inspector Helena Price from Nottinghamshire Police. Might we have a word?'

THIRTY-TWO

PARKER

FOUR WEEKS EARLIER

He knew he was treading a fine line and he had to be careful. Since he'd missed their wedding anniversary a short while ago, Luna had been on high alert. Watching his every move, asking for details of conferences and the names of hotels he was stopping at with work.

But she'd crossed a boundary when she'd turned up at the squash club where he'd met his boss, Kenny, after work one evening. After a great session on the court with lots of banter and laughs, Parker had been delighted when Kenny had suggested they call for a pint on the way home.

'We can have a chat about the sales expansion in Belgium unless you have to get back home,' Kenny had said casually. 'I've got the board of directors breathing down my neck to make this a success, so I'm looking for someone dynamic. Someone I can trust to do a great job.'

Parker had been hoping to be chosen for the lead of the new sales drive in Belgium as part of his new position. It was one of the reasons he'd agreed to tonight's squash club visit despite

Luna being on the warpath. If successful, the new project might mean a mega bonus... if only he could land the role and pull it off. It would be a sum that could help to pull him out of a deep hole that threatened to suck him in a bit further every few days.

'A drink sounds perfect, Kenny,' Parker said enthusiastically. 'The job comes first for me, so I don't need to rush home.'

'That's music to my ears.' Kenny slapped Parker on the back. 'You and me, I think we're gonna make a great team. Make ourselves a lot of money in the process.'

Parker couldn't believe his luck, could hardly keep the smile from his face. It was going to be so much easier to bag this job than he'd thought. They headed out to the car park, still chatting and laughing. But when Parker looked towards his car, it felt like the earth crumbled in an instant, out from under his feet.

Luna stood in the next parking bay, leaning against her car boot with her arms folded.

'Shit,' Parker had cursed under his breath. 'What does she want?'

His boss sensed storm clouds gathering. 'Say, we can do that drink another time, buddy. Looking at your lovely wife, it seems you might have some serious sucking-up to do.'

Parker tried to make light of it, but ultimately had to bail because he'd seen that look on Luna's face before and it meant she wasn't about to be brushed aside. If she was riled enough, she wouldn't think twice about making a scene in front of Kenny and that would be disastrous.

'See you tomorrow then,' Kenny said and turned to salute Luna. 'Nice to see you again, Mrs Vance.'

Parker felt his toes curl when Luna markedly looked away without answering.

'Hey there.' He walked over to her, kissed her on the cheek and looked back at the car. 'Where's Barney?'

'On a sleepover at his classmate's house. He told you this morning, remember?'

'Yeah, course. Well, this is nice. I didn't expect to see you here.'

'I bet you didn't.'

'What's that supposed to mean? I told you Kenny had booked us in for a couple of games.' He raised a hand as Kenny crawled by in his new Jag, grinning knowingly at Parker.

'I don't like you hanging around with him,' Luna said. 'He's divorced. Thinks he's a bit of a playboy even though he's seen the back of forty now.'

'What?' Parker snapped. She'd met Kenny once at a company presentation dinner last Christmas, but he hadn't been Parker's direct superior then. 'You barely know the guy! And he's my new boss, if you hadn't noticed. It wouldn't have killed you to say hi.'

He'd showered at the club but still felt tired and frayed at the edges. It was the worry.

'I've checked out his Facebook profile and it seems he's proud of his conquests. Likes very young, very slim brunettes, it seems. Most of his stuff is set to public view,' Luna said carefully, watching his face. 'You'd think people would be more cautious, boasting online about what they're up to. Wouldn't you?'

Parker's heart skipped a beat. Damage limitation was called for. 'Look, how about we go for a drink? It's been too long and if Barney's out all night, we can—'

She shot him a withering look and his words deserted him.

'I know, Parker, OK?' She pinned her eyes to his. 'I know what you're up to.'

'What?'

'I know what you've been doing. I found your bank statements.'

He felt himself rock slightly on his feet and put down his sports bag. 'I don't know what you—'

Luna uncrossed her arms and opened her car door. 'Save your lies,' she said curtly. 'We'll talk at home.'

She slid into the bucket seat of her Mazda sports car and slammed the door shut far harder than necessary.

Parker bent down to pick up his bag and watched as his wife drove away without a second glance. He felt vacant. Shell-shocked.

He fumbled in his fleece pocket for his keys, opened the car and loaded his bag into the boot of the new Mercedes. When it closed, he flattened his hands and leaned heavily on top of it, lowering his head.

It felt like he was clinging to a runaway train, and he didn't know how to stop it. So many lies, so many sleepless nights. Was this it? Had he come to the end of the road?

If so, there might be only one thing that could save him from losing everything he had. Everything he'd worked for.

Maybe, just maybe, it was finally time to tell his wife the very thing he'd been running from all this time. Maybe it was time to tell her the truth.

THIRTY-THREE

NICOLA

I stare for a moment at the two detectives.

'May we come in and have a word, Mrs Vance?' the man says. DS Brewster, I think he introduced himself as.

'Yes, course. I—' My mouth opens and closes and I lean back against the wall to steady myself before I come to my senses. 'Is it... it's not to do with my son, is it?' Their serious expressions set my teeth on edge. I've only just spoken to the hospital. It can't be Parker. 'You'd better come in.'

I show them through to the living room where we all sit down. The male detective takes out a notebook and pen, which I find discomforting.

Pressing my hands together in a prayer position, I wedge them between my knees to stop them trembling. 'What's all this about?'

The woman speaks then, her voice quiet but firm. 'Mrs Vance, we have received information that you may have a piece of evidence in your possession. This item is a black and gold patterned silk scarf. It's very distinctive and may be vital in a serious murder case we're currently investigating. Are you aware of the item I'm referring to?'

My heart starts up. Pummelling hard and fast behind my breastbone.

'You said you've received information?' My voice sounds confident but inside I'm dissolving.

'We have spoken to your daughter-in-law, Luna Vance, who says you visited her in hospital yesterday to discuss the item in question,' the female detective says simply. 'Do you have this scarf?'

'I... I have got a silk scarf but it's not... I mean, I found it. I don't know who it belongs to.' How could it make sense for Luna to inform the police about it? She and Parker might not be getting on, but to involve them before speaking to Parker first... she herself could be dragged into something that's perfectly innocent and mud sticks all too quickly.

'So you have got a black and gold geometric-patterned scarf in your possession?' the detective clarifies.

I touch my cheek with the back of my hand. My face feels so hot. Cal's right: I should've waited. I'm the one who's caused this problem at a time when Parker is so vulnerable and unable to defend himself. He'll never forgive me if there's a serious scandal waiting for him when he starts to recover. All caused by my snooping.

'Mrs Vance, we'll need to see the scarf, please,' DI Price says firmly.

'Of course, yes. Honestly, it's probably nothing. I just stumbled upon it and I thought I'd better ask my son and daughter-in-law about it. So I took it—'

'The scarf please, Mrs Vance,' DS Brewster interrupts.

'Right. Yes. The scarf. I'll go and get it.'

The scarf is in my car. Double-wrapped as I'd found it, but now stuffed under the spare wheel cover, as deep as I could push it down the side.

I move to the living room door and they both stand up.

I say, 'If you'd like to wait here, I'll only be a minute or two.'

I walk briskly into the hallway and pick up my keys from the console table. I've got my hand on the front door latch when I hear DS Brewster's voice right behind me.

'Where is the scarf, Mrs Vance?'

'It's... it's still in my car.' At least I think it is. I'm hot and flustered. I can't think straight. I can remember putting it in the car but... did I move it? 'I took it to the hospital.'

Silently, I curse myself. I shouldn't have told them that. 'My son and daughter-in-law are in the QMC. They had a car accident.'

'Yes, we are aware of all that.' DI Price joins him.

I open the door and step outside. Over the road, two neighbours are looking over and talking to each other over the fence. 'I won't be long. You can wait in the house.'

'If it's all the same to you, we'll accompany you to the vehicle,' she says. 'Just to ensure there are no issues.'

'What kind of issues?'

'The scarf may be essential to a major murder investigation. We're just making sure it gets to us in one piece so tests can begin,' DS Brewster says.

'Tests?'

'Yes, tests,' he says impatiently as I unlock the car. 'Is it in the glove compartment?'

'It's... oh God, I can't recall,' I say. My thoughts aren't joining up properly. 'This is all very stressful on top of my son being so ill after the accident. It's hard to think straight and I've been forgetting things.'

'I see,' he says. 'Take your time. It's important we get this right.'

I look in the glove compartment and then I open the rear passenger door and scan the back seat.

'Have you forgotten where you put the scarf?' DI Price asks.

'I'm sure it's in here. If you could give me a bit of space, that will help.'

Neither of them moves and when I walk to the boot, they follow. They're both staring at me with blank faces. There's no way I'm going to be able to conceal the fact I've purposely hidden the scarf. I might as well just get this over with.

I lift the bottom boot mat that conceals the spare wheel. DI Brewster takes a step closer and peers in.

'Are you in the habit of storing items in your spare wheel cavity, Mrs Vance?'

'No, but... I thought it might be important, so I put it somewhere safe.' My hands are shaking. If only they'd move away, I might be able to think straight.

I take a breath and push my hand down the side of the wheel. I've completely misjudged it in my stressful state. 'It's here somewhere,' I murmur, trying a few inches above. Nothing. I move further down, chafing my fingers on the side of the tyre. 'I put it right here. I know I did.'

'Perhaps you're mistaken,' DI Price says in that relentlessly calm and monotone manner that's really beginning to unnerve me.

'It was just yesterday,' I snap. 'I'm not imagining it.'

'Stand aside,' Brewster says, slipping on a pair of latex gloves. 'I'll remove the wheel.'

I feel exhausted and I haven't got the energy to argue. I move away from the car.

Brewster's large frame fills the mouth of the boot. After a bit of huffing and puffing, he takes a step back, the spare wheel in his hands.

He looks at me and then at his colleague. 'Take a look, boss,' he says.

I approach the boot behind DI Price, expecting to see the small package I'm beginning to wish I'd never set eyes on.

The detective blocks my line of sight until she turns to look at me. 'Looks like we have a problem.'

I move next to her, lean forward and push my hand into the

hole left by the spare tyre. I sweep my fingers around the perimeter and press my hand flat on the bottom but there's nothing.

The scarf isn't here.

THIRTY-FOUR

'I put it here. I know I did,' Nicola Vance says faintly, staring into the car's empty boot. Helena thinks her eyes look slightly dilated as she mutters under her breath. 'But... I've been so confused. Maybe I moved it, I don't know. I can't think straight.'

Helena turns and looks at Brewster. This is a development she didn't anticipate and a serious one at that. They might never get to know if it's the scarf they're looking for.

'Mrs Vance, where do you suppose the scarf has gone?' Brewster says.

'I don't know. I haven't had much sleep since the accident. I feel out of it. Maybe, if I get some quiet time, I'll remember what I did with it.'

Helena frowns at Brewster. This woman's thought process is all over the place. 'When is your husband back from work?' she asks.

'I'm not sure. Not yet, he's finishing off a bathroom contract.'

'Mrs Vance, I'm afraid we're going to need you to come to the station to make a statement.'

'What?' Nicola's hand touches her throat. 'When? It's just that... I'd rather wait until my husband is back—'

'Perhaps you can leave him a note or text him,' Brewster says as he stands up. 'But we do need you to come to the station right now.'

Nicola's face blanches. 'Am I... under arrest? Surely that's not right, I—'

'You're not under arrest,' Brewster confirms. 'But we have a lot of questions and you must understand, we're obliged to get to the bottom of this.'

'But I don't know anything.' Nicola takes a step back. 'I thought I was doing the right thing bringing the scarf back here. There must be hundreds of them all over the country and ... oh God.' She grabs a handful of her hair in both hands. 'I've made such a mess of everything.'

'We appreciate there's a lot happening right now,' Brewster offers. 'Your son is in hospital and you're understandably very worried about him.'

'Still, we must keep focused on the murder investigation,' Helena says firmly. 'There's a possibility the scarf is the crucial piece of evidence we've been searching for, and we need you to come to the station so we can document the facts.'

Nicola's small, slim body seems to wilt in front of them. 'I'll write Cal a note,' she says faintly. 'And then I'll get my coat.'

The detectives sit in the quiet living room listening to the tick of an old-fashioned clock on the mantelpiece, the sound of a drawer being opened and shut and a chair scraping on a wooden floor in the kitchen Helena had spotted through an open door when they arrived.

'She seems very confused,' Brewster whispers. 'But if she's deliberately got rid of it, then that's going to be a very serious matter.'

Helena nods. 'We can't assume anything. But at this stage in the investigation, the super will have our heads on spikes if we're not thorough. We need to make sure there are no loose ends. If that scarf is in the vicinity then we're obliged to find it.'

Nicola appears in the doorway. She's slipped on a padded jacket and has a handbag hooked over her shoulder. 'I'm ready,' she says. She looks so ordinary, just a woman who's trying to do the right thing. But a vital piece of evidence going missing cannot be ignored. Particularly as her son is currently under high suspicion.

The detectives stand up. 'Mrs Vance, we'll need to search the house to establish if the evidence is in here.'

'But why?' Nicola looks alarmed. 'I've told you. I put the scarf in the car because I thought it would be safe there.'

'But you also said you may have moved it. We're obliged to make sure we've covered all possibilities.'

'I see.' Nicola presses her lips together. 'And do I have the right to refuse?'

'You do, but then we'll have to rush through a search warrant request. In a major murder investigation like this, our officers will be back within the hour to perform the search. It's up to you, Mrs Vance. We can try and keep it as low key as possible if you agree to it now or send in more uniformed officers later to help make up for lost time.'

Helena can't help but admire Brewster's discreet implication as Nicola Vance's eyes swivel to the window and she considers the number of neighbours that have clear and direct sight of her front door.

'Sounds like I don't really have a choice,' she says bleakly.

THIRTY-FIVE

NICOLA

The interview room is small and stuffy. Back at home, I visited the bathroom and managed to take a couple of headache tablets but now I feel sick because I took them on an empty stomach. Or maybe I took too many in a short amount of time. I can't remember.

They've brought me to Arnold Police Station on Oxclose Lane – a place I've driven close to many times on my way into the city but never set foot in. Until now.

Ironically, even Parker wasn't interviewed here in relation to Sarah Grayson's disappearance. Once his car had been identified as the right colour and year for a vehicle seen in the Nottingham area, officers had made contact and visited him at home to check his whereabouts on that night. Parker told me they'd been and gone within twenty minutes.

'Just routine enquiries, Mum,' he'd said confidently when I'd asked him about it. 'Nothing at all to worry about.'

My poor son, having been through two operations in quick succession... it's driving me crazy I can't get to see him yet. And the thought that all this... this trouble is waiting for him the minute he can hold a conversation. Thanks to me. Thanks to his wife and in-laws who are stabbing him in the back while he can't defend himself, not giving him a chance to comment on why the scarf was there.

Behind my worries about Parker's recovery is a very worrying, repeat question in my head: if the scarf is found and it does prove to have belonged to Sarah Grayson, what the hell was it doing at my son's house?

Instead, I'm sitting here, waiting like some kind of convict. I'd tried to do the right thing – that was, speak to Luna and wait until my son was able to have a conversation to find out where the scarf came from so I could decide what to do about it. Cal had warned me and I'd gone ahead and involved other people and now... now Parker is going to be furious with me when he recovers from his latest operation.

Still, despite what I know Cal will say, I'm not the kind of person who can ignore something as important as potential evidence from a young woman's murder. If, indeed, that's what the scarf is. We just don't know that for certain yet, despite what it looks like, despite the police being desperate to find the evidence that will further their investigation.

The door opens and the two detectives file in. Brewster sets a paper cup half-filled with water in front of me.

'Sorry for the delay,' Price says, placing a thin folder down on the table. 'We had one or two things to sort out before the interview could begin.'

I nod and look at my hands.

'Right, so let's make a start.' Brewster turns on the tape and recites some information including the time and who is present. 'Mrs Vance, just to clarify, we've asked you into the station today to help us understand how you came to be in the possession of what we believe could be a very important piece of evidence in an ongoing murder investigation. Is that clear?'

'Yes,' I say.

'Can you tell us how you came to be in possession of a black and gold silk scarf that is now missing?' Price begins.

I clasp my hands together in front of me on the table. I silently will myself to focus, to try and slow this crazy roller-coaster. I'm going to speak slowly and stick to the facts. I won't be rushed.

'My son, Parker, and his wife, Luna, were involved in a car accident two days ago. We were looking after their son, our grandson, Barney. When it became apparent his parents would be staying in hospital for some time, I went to the house to get Barney some clothes and other belongings he'd need for the next week or so.'

'And how did you gain entry to the house?' Brewster says.

'I explained to the hospital I needed to get my grandson's personal belongings and they handed over Parker's keys.'

'Your son had agreed for that to happen?'

'Not exactly. I told him I was going to call at the house and he... well, he'd just woken from having an operation, so he was a bit confused.'

'What exactly did he say, Mrs Vance?'

'I think he didn't want to put me out. You know, by me going to the house.'

'That's exactly what he said, is it?' Brewster isn't going to let it go. 'That he didn't want to put you out?'

'Well, no. Not exactly. He just... he told me not to go there.'

'He told you not to go there,' Brewster repeated slowly.

'Yes, but it's not like it sounds. He probably didn't want me running around when he knew I was so desperately worried about him,' I say.

'You don't have a spare key for your son's house?'

'No.'

'Why do you suppose that is?'

I feel heat creeping into my face. 'I don't know. I suppose

we've just never got around to it. Parker's extremely busy with work and family commitments.'

'I see. And how many years have your son and his wife lived in Ravenshead?'

'Eight years, I think.'

'Eight years and yet they had never provided you with a key,' Brewster says thoughtfully. 'Was there any part of you that felt it was maybe overstepping the mark to acquire one from the hospital and then rush over there without your son's express permission?'

'It wasn't like that.' I don't like this man. He seems so personable on the face of it but he's trying to take me apart. 'Parker was confused and exhausted. I went to the house solely to get my grandson's things.'

'I can understand how Barney would need some clean clothes and perhaps some toys,' Helena says.

'Thank you,' I say, glaring at Brewster before looking back at her. 'That's all it was.'

'So when you had a key in your possession, you went straight over there?'

'I popped home first to get a suitcase for Barney's things and to tell Cal, my husband, that I was going over.'

'And what did Cal say?'

'He... he was worried they wouldn't like it. But like I told him, we have to keep things as normal as possible for Barney. I was too wired to sleep after visiting Parker and being so worried about him, so I drove over there.'

'You went straight upstairs to Barney's bedroom and got what you needed?'

'That's right. I just grabbed as much as I could and filled the suitcase I'd brought with me. Then I came out again and drove home.'

Brewster clears his throat. 'So you found the scarf in your grandson's bedroom, Mrs Vance. Is that right?'

'No, of course not!' There he is again, trying to catch me out. 'Before I drove home I decided to put their bin out. I saw the other bins in their cul-de-sac were out and thought that Parker must have forgotten to do it.'

The detectives stay silent as I take a sip of the lukewarm water before continuing. I'm trying to include just the facts like I intended but my mind keeps mixing the order of things up.

'I wheeled the bin out and I saw there was a tied black bin bag behind it. I didn't think anything of it until I saw the corner of a photo frame poking out. There was other stuff that looked too good to throw away.' I pause to take a breath and steady myself. 'I decided to bring the bag back home with me to see what else was in there.'

'So you brought the bin bag home with you.'

'Yes.'

'And was the scarf just lying there, on top of the other items?'

'No. It was wrapped in two plastic bags at the bottom. I couldn't see what was inside,' I say. 'I unwrapped it and saw it was a silk scarf.'

'Did you realise the significance of the scarf?' DI Price says.

'No, I didn't,' I say carefully. The lie nips at my throat but I swallow it down.

'That's surprising, bearing in mind our widespread media campaign.' The detective opens the brown foolscap file in front of her and removes a piece of paper. She turns it around and slides it over to me. 'Is this like the scarf you found?'

The photograph shows an identical scarf.

'It looks very similar,' I say, pushing the photograph away.

'Do you read the newspapers, perhaps catch up with news stories online, Mrs Vance?' Brewster asks.

'Yes, of course.'

'The police have been searching for this scarf since the body of Sarah Grayson was discovered in the Lace Market area of the city a month ago. To assist with this, the photograph in front of you has been widely circulated in the UK media, but with particular emphasis in Nottinghamshire for obvious reasons.' Brewster picks up the photograph and looks at it. 'Yet you claim you didn't see any of the police appeals online or in the local and national newspapers.'

'I... I thought it looked familiar. But I thought that was because I'd seen Luna wearing it.'

I'm not a liar. I'm not a bad person. And yet... these words are slipping so easily from my tongue.

I had to give my son the chance to offer an explanation. Every mother would do that! I scream it in my head and say nothing out loud.

'So you didn't think the scarf was particularly significant in any way?'

'No, I did not.'

'Perhaps you can explain why you took it upon yourself to remove it from the refuse bag then? And why you took it to the hospital the next morning in a state of panic to ask Luna Vance if she'd ever seen it before?'

My hands fly up to cover my face. My head is pounding. 'I don't know! I panicked... I thought I recognised the scarf, but I wasn't sure where.'

'Mrs Vance.' Price's voice is calm and measured compared to Brewster's abrasive manner. 'A month ago, your son, Parker, was questioned by officers as part of routine enquiries in connection with his vehicle. Officers were satisfied he was not in the vicinity of Sarah Grayson's disappearance that night. But I think you might have known exactly the significance of the scarf and took it away with you in order to try and protect him.'

'No! You can't just put words in my mouth like that. Parker would never do anything to hurt anyone, I'd bet my life on it. He had an alibi for that night. If anyone knows anything about that scarf, it's Luna. Parker said as much himself.'

The interview room falls silent. I hear faint footsteps in the corridor, a sharp click from the digital recorder.

'So you did speak to Parker about the scarf?' Helena says, leaning back in her chair.

'I... I might have mentioned it to him. But he told me when he was questioned about his vehicle that he had nothing to do with it all.'

'We have a witness sighting of a man talking to Sarah shortly before she died,' Brewster said. 'We'll be showing her your son's photograph – among others – and asking her if she recognises any as the man she saw.'

'Parker told us he'd never met Sarah Grayson,' I say curtly. 'So it can't have been him.'

'I think we need to go back to the beginning.' Brewster steeples his fingers and looks over them sternly. 'And this time, Mrs Vance, we need the whole truth with no omissions designed to protect your son.'

THIRTY-SIX

After the interview, I walk out into the police station reception area. There are a handful of people waiting there who look up at me curiously. They seem distorted, as if I'm viewing them through a looking-glass.

Slowly, I walk to the entrance door and stand there in the buffeting wind gulping air. The passing traffic noise echoes in my ears. I lean back on the doorframe and close my eyes. The last time I felt so drained of energy was when I'd finished my cancer treatment and we went to the Lincolnshire coast for a few days.

It had been May, I think. Yes, late May. The sun was shining, the smell of the sea air and the call of the gulls above us... walking along the promenade that first day, I'd been so grateful for my life, for my family. I'd promised myself this was a fresh start. I was going to live life a different way. Start doing some of the things I'd dreamed about: travelling, learning to play the piano. Speaking my mind more instead of floundering in the face of causing upset.

Now I realise thinking about it was how far I got.

I hear a shout and my eyes spring open. I can see someone

waving across the road and a whimper rises in my throat. I stumble forward. 'Cal!' I whisper.

In seconds, he's right in front of me, his face a mask of concern. I fall heavily towards him and he holds me tightly, keeping me upright.

'Christ, Nicola. What have they done to you?' He grasps my elbow, his other arm firmly clasped around my shoulders. 'Let's get you home. Where's Barney?'

'He's... he's safe. The hospital... I need to see Parker, need to—'

'I rang the hospital and he's stable after his operation. There's no more news than that yet, love, and they've said it's too soon to visit. You need to rest or you're going to collapse.'

I nod, remembering my own conversation with the hospital this morning. My head is full of white noise. Nothing is making much sense. But there's something I must ask him.

'Did you move the scarf from the car, Cal?'

'The car?'

'Yes, I thought I put the scarf in the car because I didn't want it in the house, but when the detectives looked there, it had gone. And now I don't know if I just imagined it.'

Cal shakes his head and opens the car. 'I thought it was still in your handbag.'

I shake my head. 'I'm losing it. I thought I put it in the car but then... I don't know whether I brought it back in the house. I just can't remember. My brain has turned to mush.'

We get into the car.

'Hey, look at me.' His voice softens. 'You're not losing it, Nicola, you're just buckling under all this stress. Give yourself a break. We can look for the scarf when we get home. It's going to come to nothing anyway. Parker has his faults, but he doesn't go around murdering young women and hiding their belongings at home. We both know that.'

He starts the car and we pull away. A knot pops up in my

throat as I suddenly remember. 'Oh God. They're searching the house.'

'What?' He looks at me, his knuckles shining white on the steering wheel before looking back at the road.

'They said they had to search the house for the scarf.'

'This is... it's crazy. Coppers crawling all over the house... what will the neighbours think? When are they doing this search?'

'Maybe they're already there... I don't know, Cal.'

Two red spots appear on his cheeks. 'You know, all you had to do was to keep quiet until Parker woke up properly. A day or two, that's all. But you had to start blabbing to other people.'

He's angry and I can't blame him. I've made a mess of everything.

Cal doesn't ask me any more questions on the way back home. He falls quiet, a muscle in his jaw pulsing as he stares straight ahead and drives.

My heart sinks when we turn into our street.

'What the bloody hell...' Cal curses, face like thunder. He parks as close as he can to our driveway due to a large white van with 'Scientific Investigation' emblazoned on the side with police blue and yellow livery. In front of that, parked across our gates, is a police car.

I glance across the road at the neighbours all busy in their gardens despite the drizzle. Pottering around in one spot with their eyes firmly trained on our front door, which is currently wide open.

Cal glares at me. 'See what you've done?'

My eyes sting and I blink rapidly to get rid of the tears but I don't retaliate because he's right. There's no proof that scarf belonged to Sarah Grayson and, whatever my suspicions, I should have spoken to Parker properly about it once he was in a fit state.

'Cal, I—'

Before I can finish, Cal opens his door and gets out of the car, slamming the door hard behind him. The neighbours forget their unconvincing 'busy in the garden' performances and blatantly gawp at the sight of Cal's angry tirade at the young officer standing outside the house.

This exchange continues for a couple of minutes until Cal returns.

'What's happening?' I say in a small voice, twisting the cuff of my jacket into a point.

He doesn't look at me, just stares at the house. 'What's happening is that there are God knows how many police officers tearing our home apart to look for a bloody scarf.' He pinches the top of his nose. 'Which apparently you gave them permission to do. Without a search warrant. You've really gone and—'

Cal's words fall away as a uniformed police officer carrying a large plastic bag emerges from the house. He's followed by two female officers.

'Christ, what've they got in there?' Cal growls.

I open my door and get out, ignoring Cal calling out. 'Nicola, what are you doing? Get back in the car!'

I approach one of the female officers.

'I'm Nicola Vance and this is my house.' I look at the bag. 'What's in there?'

'The supervising officer will be out in a moment to speak to you, madam,' she says. 'You'll get a full list of what's been taken today.'

'Can you tell me if you found the scarf?'

'Sorry, I'm not able to discuss that with you. As I say, you can speak to the—'

'Nicola!' Cal shouts across to me from the house. 'We're needed inside.'

The supervising officer is a tall, thin man in his early forties who is losing his hair. 'Thank you for agreeing to the search,' he says, looking at us both in turn. 'We've tried hard to minimise disturbance in all the rooms.'

He offers Cal a clutch of paperwork but I take it from him instead.

'This is an initial list of what we've taken. You'll get updated paperwork in due course.'

I scan down the list and there it is: one silk patterned scarf – black and gold.

'You found it then,' I say coolly. 'The scarf. I don't know why you need all the other stuff.' Clothing... items that have nothing to do with all this. Taken from the back bedroom, it says here. Parker's old room. 'What will happen to the scarf now?'

'DI Price will no doubt be in touch with further details,' he says, putting on his cap. 'But it will more than likely be sent for tests.'

'What sort of tests?'

'DNA and other evidence.'

A chill travels up my arms and I wrap them around myself.

'Can we go back inside our house now?'

'Certainly, Mrs Vance. We're all done here,' he says.

I turn and walk inside my house while Cal speaks to the officer. I wish he'd come inside and let them go. I just want them to go away and leave us alone.

I close the front door and stand in the middle of the hall-way. It smells different: sort of earthy and ripe. It feels different, too. Like the house itself is trying to settle after all the upheaval. I'm itching to throw open all the windows but I'm too exhausted.

When Cal gets back in and heads for the kitchen, I sit quietly on the sofa and stare at the soft grey sky outside the window. Listening to the comforting sounds of cups and spoons chinking down the hall. The neighbours have all gone inside now. The show's over, but they'll dine out on all the upset for weeks yet, I'm sure.

Cal comes back in with tea and places the mugs down on the coffee table. 'Thank God I had my laptop with me in the van. If they'd taken that I wouldn't have a clue where I'm supposed to be or what job I'm working on.'

'Sorry, Cal,' I say in a small voice. 'I don't know why I agreed to such a thing.'

'I don't suppose you had a choice. But when I left for work this morning, Barney was here and there was no sign of the police,' he says calmly, sitting down. 'So what the hell happened?'

I start with the Barton-Jameses turning up, insisting they take Barney back to Helmsley with them. 'When I refused, they produced the paperwork to say Parker and Luna have given them legal guardianship. Then Marie said I should go to the police about the scarf.'

'What did you say to that?'

'I said I wasn't going to do that until I'd had a chance to speak to my son. Then barely an hour after they left, those two detectives turned up. They said Luna had reported me and insisted I go down to the station with them.'

Cal's cheeks inflame. 'I came back and found your note and then I saw your text. I drove straight to the police station and asked to see you, but they said I had to wait until you were finished speaking to the detectives. So I waited in the car.'

'The police are coming for Parker, Cal. I know it,' I say, taking a sip of strong, hot tea. 'They think he killed Sarah Grayson.'

'That's what they said?'

'Not in so many words, but I know it. I saw that girl's poor mother on television pleading for the public's help to find the scarf. She said someone must know something and...'

'Go on.'

'Well, I'd never admit it to anyone else, but it got me thinking. Is it possible that Parker *might* know something about what happened to her?'

I expect him to get annoyed, but Cal looks at the floor before speaking. 'I know you're not going to like this, but I keep finding myself thinking... is it possible that in a moment of madness, Parker lost it and did something terrible? He's been under pressure and we haven't realised until now.'

I cover my face with my hands. 'I can't stand it. No, he'd never... he could never do that, Cal. Surely not.'

'Jeez.' Cal blows out air. 'I don't know.'

'When I showed Luna the scarf, told her what I thought it was, I think she saw an opportunity to implicate Parker.'

'Why on earth would she do that?'

'Think about it. It'd make things so much simpler if they're splitting up. She'd get full custody of Barney for one thing. If Parker went to prison, she'd be left to get on with her life with minimum interference from him.'

'It's a bit extreme, isn't it? Trying to frame someone for murder to make your life a bit easier!'

'We don't know the full story yet, do we? We'd no idea their marriage was in trouble until I went to the house.'

'What did Luna tell the police, exactly?'

'I don't know, they didn't say. But she's put herself in a good light reporting him. Showing she's got nothing to hide.'

'So what now?'

I sit up straighter. 'We have to get back to the hospital to see Parker the minute they allow us to. We've got to get the truth out of him before this thing gets any worse. He needs to know that Luna has gone to the police.'

'If the scarf comes back from tests showing it did belong to the murder victim then both Parker and Luna are in the firing line,' Cal says.

'I think she knows far more than she's letting on. If that

scarf belonged to Sarah Grayson, then I found it on their property. So one of them knows the truth.'

Cal's expression darkens. 'Maybe both of them know what happened.'

I throw my hands up. 'We've got to believe in Parker's innocence until we're convinced otherwise. I'm his mother; I have to be on his side. I'll give him the chance to tell me everything. In the meantime, I'm not going to just sit back and let his wife and in-laws hang him out to dry while he's unable to defend himself.'

The house landline rings before he can reply and he walks into the kitchen to take the call.

They're brave words I've just said, but inside it feels like small pieces of me are breaking off bit by bit. I pick up my tea and stare into the depths of the brown liquid. Despite my loyalty to Parker, I'm starting to fill with a creeping horror. I can't rule out, no matter how much I protest, that there's a possibility my beloved boy, my clever, handsome son might be involved with something so evil, so base. A young woman's life snuffed out in the cruellest, most violent way when she had so much to live for. An act that has left her grieving mother and her child to somehow try and carry on without her. How could I live with that knowledge?

I take my empty cup to the kitchen to find Cal just finishing a telephone conversation in the hall. He looks at me, a haunted expression on his face.

'That was the hospital,' he says faintly. 'There's been a setback in Parker's condition.'

'What kind of a setback?' I reach behind me to hold on to the worktop.

'They say we should get there as soon as possible.' Cal's face sags. 'It's serious.'

THIRTY-SEVEN

PARKER

FOUR WEEKS EARLIER

Parker drove out of the squash club and turned left, taking the long route home instead of following Luna in her Mazda.

Despite his kneejerk reaction to tell her the truth, he couldn't face her yet. Driving home was the only thinking time he had available before she'd try to force him to deny or admit her allegations. The thought of having to come clean at last seemed less palatable with each second that passed.

Was it ever a good idea to lay yourself bare, warts and all? He thought not. When Luna had turned up at the squash club car park, he'd felt the time for lying and cheating had come to an end. But now, the familiar feeling that he could get himself out of any tight spot was returning with a vengeance. What was he thinking of, confessing all? He could solve his problems. He just needed a little more time.

Parker had always been a good judge of people. He had the useful ability to weigh them up within a couple of minutes or even less. It was a skill that had helped make him an excellent salesman. His understanding of Luna went far deeper than she knew and despite her bravado, he knew that if she had all the answers, if she knew everything there was to know, she would never have stood there calmly demanding they talk at home.

On the contrary, she'd have had him by the balls the second he'd exited the squash club with Kenny. He'd been on the end of her psycho side before when she'd got into her head he was up to something. No. Bank statement comment or not, she was bluffing. She knew some stuff but not everything. She was trying to make him believe she had the whole pie.

Still, when he thought about how all this had started and the speed with which it had escalated, it was enough to make him blurt everything out in one go just to relieve the weight on his shoulders. At least he'd felt that way when Luna put him on the spot in the car park.

Now his head had cleared, he realised the best thing he could do for his family was to calm down and think logically. Think strategically for the future, not just react to the panic of today.

He would use the ten minutes remaining in his journey home to think over the last few weeks and devise a plan that would finally get him out of this mess.

Whatever it took and no matter how unpleasant, he was prepared to do it. He'd proven that to himself before.

THIRTY-EIGHT

NICOLA

After the call, we race to the hospital in Cal's work van because my car needs petrol.

'I should have been to see him before now,' Cal keeps repeating. 'If anything happens before... I could never forgive myself.'

'Don't think like that. You were looking after Barney until today,' I tell him. 'That's what Parker would want you to do.'

He's quiet during the drive over, which suits me as I feel exhausted. So many dark thoughts are tunnelling through my mind and I can't focus on any one of them.

Thankfully, there is no queue at the car park. Cal takes a ticket at the barrier and, together, we hurry into the main building, through reception and manage to get the last two spaces in the lift. The hospital itself is busy, people walking in all directions, patients wheeled by attached to tubes and wires... incredibly, everyone seems to get to where they are going.

When we emerge from the lift and start our long walk through the corridors to critical care, I glance at Cal. His eyes are downcast, his face pale and drawn. I wonder if he's berating himself about his antagonistic relationship with Parker for the last few years. Sometimes, it takes a serious, unexpected incident like this to snap a person out of a stubborn attitude. Parker and Cal have never really enjoyed 'dad and son' activities like sharing a pint at the local pub, shouting at the footie on the television at home, or visiting the legendary Trent Bridge to enjoy the cricket. Not for the last few years, anyway.

Finally, I see the signage for the critical care unit in front of us.

'Oh God,' Cal mutters, staring up fearfully at the bold lettering. 'How did it come to this?'

I reach for his hand and squeeze it. 'It'll be OK. We must believe that.'

I buzz at the door and say our names. 'We're Parker Vance's parents.'

There's a few moments' wait and then the door buzzes open. I walk up to the reception desk.

'Nicola and Caleb Vance. We got a call to say we could see our son. That he's very ill and...' My voice falters. The reception clerk nods in understanding and taps at his keyboard. I feel Cal's firm, warm hand on my shoulder.

'If you'd like to take a seat, Mr and Mrs Vance, someone will come and get you in a little while.'

I look at Cal and he steps forward to speak. 'We were under the impression time was of the essence and we'd need to see him straight away?'

'It shouldn't be long,' the clerk says. 'We only allow two people at a patient's bedside; so soon as he's free, someone will take you through.'

'What's that? Are you saying there's someone with him now?' The clerk shifts in his chair as my tone changes. He looks around as if he's going to consult someone but there are no other staff members close by. 'We're his family. My husband and I are the only visitors he should be having. So who's in there now?'

'It's... the police, Mrs Vance,' the clerk says, lowering his voice discreetly. 'Two detectives are currently speaking with him. A nurse is present to ensure he doesn't get upset and—'

'They've no right to be in there when he's so ill!' I look wildly past reception. 'I want to see my son. Right now!'

'Keep your voice down, Nicola,' Cal whispers in my ear. 'You'll get us thrown out.'

'Let them try!' I say loudly, glaring at the clerk. 'We insist on seeing our son right this minute. Whoever let those two detectives through when he's so ill needs firing!'

The ward manager who'd helped me a couple of times by enquiring how Luna is approaches. She's fiddling with her name badge as if she's just starting her shift. 'Can I help, Mrs Vance?' she says, concerned.

'The police are in there questioning my son and that can't be right. He's not well enough.'

'We got a call about forty minutes ago to say Parker is struggling,' Cal adds. 'He's in no fit state to be grilled. We'd like it to stop.'

'Let me look into this,' the ward manager says calmly. 'Please, take a seat while I find out what's happening.'

I tug at Cal's sleeve and he sighs, follows me to the hard plastic row of seats.

'I don't know why it's so bloody hard,' he hisses. 'They just need to ask those detectives to leave.'

'Luna's the one who got the police involved in the first place.' I meet the gaze of a couple opposite who are staring at us. When they fail to look away, I realise they're in a zombie-like state of staring but not really seeing. No doubt dealing with their own trauma.

A few minutes later, the ward manager appears again, followed by Price and Brewster, the two detectives that had interviewed me earlier. I stand up.

'Nicola, leave it,' Cal says.

'You had no right to come here when my son is struggling,' I address DI Price. 'It's not right. I answered all your questions earlier.'

'Hello again, Mrs Vance,' she says with a tight smile. She looks expectantly at Cal and he stares back at her and doesn't offer his name. 'We just had a very quick word with Parker. We'll be back for a longer chat when he's stabilised.'

DS Brewster nods and they're off again, striding through the fluorescent corridor towards the exit.

'Don't come back until he's fully recovered,' I call after them, causing Cal to squeeze my arm gently.

'Leave it, love. The main thing is they've gone and now we can see Parker.'

I blow out air and nod. Every inch of my flesh aches; it seems to permeate through to my bones.

Two nurses rush by us following a doctor as I try and catch the ward manager's eye again. She glances at me and then turns her back, walking quickly away, back into the unit. I approach the reception desk. 'We'd like to see our son, now the detectives have left, please.'

The clerk looks hassled, narrowing his eyes as he studies his monitor. He clears his throat. 'If you can take a seat, Mr and Mrs Vance, it shouldn't be too long before someone can give you an update.'

'We don't want an update. We want to see him.' Cal pulls himself up to his full five foot ten and squares his shoulders, and I'm struck by how his shoulders had seemed so much broader when we met all those years ago. I feel a flood of affection for how he's fighting for us. Fighting for Parker. 'You called us, remember? That's why we came rushing over here.'

The clerk nods, uses a sympathetic tone but I can't discern the words because I'm watching a second doctor rushing into the critical care unit pushing his pager back on his belt. I'm observing the ward manager, who has been so helpful to me up until now, return to the front desk. Her face is pale and her eyes evasive as I will her to look back at me.

The clerk glances at his monitor and he stops talking. Bile begins to rise in my throat.

'Is... is Parker alright?'

The first doctor I saw walks briskly over to us. 'Mr and Mrs Vance?'

'Yes?' I manage to say, my throat suddenly raw.

'I'm afraid we're going to need to take immediate action—'

'He's just been talking to two detectives!' Cal's face darkens. 'What's wrong with him?'

'Parker's body is beginning to shut down. I'm afraid we're going to put him into an induced coma to give him the best chance of fighting the sepsis.'

THIRTY-NINE

Cal holds on to me as we leave the hospital. I feel my legs might give way any moment. I stop walking.

'I can't go. I can't just leave him like this.'

'Come on, Nicola, you heard what they said. We should be able to come later today if he stabilises. The doctor sounded confident, didn't he?'

I sniff and manage a miserable nod. The doctor had said, 'It sounds very dramatic, but an induced coma is the safest state for your son to be in right now. It takes all the stress from the body, protects the brain and allows it to recalibrate to prevent organ failure.'

I'd asked him if speaking to the detectives had caused the problem to worsen. 'I don't think that's very likely,' he'd said. 'The doctor who gave permission to the police considered your son was fit to chat for a few minutes given the seriousness of their enquiries. Sadly, he took a turn for the worse.'

I'd nodded but I wondered if the staff would tell me the truth anyway. Now, I can feel my face burning and I'm skittish. I can't keep still. Can't focus.

'I think if we can grab a few hours' rest then we can come

back later.' He stops by a wooden bench. 'Sit here and I'll get the van with you being unsteady on your feet.'

Cal walks off and I sit down, thinking again about the fact the hospital let the police in to speak to Parker. Movement across the car park makes me look and that's when I see them.

I stand up and despite my legs feeling weak, I start to walk towards the tall woman who is pushing a wheelchair.

'Luna!' I shout. 'Wait!'

Marie twists from the waist, sees me and starts to stride faster with the wheelchair.

When I catch up, Marie stops pushing the chair and spins around.

'What is your problem, Nicola?' She looks around us, at other people who are heading for their cars, breaking their step and taking an interest in our increasingly loud conversation. 'Stop causing a scene!'

I ignore her and move in front of Luna.

'Why are you trying to ruin Parker? Why did you go to the police when we don't know the facts yet?'

Luna looks down at her hands and says nothing.

'You had no right to get the detectives involved when he's so ill. You should be ashamed of yourself.'

'Don't say anything, Luna, darling.' Marie glares at me. 'Please move out of our way, Nicola, or you'll leave me with little option but to call the police.'

Cal comes running up, breathless. 'Nicola, what's happening?'

'I'm asking Luna why she's framing Parker for something he's had nothing to do with,' I say simply, shrugging off Cal's restraining hand.

'You know nothing about our life, Nicola,' Luna says, her voice calm and quiet. 'You think you know Parker, but you don't. You really don't.'

'I know you're sleeping apart,' I snap. 'I know he asked to

speak to me privately the morning after the dinner dance and he didn't want you to know about it.'

She looks away, but not before I see a strange look cross her face.

'What kind of a person betrays their partner when they're fighting for their life?' I continue. 'How do we know *you're* not the one who'd tried to destroy the scarf?'

'Now you're just being ridiculous!' Marie interrupts again.

'I hope you're satisfied.' I round on her. 'I won't let you airbrush our son out of your lives this way by lying to the police. You've never liked him. He's never quite been good enough for her, has he?'

'Come on, Nicola.' Cal takes my arm. 'Don't bring yourself down to their level. Let's go home.'

I look at Luna and then at her mother. 'Parker wanted to speak to me about something and I'm going to find out what it is. See why you were so keen to tell the police Parker had some involvement with that scarf.'

Marie lifts her chin. 'Are you threatening us, Nicola?'

'Not at all. I'm just telling it like it is. If you take Parker down, I'll make sure you go down with him,' I say and look at Luna. 'So don't get too comfortable in your nice private hospital.'

Luna looks at me and then at Cal. She smiles and her mother starts to push her in the opposite direction.

Back in the van, Cal is quiet for a while. Then he says, 'Maybe you shouldn't have said some of that stuff. Marie and Joe could make life very difficult for us.'

'I'm sick of keeping quiet, Cal. We've done it for too long.'

'They have money, a legal team. They could break us as easily as that—' he snaps his fingers '—if they wanted to.'

'I'm not running scared anymore. Frightened of offending them in some way.' I stare out of the window at people going about their business. Doing everyday things, their lives just ticking along undisturbed. 'Not challenging Parker and Luna about never coming to see us. The way she went to the police behind our backs. I'm finished with excusing it all.'

Stopping at the traffic lights close to home, Cal turns his head to watch me. 'So what are you planning to do instead?'

'I'm going to find out what's been happening in their lives. Parker kept us at arm's length and I'm wondering why that was. What was he trying to keep from us?'

'Sounds a bit dramatic,' Cal mumbles, accelerating when the lights turn green.

'He wanted to talk to me about something the morning after the dinner dance. Didn't want anyone else to know.'

'And he gave you no hint what it was about?'

'No. He said it was important to tell me everything, right from the beginning. That's what he said. *Right from the beginning.*'

'Hmm. Could be something quite innocent. Maybe he wanted to talk about work or Barney's schooling.'

I glance at Cal. 'You didn't see what he was like, Cal. He seemed worried about something. We made a definite time when Luna was at home and you were at work.'

'Charming!'

'It was something important, I know it was.' I hesitate. 'What if it was to do with that scarf?'

Cal had left the gates open so now he pulls on to the drive before turning off the engine. He unbuckles his seat belt and looks at me. 'I worry about you, Nicola, getting stressed out like this. It's not that long ago you were being told by the hospital to avoid stressful situations to give yourself the best chance of recovery.' We both get out of the van. 'If you put the kettle on, I'll make you a cuppa when I come back in. I just need to get the last tools out.' He kisses me on the cheek. 'We just have to pray that Parker will recover. There'll be no guesswork then; you can just ask him what he wanted to talk about.'

I nod, but when I'm inside the house with the door closed, I walk quickly into the kitchen, take out my phone and call the hotel they were staying at on Friday night.

The call is picked up within a couple of rings and I explain who I am. 'My son and his wife attended an event at your hotel Friday evening but they checked out in the early hours and sadly, had a car accident on their way home.'

'Oh dear, I'm so sorry to hear that. I hope... they're both OK?'

'Not really, no,' I say to a slightly awkward silence. 'I'm trying to piece together a timeline of what happened, so I can better understand why they checked out early instead of stopping over. It's just a couple of questions I have if you don't mind.'

'Of course,' she says, sounding genuinely concerned. 'We'd be glad to help in any way we can.' She asks for their names, which I provide.

'Firstly, can you confirm who arranged the dinner dance they attended? I assume it was probably the company my son works for. And secondly, I wondered if they said anything at the desk about why they had to check out so early. Whether they gave an excuse?'

'I wasn't working Friday evening but I believe my colleague was. I'm just going to put you on hold for a moment. Is that OK?'

'Thank you, that's fine,' I say. For the first time, my heart feels just a tiny bit lighter. I'm grateful for her compassionate manner, grateful enough I don't mind the toneless sounds that start playing in my ear.

If it is Parker's company who arranged the event, I will give them a ring. Doubtless there would be lots of other staff there and someone might be aware if Parker and Luna had a problem and said they were checking out early. It just doesn't make any sense they'd go way before breakfast with no explanation to anyone.

It's less than a minute before the receptionist is back.

'Mrs Vance, thanks for waiting. I just want to check it's definitely Friday evening we're talking about?'

A chill starts to rise from the bottom of my spine. 'That's right. Friday night.'

'Right. The reason I'm asking is that although your son and his wife checked in, there was no event held here over the weekend. The last dinner dance we held here was at Christmas.'

My ears start to pound. I must have made a mistake.

'I... I don't understand. My son told me the event was being held there and that's why they chose to stay over. They were both so excited to attend the dinner dance, they even sent me a photograph of them all dressed up before they came down.'

Just about to make our entrance!

'That is very strange,' she agrees. 'My colleague said there was nothing out of the ordinary at check-out. They wouldn't need to give a reason for leaving early because it's auto-checkout with full pre-payment. That means guests simply drop their keys into a night box and are free to leave the hotel at their convenience. And I can see on the system that they did leave their room keys.'

'I just... I don't know what to say.'

'I'm so sorry, Mrs Vance,' the woman says, her voice full of sympathy. 'Is there anything else I can help you with? Anything else you want to ask?'

I can hear voices in the background and I realise she's probably got guests arriving at the desk that she needs to deal with.

'No, no. That's all I wanted to know. Thank you.' When the call ends, I walk over to the kitchen window and look out at the lawn Parker used to kick a football around on. He'd be out there from when he got home from school until I called him in for his tea and bath.

Life was so simple back then. I knew my son better than he knew himself but now... now, I feel like I barely know him at all. He kept us out of his life and the details he did share were carefully selected to make me think my worries were in my own mind. He's been playing me for some reason, kept stringing me along to think everything was fine.

I'm only just entertaining the possibility that everything Parker has led me to believe so far about his life is a lie.

He's told me lie after lie, after lie.

What I don't know yet, is why.

FORTY

SARAH

NINE MONTHS EARLIER

Since she'd moved out of her mum's house and into her own place, there was no denying that Sarah's life had taken a definite turn for the better.

She dressed herself and Millie in designer clothes, she made sure they enjoyed at least one nice outing together at the weekends and more in school holidays. It might be a visit to the petting farm, or perhaps the cinema and then TGI Fridays afterwards. Always the sort of outing she knew Millie would love.

Sarah stocked her fridge and cupboards full of the best organic food and enjoyed ordering sundries online just so she'd get parcels every day. Yesterday she'd ordered a craft set for Millie and a pretty blanket for her mum. It didn't matter that they were small things. It felt like the more she bought, the more money she spent, the quicker she could fill that little dark space inside herself and chase away those feelings of never having, or being, enough.

But since her fortunes had changed, another problem had crept in unnoticed until now. Sarah's tastes and purchasing habits had outgrown even her supercharged new income. There was the hefty mortgage and associated living costs together with high food and eating out bills and her insatiable appetite for designer clothes and handbags. There were also pricey new fitted wardrobes in both bedrooms, the glossy white kitchen and appliances she'd had installed before they moved in, and the luxurious soft grey carpets throughout she'd replaced the wooden floors with so they could be hoovered into triangular patterns like she'd seen on Instagram. On top of the thousands it had all cost, she'd paid a premium to get the work done quickly to allow them to move in well before Christmas.

She'd gone out for drinks with a couple of the other girls she worked with. One had just bought a brand-new sports car and the other had spent twenty grand on cosmetic procedures. After a few cocktails, Sarah had confided in them.

'My lifestyle is great, but my income is lagging behind!' she'd said lightly. 'Any tips on how I can increase my client numbers quickly?'

'It's not so much getting more and more clients, you should be focusing on upselling to your best ones,' one said.

'We all have one or two super-clients, as I like to call them,' the other remarked. 'You know, the ones who are logging on and viewing your pics and stuff every day. They're the ones who'll pay a lot more to sign up to the direct messaging and tailored pics.'

Sarah had nodded. She had such a client. A guy called Jack who looked gorgeous in his profile pic. He had dark hair, broad shoulders and a pearly-white smile. His photo showed him standing next to a Lamborghini sports car. He spent a lot of money with her already.

'The pay's great but if you really want the big money, you've got to diversify,' the girls agreed over cocktails.

'Diversify?' Sarah had frowned.

'You need more than the basic income stream to support the lifestyle you have. And for all the forum keeps urging us to increase our client numbers, the real money comes from private clients. Wealthy private clients who want to be your sugar daddy in return for... favours.' The girls winked and giggled.

Sarah had shaken her head firmly. 'That's not for me. I don't want to go there.' She'd chosen her words carefully, mindful that the other two women obviously welcomed this line of work. 'I just need to earn a bit more.'

'There's a compromise, but you won't make the really big money.' One had sniffed and drained her cocktail glass.

That's when they'd talked to her in detail about the private messaging, sending clients personalised photographs and videos tailored to their personal tastes. It sounded like a halfway house between the lightweight stuff she was doing now and... well, the stuff *they* did.

When Sarah showed interest, the other girls hit their stride.

'You might get lucky and find your prince.' One grinned, sipping daintily at her drink.

'Run off into the sunset together and leave your webcam behind. But be warned; generally, they're all married with kids or still live with their mother.'

Sarah had grinned. 'Don't worry, I'm not looking for a relationship.'

'Most of the super-clients tend to be older – the sort of guys you wouldn't look at twice in a bar.' The other had laughed. 'That's where you close your eyes and think of England, so to speak.'

'Better still, close your eyes and think of your bank balance!' The other women had hooted with laughter and even Sarah, thawing a little thanks to her second Cosmopolitan, had allowed herself a little chuckle.

They'd ordered more drinks and Sarah had changed the subject. She needed time now to think around the problem.

She liked the idea of focusing on specific clients and she had the perfect man in mind.

FORTY-ONE

NICOLA

When I finish the call to the hotel, I see Cal has disappeared down the garden to potter around in his shed. I walk into the living room still musing over why Parker and Luna would tell a lie over something as simple as attending a dinner dance.

I see through the window there are people outside the gate. Two women and a man just sort of standing there, talking. Every so often, they look at our house before turning away again.

I stand just behind a curtain for a while and when two more people join them, one carrying a camera, I know it's the press. I shiver. What are they doing here? Surely the Barton-Jameses wouldn't stoop so far as to leak details of what they've told the police about Sarah Grayson's murder. It's all speculation as yet. Nothing has been proven about who the scarf belongs to.

There's only one way to find out what they want and to try and get them away from the gate. I open the front door and walk down the drive. I see a neighbour across the road polishing his car... rubbing at the same spot again and again while gawping shamelessly at the house.

'Mrs Vance? Mrs Vance, what are your views on your son

being involved in the disappearance and murder of Sarah Grayson?'

Another: 'Did your son murder Sarah Grayson? Did he keep her scarf as a trophy?'

'Listen to me.' I clap my hands sharply and they fall quiet. 'I need you to move away from my property. My son isn't here, he's in hospital. Can you just—'

'Is it correct that you found the murder victim's missing scarf, Mrs Vance?' A young woman, probably in her late twenties, pushes some kind of recording device close to my face.

'Stop that, now!' I instinctively raise my hand to push it away and it clatters to the floor. Something snaps off and bounces into the gutter.

The guy with the camera steps forward. *Click-click-click.*

'I'm sorry, that was an accident. I didn't mean to—'

'Is it true you're banned from seeing your grandson?' The same young woman has an added streak of meanness now I've crossed her. 'Because a source is saying you knew about the scarf and you protected your son. He was questioned by police at the beginning of the investigation, is that right? His car was spotted in the area where Sarah's body was found.'

'No! That's completely untrue!' *A source says...* I've read that phrase so many times in the media. It's just a way of getting away with saying stuff that hasn't been corroborated. 'The police haven't even confirmed the scarf belonged to Sarah Grayson yet!'

'Nicola!' I hear Cal call from the front door. 'Come inside. Don't talk to them!'

I turn and walk back to the house. They're still shouting awful things, accusatory things about Parker. About me. Out of the corner of my eye I see Amira from next door dash back inside the house without speaking or acknowledging I'm there. Amira, who always brings us gifts of homemade food on birthdays and holidays and whose front hedge Cal cuts when he does our own.

'Come on, love, you shouldn't have gone out there. They're the lowest of the low.' Cal helps me back inside. My legs feel shaky and I sit on the stairs to gather myself.

'They're saying I knew, Cal. They're saying I knew about the scarf and they...' My voice breaks but I have to say the words. 'They're calling our son a murderer. They really think he did it.'

'They are full of hot air, Nicola. They can't print anything without any evidence, they're just bluffing.'

'I rang the hotel... there was no dinner dance there.'

'What?'

'Parker told us they were going to a dinner dance but there was no such event on. So why were they there?'

Cal throws his hands up. 'Who knows, Nicola? To be honest, that's the least of our problems.'

'But the things the press are saying... that's what they really think, isn't it? That's what everyone is going to think if that scarf turns out to belong to... oh dear God.'

I stand up and walk down the hallway.

Cal holds me while I sob into his chest.

'I know, love. I know. But listen, once Parker gets over this sticky patch and starts to recover, they'll have no power then, will they?'

'It's a bit more than a sticky patch, Cal.' I pull away and look at him, rubbing at my sore eyes. 'What if he doesn't recover, doesn't wake up from this coma? What then? They'll be able to say what they like about him.'

'We can't think like that.'

'We'd be stupid not to consider the worst-case scenario. You know that's true.' I can't bring myself to say it, but I can see from his grim expression that Cal knows exactly what I mean. 'If the worst did happen and we lose Parker, the Barton-Jameses already have Barney. We might never get to see our grandson again.'

'Luna will be recovered soon, I'm sure. Then she'll be taking care of Barney again.'

I let out a harsh laugh. 'What makes you think she'll be any different to them? She's already stabbed Parker in the back, going to the police while he's so ill. What kind of woman do you think she is?'

Cal lets out a frustrated sigh and runs a hand through his hair. 'We have to give her the benefit of the doubt until we know otherwise, or things will start to seem hopeless.'

I can't even reply to that. I'm already feeling more despairing than I've ever done in my life and there's good reason for it.

Cal's phone rings and he moves away to take the call. I return to the living room and pull the curtains closer together, putting my head in my hands. I just don't know which way to turn. When I open my eyes my gaze falls on a framed photograph on the console table. It was taken at the coast when Parker was around the age Barney is now.

His face is tanned, his smile bright. In fact that goes for the three of us. A family. Together. Committed to each other. Things have changed, life got in the way, but strip it all back and that photo is the bedrock of the person Parker is today. That's how he's been raised.

It's true I feel confused, angry and upset with my son. But despite acknowledging he's repeatedly told me lies, I look at the happy boy in that photograph and I cannot accept he had anything to do with that poor girl's death.

Marie and Joe are piling more and more against Parker – against us. Meanwhile, they're shielding Luna, keeping her safe from harm and getting ready to move her over a hundred miles away. They're in the process of building a brick wall around her. Currently, the police seem to be taking everything they say as the truth and Parker is unable to defend himself, tell his side of the story.

I've felt so hopeless up to now, but seeing the press so eager to jump to conclusions like that... something shifts inside me. Honestly, I can't be certain Parker knows nothing about Sarah Grayson's murder. But I know my only chance of finding out more is to get a grasp on what's been going on in Parker's life. It won't be easy because he's always kept his life private from us. Even more so this past year and I must now face he's told blatant lies to cover up... what? I don't know.

Before the accident, Parker had already said there was something he wanted to talk about. To offload. For the first time since he's been married, he'd turned to me for help.

I need to find out why he looked so worried when he asked for a chat with me. We might not have seen much of our son in the last few years, but I'm still the person Parker planned to turn to before the accident changed everything.

He didn't choose his wife or his dad. He didn't choose his in-laws, either.

My son chose me for a reason.

FORTY-TWO

NICOLA

MONDAY

Only a few weeks ago, I read various articles and reports about the murder of Sarah Grayson like everyone else did. I had a sense of horror with the utmost sympathy for Sarah's family. How must they feel? Did they have any theories of what might have happened that awful night?

The one good thing to come from all my interest in the case is that I now have a good overview of that night and what happened.

I decide to start with Sarah's widowed mother, Julie Grayson. The woman I watched baring her grieving soul on national television when she begged for help.

Please, someone must know something. If you suspect your partner, your son, your work colleague... if you knew this pain, this hopelessness, you would help us!

Cal is still trying to rearrange his existing jobs for the next couple of weeks, so I leave a note that I've had to pop out and I get in the car.

The press named the town Julie lives in, but the hairdresser

I visit lives just a couple of streets away from her and so I roughly know where her house is although not the number. The press reported that after Sarah moved into her new flat, Julie Grayson was living alone, but after the death of her daughter, she's now raising her grandaughter, Millie. I know the area, know exactly where the street is. But I don't know her full address. Still, the case has drawn such attention, I know I'll easily locate her by asking one or two people nearby.

In the event, I don't need to ask anyone directions. I park further down the road, zip my jacket up and stuff my hands in the pockets. When I start walking down the long street, I see a woman who looks like Julie Grayson at a distance – small with jet black hair – letting herself into a house about halfway down.

As I enter the front gate of the modest semi-detached property, someone calls out: 'Are you visiting Julie Grayson?'

I turn round and see two people, one snapping pictures of me with a big camera. The recent negative press and speculation about Parker's role in what's happened seems to have reignited a fresh interest.

Someone else calls from across the road: 'What's your name? Did you know Sarah?'

Then more people, seemingly appearing from nowhere, start running towards the gate.

Behind me a cacophony of shouting starts up. I ring the doorbell and wait, praying Mrs Grayson answers.

I ignore all attempts to engage me in conversation, but my blood turns cold as I hear someone say: 'She's Parker Vance's mother!' I'd seen a couple pictures of myself online, mouth open and eyes wide, snapped when I'd knocked the reporter's equipment to the floor by mistake. I'd been shocked and apologising, but the photos make it seem as if I'm yelling in temper. Now everyone out here seems to recognise me.

So many people are shouting together, I can only catch odd words and phrases.

'Is your son guilty?... murder... scarf... why are you here?'

I ring the doorbell again, leaving my finger there. Beside where I'm standing, a net curtain trembles slightly and I catch sight of a pale hand in a narrow gap. At the top of the bay window, I notice that a smaller top window is slightly open.

'I'm not a reporter, Mrs Grayson,' I call, outside the glass. 'My name is Nicola and I live in the next town. I'm here because I'd like to speak to you. I'm in a similar position with my son... I'm trying to find out the truth of what happened to Sarah.'

The voices behind me die down as they strain to hear what's being said.

The curtain doesn't move and the front door remains firmly closed. Behind me, the volume of the press voices ratchets up a notch.

'Has Parker confessed? Did your son kill Sarah Grayson?'

I turn to the window again. 'I'm hoping we might be able to help each other, Mrs Grayson. I won't stay long, I just need to speak with you. A few minutes of your time, that's all I—'

The door opens and the woman I've seen in a hundred press photographs, and who I've watched crying on television and begging for information on her murdered daughter, stands in front of me. She is smaller than she looked on TV and has a gentle air about her. Her grey eyes seem far away in another place. I can't even begin to imagine the horror she has been through during the last five weeks.

The press interest explodes at the sight of her and I have to lean forward to hear her speaking.

'You'd better come in,' she says in a soft, sad voice. 'This lot will eat us alive given the chance.'

I step gratefully inside the house and she closes and locks the door behind me. The small hallway is scattered with mismatched wood: dark floorboards, a mahogany bannister and a light oak console table bearing a lamp. There are far too many framed photographs of a young, attractive red-haired woman I recognise as Sarah packed on to the small dusty table top.

'Come through to the kitchen,' Mrs Grayson says. 'I want to stay as far away from the baying press as possible. What did you say your name was?'

'Nicola,' I say, purposely omitting my surname. The papers are all quoting my son's full name along with words and phrases like 'allegedly', 'believed to be' and 'possibly' to cover themselves. I fear that the second she realises who I am, I'll be out on my ear with the door slammed in my face. She'll never speak to me again. 'I live in the next town.'

She nods. 'I'm Julie, as you seem to know.' She leads me into a small, clean kitchen with pine units and a freestanding compact table and four chairs. There's a cork noticeboard on the wall covered in photographs of Sarah, many with her daughter and her mum. The two women don't really look alike with their different colouring, but Julie does have a small neat nose like I've seen in the pictures of Sarah.

Julie directs me to sit down at the wooden table and I accept her offer of tea.

'You mentioned your son,' she says, filling the kettle. 'Have you lost him in similar circumstances?'

'No. That is, not yet. I... he was involved in a serious car accident with his wife at the weekend and he's currently in a coma,' I say. 'It's touch and go whether he'll make it.'

'Oh no. I'm so sorry.' She takes two mugs out of the wall cupboard, pops a teabag in each and sits down opposite me. 'I thought you meant you'd lost him, like I've lost Sarah. Her daughter, Millie, she's out with her great-auntie today – my late husband's sister. She's still so young, doesn't really understand what's happened at all. She keeps asking where her mummy is and every time she does, my heart breaks a little bit more.'

I want to reach over and squeeze her hand, but it's inappropriate. I don't know Julie at all but I know a disproportionate amount of information about what's happened to her daughter. I know I must come clean and tell her the truth, but I feel so nervous. I'm desperate for her to hear what I have to say before she throws me out.

'I can't imagine how you feel. It must be beyond heartbreaking,' I say as she rises to her feet when the kettle clicks. She pours boiling water into our mugs and stirs each one with a teaspoon.

'It's a feeling I pray no other mother ever has to go through,' she says, almost absent-mindedly as she stirs. 'But the pain is made worse still by the fact they haven't arrested anyone yet for Sarah's death.'

She adds milk to the mugs and brings them over, placing one down in front of me.

'The police tell me that might change very soon though,' she says, sitting back down at the table. 'I think they may have found their man. Have you seen the reports?'

'Yes. That's why I—'

'The police have been here. Shown me photos of some man who's in hospital. A man who they can't question or arrest until he's well on the road to recovery, apparently.' Her face darkens. 'Well, I hope that never happens. I hope he rots in hell.'

At that moment, I know I can no longer deceive her.

'Julie, I need to tell you why I'm here. It's a lot to ask, I know, but I'm begging you to hear me out.'

'I'll hear you out,' she says, sipping her tea. 'God knows I know everything about getting the grief off your chest. Although I'm not sure it's done me any good.'

'The man in hospital, his name is Parker Vance.'

She looks surprised. 'That's right. Did you read it in the newspapers? They questioned him, you know, but he had an alibi for the night Sarah was murdered. He had the same car a witness spotted driving around the area, but he's changed the vehicle now. If that's not a guilty reaction, I don't know what is.'

'I know his name because he's my son,' I say quietly. Underneath the table, my hands have bunched themselves into tight fists. I screw my nails into the cushion of my palms as I stare down at the table. 'I'm sorry, Julie. I couldn't tell you before because you wouldn't have given me a chance to explain—'

She pushes her chair away from the table but she doesn't stand up.

'Parker Vance is your son?'

I nod. 'And I truly believe he's innocent. I'm trying to find the truth.'

'I'd like you to leave, Nicola.' She doesn't raise her voice and it seems more powerful because of it. 'I'd like you to go now.'

'Julie, please. Yes, I'm his mum, but I know he's not capable of doing anything like that. I—'

'The detectives told me you found my Sarah's scarf, but you didn't tell them. At least your daughter-in-law had the decency to report it.'

'No! It's true I didn't go straight to the police, I took it to the hospital to ask Parker and Luna about it. We still don't know if the scarf belonged to Sarah. But I did recognise the design from the press coverage and I—'

'Where did you find it, the scarf?'

I take a breath. 'I found it at Parker and Luna's house. I stumbled on it by accident.'

'One of those reporters outside told me they'd tried to get rid of it. Put it out with the rubbish.'

I look at her. Who has told the press all this? I already know the answer to that; it can only be the Barton-Jameses.

'Julie, I won't protect my son if it's proven he had anything to do with your daughter's death. But until that happens, until the police prove his involvement, I have to help him the best I can because he's in no position to help himself.'

She looks at me steadily. 'And neither is my Sarah in a position to do anything because, thanks to your son, she's gone forever. She's cold and dead, lying not in a comfy hospital bed but on a mortuary slab covered in post-mortem scars.'

I shudder inwardly at her brutal language, at the pain I can see etched on her face. I shouldn't have come here. She's too raw, too angry inside. I can totally understand that – of course I can.

'I can't bury her yet, do you know that? They won't release the body because there might be more forensics required. More cutting and prodding at my beautiful girl who just a few weeks ago was so full of life.' Her voice breaks. 'All because the bastard who did it is too much of a coward to come forward.'

'I'm so, so sorry for your terrible loss, Julie. I really am,' I whisper, squeezing my eyes closed against the horror of it all.

She looks at me for a moment and I think I see a look of sympathy pass over her face.

'Two detectives came to see me last night. They told me about this man, your son. They said he was in hospital but that evidence had come to light from a new source. That they're now treating him as a suspect.'

'They're wrong, I swear. He—'

'Wait.' Julie raises her hand to quiet me. 'They showed me a photograph of him, your son, and I was able to identify him as the man I'd seen Sarah speaking to in the park close to her flat, a few weeks before she went missing.'

She waits for a reaction, but I feel frozen. They told me they were going to do this but... I realise that it's only since I found the scarf that the police have suspected Parker. The routine enquiry about his car had been a separate strand of investigation. As his alibi had checked out, they'd no reason to suspect him and show his picture to Julie Grayson back then.

'Is it possible you were mistaken about seeing him at the park?' I say carefully. 'Parker told me he'd never met Sarah.'

'It was him,' Julie says shortly. 'Sarah's new flat overlooked the park. I collected Millie from school one day and let myself in. I had a good view of Sarah and a man standing at the entrance to the park. They were talking, discussing some paperwork... possibly arguing. He looked up at her flat window, so I saw his face. The man was your son.'

'Did you ask Sarah who he was?'

'Yes, but... she just brushed me off. Said he was just a guy she knew and that I worried too much.'

She walks across the kitchen, opens a deep drawer and picks up what looks like a pad of crinkly tissue paper. She brings it back to the table and lays it down, flat. She starts to unwrap the paper carefully, almost reverently. When the last piece is peeled away, she sits back and I look at the item folded neatly inside.

'Sarah loved to wear scarves. She has a drawer full of them upstairs, but this one is special. This is the one she wore the day before she went missing.' She reaches for the scarf and I force myself to keep my breathing steady. It's identical to the scarf I found but blues and yellows instead of the black and gold colour scheme of the one I found at Parker's house. 'The one you found... does it look the same?'

She takes the corners and shakes it out, the fine silk fabric billowing into the air. I battle nausea as my nostrils fill with a sweet, floral perfume, identical to the scent that was on the scarf I found.

And then I know. At that moment, even without any conclusive test results yet, I know without any doubt whatsoever that the scarf I found at my son's house did belong to Sarah Grayson.

FORTY-THREE

SARAH

NINE MONTHS EARLIER

DIRECT MESSAGES – FANTASYFORUM

To: Emerald (Sarah Grayson)

From: Client #31 Jack Benedict

EMERALD: Hey, thanks for increasing your credits, Jack. I appreciate your support.

JACK: You're very welcome. So great to be in direct contact with you. You brighten up my day, do you know that?

EMERALD: That's so nice of you to say. Will be great to chat on here and, who knows, if you want to take it off the platform, we can always come to a private arrangement. Just let me know if you're interested...

JACK: Can you send more details of that? Definitely interested!

EMERALD: Sure. Can you click the link below in the next ten minutes? It's just a way I can verify who I'm dealing with. There are a lot of weird people on here!

Link to: Emerald19374@gmlz.com*

JACK: I can imagine! Thanks, sweetheart. Email on its way.

Jack's email arrived three minutes after she sent the direct message. One of the girls she'd been for cocktails with had recommended taking any private messages on to email.

'First, it gets rid of the forum's mandatory fee for each customer, and secondly, if you post a link, they'll forget themselves in all the excitement and reply to it straight away. If they do that, the email client will pick up their default email which is most likely not the false one they usually use when communicating with you.'

The other woman had grinned. 'Sorts out the wheat from the chaff when that happens. I had one guy swear on his mother's life he was Brad Pitt. His email revealed he was actually Fred Smith from Halifax.'

Sarah had enjoyed the joke but actually it had been a brilliant tip because Jack had unwittingly replied from a business email and she was just about to check it out. Hopefully she'd soon discover exactly who 'Jack' was and, once she'd discovered that, the sky was the limit in terms of extra income.

Best of all, she'd had her own idea based on what the girls had told her. An idea that should be far more effective in extracting money from this client than a few erotic photographs.

'I suppose you could say we're in a bit of a fix, boss.' Brewster is busy tapping away at his keyboard as Helena approaches. 'On the one hand, we've made a great deal of progress, but the main suspect is in a coma and until such time as we can get a DNA sample from him, our hands are tied.'

'True, but let's not under-estimate how powerful it is that Julie Grayson has now identified Vance as the man she saw in the park with her daughter a couple of months before she disappeared.'

Mrs Grayson had told police she'd seen her daughter with a man in the park a few weeks before her death, but she didn't realise any significance at the time. She didn't know who Parker Vance was but she'd had a clear view of his face that day. Following the discovery of the scarf in Nicola and Cal Vance's home, Helena and Brewster had taken three photographs round to Mrs Grayson. She'd pointed immediately at the middle one – Parker Vance – and said firmly, 'That's him. No doubt in my mind; that's who Sarah was talking to.'

'That's true, but there are other things we can do,' Helena says. 'Because we only made routine enquiries about his vehicle and were satisfied with his alibi, we haven't looked at Vance in any detail yet, at all. We'll need to speak to his employers again to find what the exact timeline of this conference was. We need to know the last time he was seen in the evening of her murder and how early he was sighted the following morning.'

'See if he could have feasibly got back, killed Sarah and returned to the conference,' Brewster murmurs.

'Exactly. We need to speak to Luna Vance in greater detail, too. Find out what her thoughts really are about her husband... and in the meantime, let's chase up his phone records.'

Brewster nods. 'I'll get on to that right away. There's Nicola Vance to think about, too. The issue of whether she knowingly withheld evidence when she found that scarf, even though it was only a short time.'

'Agreed. So, what next?'

'I've already arranged for us to speak to Luna Vance early afternoon, boss. The Barton-Jameses are waiting for the go-ahead from us to move her to a private hospital. They're claiming Luna did us a big favour reporting the recovery of the scarf and so we should reciprocate.'

'It doesn't quite work like that. We're not in the business of doing favours.' Helena frowns. 'I think, under the circum-stances, we need her to stay put until we're satisfied she's the innocent party here. We need a better picture of the Vances' relationship leading up to the time of Sarah's death.'

'I'll sort that out pronto.' He turns back to his computer as a notification dings.

Helena nods, distracted. 'It feels like we're missing some-thing big here, Brewster. We need to find the piece that opens up the big picture.'

Brewster turns and looks at her. 'I think we might just have it.' He points at his monitor. 'We've just got the initial DNA results through. A match for Sarah Grayson. It's her scarf, boss.'

Helena feels her chest lift. They'd sent the scarf Nicola

Vance had found for testing with an initial subset of markers rather than a full specification. This would give them a very strong indication of whether a suspect was indeed guilty before more in-depth tests were done before court proceedings. This interim level of testing had been done in the interests of speed – extensive DNA testing was notoriously slow – and because they had a definite suspect in mind: Parker Vance.

'All we need is a sample from Vance to prove we've hit the jackpot, but my gut tells me we're much closer now.' Brewster punches the air.

'Let's hope so because Sarah's family are desperate for a conclusion,' Helena remarks, noting her partner's enthusiasm. 'Best to remain cautious, Brewster. *My* gut tells me we're not quite out of the woods yet.'

At the ward desk, Brewster gives the receptionist their details.

'Please take a seat, DS Brewster. Someone will be out to take you through to Mrs Vance's room shortly.'

Brewster raises an eyebrow as they move over to the seating area. 'Sounds like the Barton-Jameses have managed to somehow get her into her own room in an overcrowded NHS hospital. You can't keep some people down, eh?'

Helena nods and pulls up notes on her phone. 'Obviously, we're going to take it easy with Luna Vance today. Although she's not in as bad a way as her husband, it seems she has some quite serious challenges to overcome. Not least a broken pelvis and they're having problems regulating her blood pressure.'

'Hmm. The doctor emphasised if she got upset in any way we'd have to leave. Don't fancy going back to the station before we've barely started. The super's not going to like that one bit.'

'Essentially, we're after a feel of what's been happening in the family, particularly in their marriage. We both agree there are some strange vibes in the air, some people not saying what they mean. Now we know a bit more, there's the possibility of others using this situation to lay the blame entirely at Parker

Vance's door. The doctor I spoke to told me he's still in a very bad way. They're not going to let us near him for at least the next forty-eight hours and obviously we've no room to push on that issue.'

Helena nods, understanding that in cases where a suspect is seriously ill, the person's welfare must be determined by a medical professional before police are granted permission to begin questioning. Parker Vance, currently unconscious, is not in a fit state at this point in time.

'Hello, are you the detectives?' A smiling young nurse stands in front of them. 'I can take you through to see Luna now.'

'Thank you,' says Helena. 'How is she?'

'Well, it's early days, of course, but signs of improvement are there. She's been relaxing and is still on quite a bit of medication, so the doctor has asked me to emphasise that you shouldn't stay too long and keep your questioning light.'

'Of course,' Helena says.

The nurse leads them down a corridor. At the end, they turn left and the nurse stops in front of a door.

'This is Luna's room and she knows you're coming. I'll leave you to it and I'll be back in about fifteen minutes. If she's happy to chat longer that's fine, but we'll see how it goes.'

'That's fair enough,' Brewster says. 'Thank you.'

The nurse opens the door and Brewster throws Helena a look. Marie Barton-James stands beside her daughter's bedside. She's dressed in starched dark denim jeans with a white blouse and several long, grouped gold necklaces. Her hair and make-up look immaculate as if she's just visited a salon. Beside her is a man in his early fifties, dressed in a grey pinstriped suit. A pale, bruised Luna stares vacantly at the wall, lacing and unlacing her fingers.

The nurse leaves the room, closing the door softly behind her and Marie smiles tightly at the detectives. 'DS Brewster, DI

Price. I've taken the liberty of asking our solicitor, Brian Bayley, to sit in on your interview.'

'That's fine, Mrs Barton-James. We have a few questions, but we're not here to conduct a formal interview.'

Marie gives a tight smile. 'Starts off like that, but we don't want things spiralling out of control, do we?'

Helena does not reply but smiles at Luna. 'Hello, Luna. Thank you for agreeing to speak with us again. How are you feeling?'

'A little better, I think.'

'She'll feel better when she can focus on her recovery and stop answering questions about something she knows nothing about,' Marie says curtly.

Brewster sniffs and takes out his notebook. 'We wanted to speak with you, Luna, to try and get a picture of how things were for you before the accident. You'll appreciate Nicola Vance has given us some information and—'

Marie gives a harsh laugh. 'I wouldn't believe a thing that woman says.'

'And as you'll appreciate, Luna, we're obliged to try and corroborate some of that information,' Brewster says, without acknowledging the interruption.

'Yes, of course,' Luna says. 'If I can help, I will.'

'Thank you. So, first of all, can you just confirm what happened on Friday evening... in particular how you came to travel home so unexpectedly?'

They had checked out the couple had actually stayed at the hotel and that they had used the automatic check-out facility to leave in the early hours of the morning. Beyond that, the staff had been unaware of any other problems with their stay, but Brewster had also requested they send full guest records of that evening for closer inspection.

'After the event, we got back to our room and went to bed, but Parker couldn't seem to rest. Then he got up, began pacing around the bedroom and said he felt unwell and wanted to go home.'

Brewster raises an eyebrow. 'And this was in the early hours? Had you both been drinking?'

'I'd had a few glasses of champagne, but Parker had stuck to soft drinks all night.'

'That's very disciplined of him when you were intending to stay over at the venue.'

'He's not a big drinker, never has been. And he said he had several things he wanted to get done on the Saturday.'

'Did he mention what those things were?' Helena asks.

'No doubt getting rid of the scarf he'd hidden away,' Marie mutters.

'You know that for a fact, do you, Mrs Barton-James?' Brewster turns to her, his pen raised above the notebook. 'Because we're only dealing with facts here. Any deviation from that is most certainly not helpful.'

Marie glares at her solicitor, who looks away and shuffles a few papers.

'He didn't say, but he'll have meant work. He's recently been promoted and he's putting in a lot of extra effort.'

Brewster nods. 'So it was agreed you'd go home. And Parker drove even though he said he felt unwell?'

'Yes. Once he'd got dressed and I'd packed our things, he said he was feeling a little better just knowing we were going home.'

'Can you tell us exactly how the accident happened, Luna?' Helena says softly.

'It was so quick, I... I can't remember anything until the paramedics were suddenly there but before, we were just talking and Parker seemed to be getting more and more agitated. He said he had something to tell me. That he was so, so sorry but it was something terrible. I felt sick. I said, "Just tell me" and he said he would but it had to be when we got back home. He said he wanted to tell his mother what he'd done, too. We... we started arguing.'

'About?'

Luna looks up at the detectives. 'I was convinced he was having an affair. I didn't know with who but... I started off suspecting it months ago and I wrote down a list of things that were happening – stuff that seemed out of the ordinary. Him lying when he'd been in the office all day when I knew from the receptionist he'd met someone for lunch, more overnight conferences than ever. I knew the signs. But he denied it all.'

'What happened next?'

'I fell asleep. I've not been sleeping well for some time. A jolt woke me and I told him to pull over and tell me what was wrong. But he wouldn't stop the car. He was staring at the road, gripping the steering wheel like a mad man. I can remember looking at him, noticing the sweat on his upper lip and forehead. He was driving faster and faster and then... then the car was just spinning out of control. They tell me I was unconscious for a short time.' She looks down at her bruised hands and Helena notices one long nude fingernail has been torn off and left crusted blood covering her natural short nail bed. 'I'm sorry, it's not much help, I know.'

'Parker caused them to crash, basically,' Marie says. 'There was no other vehicle involved and it was a clear night with good conditions.'

'He didn't do it on purpose, Mum.'

'Well, as you've said, you can't remember, darling. Who knows what was going through his mind... although we can probably guess.'

'What do you think he wanted to tell you when you both got home?' Brewster says.

Luna sighs. 'With everything that's happened since... the scarf being discovered... I can only think he might have wanted to confess.'

'I'd say he did,' Marie says bluntly. 'He knew he was going to be found out. Wanted to tell Luna and his mother before the police did.' She looks at her daughter. 'Go on, tell them. Tell them what you really think.'

'Mum!' Luna rubs her forehead before addressing the two detectives. 'It was just... the way he was speaking about something terrible he'd done... I think... well, I think he might have wanted to tell me he'd murdered Sarah Grayson.'

'No doubt about it in my mind!' Marie declares triumphantly as Luna stifles a sob.

'We have some personal questions to ask you, Luna,' Helena says, glancing pointedly at Marie Barton-James. 'Perhaps you might like some privacy while we do that?'

'Luna has agreed for both me and Mr Bayley here to be present throughout your visit,' Marie says firmly.

Helena notices Brewster's foot tap-tapping on the floor. A sure sign his patience is being tested.

'It's fine,' Luna says wearily. 'Let's just get it over with.'

'Nicola Vance mentioned you and your husband have been sleeping apart and your house was up for sale.'

'That insufferable woman,' Marie hisses.

'Mrs Barton-James. If you insist on remaining in the room, then please do not interrupt,' Brewster says in an authoritative tone.

Two indignant spots of red blossom on Marie's cheeks and Helena notices a muscle twitching in her jaw as she forces back a retort. Mercifully, she falls silent.

'We've been sleeping apart for a while,' Luna says quietly. 'Parker has been bad-tempered and anxious. He's even been snapping at Barney the last few weeks, which is unusual. I'd put it down to the pressures of his new job. He's had a chunky increase in salary, but has also gained a lot of extra responsibility and feels the pressure to make his mark in the company.'

Marie opens her mouth to speak but closes it again when Brewster gives her a look.

'Some might say it's surprising the two of you went for a nice night away to a hotel when you were having problems,' Brewster says. 'The picture you're building is that you had grown very much apart.'

'Well, that was just it. We'd had a long talk and I'd said I wanted to move back to Yorkshire. Make a fresh start together. Parker suggested we make a big effort, get out of the house and spend an evening together to talk things through.'

'And did you discuss your problems? Did Parker admit it was work issues?'

'No, that's just it. If he'd opened up a little, we could've solved it but he's not wanted to talk. He just makes an excuse or finds something to do when I try.' Luna hesitates and glances at her mother in a way that makes Helena wonder if she's been coached in her responses. 'I mean, that hasn't stopped me forming my own opinions. I still have my suspicions he's been having an affair.'

'But you have no proof of that?' Brewster says.

'No. Apart from the behaviour I've described, but earlier in the night he did make a cryptic comment he wouldn't elaborate on.'

'And that was?'

'He said, "I've done something incredibly stupid, and I don't know what the hell to do about it." When I asked him what he meant, he tried to backtrack. Said it was nothing, but of course it unnerved me.'

Helena watches as Luna scratches the side of her nose. Is she telling the truth?

'Had you and your husband discussed the disappearance and murder of Sarah Grayson in any detail up to this point?' Brewster says gravely.

There are a few moments of silence where Helena could swear the room grows cooler. Luna and her mother exchange glances. The solicitor shifts in his seat.

'Not really, not in any great detail,' Luna says. 'I mean, we obviously spoke about it when Parker was routinely questioned about his car.'

'And you confirmed to officers that he was working away at a conference the night Sarah Grayson disappeared,' Brewster says. 'That he didn't return home at any point that evening.'

'Yes. That's what he told me. He was in Newcastle at a conference the evening Sarah went missing and he certainly didn't come back home until the next day.'

Helena watches Luna carefully. The way her fingers are tapping a beat on the top of the bed sheet. Her newly heightened colour. The way she takes a sip of water to avoid saying more.

'Where did you go that night?' Helena says carefully.

'Mrs Vance has already appraised your officers of her and Mr Vance's whereabouts on that evening,' the solicitor says loftily.

'It would be helpful to recap, if you didn't mind, Luna.'

'Parker was away for the night as we've discussed. He left me and Barney at home about 8 a.m. Friday morning and it was the last time I saw him until Saturday afternoon. He stayed at the Mal Maison in the Quays that night, but I'm sure your officers will have checked all that out.'

'Did you speak to your husband during his time away?'

'Yes. I spoke to him a few times and texted him too.'

'So there is still no doubt in your mind he couldn't have come home early and returned after he'd seen Sarah Grayson?'

Luna sighs and glances at her mother.

'Well, that never occurred to me until... recently. But now, when I think back, he did seem a bit quiet when he came home on Saturday. I mean... it was possible he could have done so, I suppose.'

Helena can feel, rather than see, the change in Luna's demeanour. Although the younger woman appears to be calm, something about her feels skittish. And her staccato speaking pattern suggests to Helena that she feels nervous discussing the matter.

Brewster seems to have picked up on it, too.

'It feels like you have rather more doubts about your husband's whereabouts than you did five weeks ago when you were questioned,' he says.

A guarded look passes over Luna's face. 'I've had the benefit of hindsight now, haven't I? I'm taking into consideration his out-of-character behaviour. I thought you'd want me to do that.'

'Thank you,' Helena says, mindful of the time and the nurse's warning. 'Not much longer, now. If we can just discuss the scarf that Nicola Vance found in a rubbish bag outside your property. She came to the hospital to ask you about it.'

Luna puffs her cheeks and blows out air. 'That was a shock. I didn't know anything about it being at the house although it looked familiar from the police campaign to find it.'

'You'd followed the campaign?'

'I took an interest in the case with it being local and because of Parker being questioned about the car, yes. Of course I did.' Luna widens her eyes. 'But it's still a big leap to accept when someone says they found it at your house.'

'We understand the scarf was found at the bottom of a bin bag full of your own unwanted items,' Helena says.

'Apparently so.' Luna smooths the bed sheet. 'I suppose we just have to take Nicola's word for that, don't we?'

Helena shuffles to the edge of her seat. 'You think she might be lying about that?'

Luna shrugs. 'Who knows. If she found it amongst Parker's things I can't imagine her shopping her darling son. But still, I didn't really think it could be *that* scarf. You know, the murder case one.'

'I see,' Brewster says. 'And yet you alerted police almost immediately to the fact that you believed Mrs Vance had crucial murder investigation evidence on her person.'

'When Luna told me that mad woman had tricked her way into the ward,' Marie says, affronted, 'asking her if she knew about a scarf that allegedly belonged to a murder victim. I told her we should notify the police without a second thought. I'd imagine that's what you would have expected us to do as law-abiding citizens.'

'There's something else we need to ask you about, Luna,' Brewster says, markedly ignoring her mother. 'We have a witness statement and now, a positive identification that your husband met Sarah Grayson in the park next to her house a few weeks before she went missing. Are you aware of this?'

Luna glares at him. 'What do you think? Of course I wasn't aware of it. What kind of a question is that?'

'You seem angry rather than surprised,' Brewster says mildly.

'I'm shocked. Upset. Who is this witness?'

'Julie Grayson, Sarah's mother,' Helena says. 'We already had her statement, but following the discovery of the scarf, she identified your husband as the man her daughter was talking to.'

Luna stares at the wall and doesn't reply.

'Do you have any comment on this development?' Brewster says. 'Does it fit with your husband's movements around that time?'

'Maybe that's who he was having an affair with,' Luna says faintly. 'Sarah Grayson. Perhaps that's who it was.'

'I don't know what you're hoping to achieve here or what sophisticated investigation techniques you're using,' Marie says.

'But from a purely common-sense point of view, I think it's clear that Parker has been lying through his teeth to both the police and my daughter. It's obvious to all of us, I think, that it's more than possible he may have murdered that poor girl.'

FORTY-SEVEN

LUNA

Luna had been so completely immersed in sourcing affordable outfits to photograph for her followers, she hadn't heard Parker get home. It was only when Barney called, 'Hi, Dad!' that she looked up and saw her husband standing there, rugged and handsome in the doorway.

She'd caught an expression on his face she had rarely seen in their nine years of marriage. It was a look of pure dread. Of nervous anticipation of what was to come. She didn't know what it meant, just recognised it was there. Parker had turned to see her looking and the expression had instantly melted from his face, but his cheeks remained flushed.

She raised an eyebrow. 'Good day?'

'Tiring day,' he'd replied. 'Too many meetings and not enough fresh air.'

She'd closed her laptop and walked over to him, but he'd waved his hand in front of his face. 'Don't get too close. Desperate for a shower doesn't cover it.'

She'd pressed her face closer to his, inhaling. His citrussy aftershave, the faint, not entirely unpleasant, tang of fresh sweat and... something else. Something slightly different, but that she could not identify before he gave her a peck on the cheek and disappeared upstairs to get showered and changed.

He'd taken his time coming down and the fresh linguine had turned a little sticky and the tomato sauce slightly too cool.

'Sorry,' he said, waving his phone as he entered the kitchen. 'Had to take a call.' He nodded at the pasta. 'That looks delicious.'

There was a false energy about him, as though he was trying his hardest to summon a performance of who he usually was. Later when they took their glasses of Merlot into the lounge to watch TV, he sat in the armchair not looking at the screen, a wretchedness creeping into the tiny, feathered lines around his eyes and mouth.

He was desperately worried about something. Something he didn't want to share with her.

When Barney went to bed, Luna sat next to Parker on the sofa. She swallowed down the slow-bubbling fury building in her chest and twisted to face him. 'I know something's wrong,' she said carefully. 'I want you to be honest with me. Are you having an affair?'

'God no!' He looked genuinely taken aback. 'No. Absolutely not.' He pulled gently at her wrist until she gave him her hand. 'I know I've been... distracted. Stressed. But I swear to God it's nothing to do with anyone else.'

She looked at him. Wanted to believe him. But the doubt within her twisted like a knife. It was always so impossible to convince, destroying any faith she had in him. Whispering possibilities to her constantly.

Make him tell you what's wrong.

'Tell me then,' she said, a dull thud starting in her temple. 'If it's not someone else, what is it? It's not just "work" so don't bother fobbing me off with that. I'm not an idiot, Parker, I know you. I know it's something bad. Very bad. Just be honest.'

She'd expected a battle. Expected a litany of denial and his usual flannel about 'just feeling a bit low, just got a lot on'. But Parker's face crumpled in front of her eyes.

'I'm so sorry, Luna.' He rubbed the back of his hand roughly across his wet cheeks and he looked at her pleadingly. 'I've done something incredibly stupid, and I don't know what the hell to do about it.'

Her heart swelled in her chest, a wash of dread and fear threatening to overwhelm her. 'What is it?' she whispered. 'You need to tell me everything.'

And so, he did. He told her everything.

When he'd finished, Luna couldn't look at him. The very sight of him sickened her.

'Move into the spare room tonight,' she said coldly. 'I can't bear for you to touch me again.'

FORTY-EIGHT

NICOLA

NOW

I sit in the car outside the fancy steel and glass office block and look at the notepad in front of me. At the name: *Kenny Hocking, Sales Director, Carter Home Interiors.* Parker's new boss, whose name had been mentioned when he'd told me about his promotion.

I know if Parker was able to, he'd forbid me to do what I'm about to do. To talk to Kenny, involve him in Parker's personal business. At one time I'd have listened to him, but a hell of a lot has changed in the last couple of days.

I've spent my whole life keeping quiet, saying the right thing, swallowing down my feelings. All because of an illogical fear I might make things worse, might upset someone... I've worried about everyone but myself.

I made a vague excuse to Cal about needing to catch up on stuff out and about today. He's out working anyway, so it doesn't really affect him and he showed little interest. I've decided not to tell him what I'm really doing until I have a bit more information.

Since speaking to Julie Grayson, my shock and disbelief has crystallised into stone-cold fury. Fury with my son for keeping so much from me, for lying to possibly save his own skin. I've been so gullible. Determined to protect him, to hear Parker's side of things before getting the police involved but enough is enough. My world as I know it has changed shape. If my son has anything to do with the death of Sarah Grayson then it isn't my place to protect him. He must face the consequences of his actions and own up to what he's done. There's no other way. Such is the life law; a terrible deed can never be erased nor forgotten.

The smell of perfume on that second scarf... the absolute certainty of Julie Grayson that my son is the man she saw in the park with Sarah a few weeks before she died. It's taken this to open my eyes. To see how I've been lied to, misled, and treated like a fool.

I slide the notepad in my handbag and get out of the car. An icy wind brushes my face and I feel glad I wore my padded jacket for the short walk across the car park. In the foyer, I give the receptionist my name. 'I need to speak to Kenny Hocking urgently. My son, Parker Vance, works for him and—'

'Oh yes, we've heard about the accident, Mrs Vance,' she says, concerned. 'How is Parker? We'd like to send some flowers and a card if—'

'He's in a bad way. In critical care.' I sound cold, but I can't let my guard down here or I'll fall to pieces right in front of her. 'I must speak to Kenny... can you help?'

'Of course.' She gives me a sympathetic smile. 'Take a seat and I'll call Kenny's office now, see if we can squeeze you in between his appointments seeing as it's urgent.'

I thank her and sit down on the modern, low seating. I look around. Everything is white and grey in here. The floor, the ceiling, the walls and the cushions. The business magazines on the glossy white coffee table look like they've never been touched. Everything feels sterile. Synthetic.

I check my phone. Hours are rolling by with no news of any improvement in Parker's condition. Up until now I've felt disloyal even considering he might know something about Sarah's death, but that time has gone. I know there are inconsistencies and lies covering up the facts and if I'm ever going to sleep again, focusing on finding out the truth has to be my priority now.

Double doors open at the other end of the foyer and a tall, well-built man wearing a suit appears. He has a tanned face and swept-back brown hair and he strides towards me holding out a hand.

'Mrs Vance? I'm Kenny Hocking. So lovely to meet you, I only wish it were in happier circumstances. How is Parker?'

'He's... not good. He's had two operations and... oh...' I swallow the lump in my throat, feeling suddenly tearful. 'It just feels like everything's falling to pieces.'

'I understand.' Kenny squeezes my hand and ushers me forward. 'Tell you what, come up to my office and we can have a chat.' He turns to the receptionist. 'Can you ask my secretary to get us some coffee organised and delay my next appointment? Thanks.'

Kenny guides me through the double doors and I'm surprised to see the ground floor consists of one big open space with lots of people working at computers or walking around talking animatedly on their phones.

'This floor is our hot-desk space for the sales teams,' he says. 'But we'll take the lift up to the office suites.'

In the lift he presses floor five and asks me about Parker's condition. I explain about the gastrointestinal bleeding and the operations. 'He took a turn for the worse and contracted sepsis. They started with antibiotics and now they've put him into an induced coma.' My voice wobbles as I add, 'There's a chance he might not pull through.'

His face blanches. 'Strewth. Sorry, I – it's just a shock. Something so serious happening out of the blue like that.' The lift stops and the doors open smoothly. We step out on to a carpeted landing. 'My office is just down here.' It's much quieter up on this floor and there are photographs on the wall. I falter as we pass one of a younger Parker shaking a man's hand and holding an elaborate glass award in the other.

'Salesman of the year,' I say faintly.

'That's right! He won it two years on the trot. Parker was always destined for the top tier.'

He'd been so proud. Brought the trophy to show us the first year. 'We only see him when he wants something or he's showing off,' Cal had said scathingly. He'd found something that needed doing in the garden shed and had left me to tell Parker how proud we both were of him. 'I never knew he won it the following year too,' I say sadly. Parker hadn't bothered to tell us that.

'This is Parker's office.' Kenny reaches in front of me and opens a light oak door with a pale gold name plate. *Parker Vance. Regional Sales Director.*

I step inside and walk over to the mahogany desk with its green leather writing insert. It feels very different up here to the impersonal ultra-modern décor of the foyer. This space is classically furnished with rich, dark colours offset by floor-to-ceiling windows that showcase the skyline of Nottingham including the thousand-year-old castle.

I walk around the other side of the desk where Parker sits and run my fingers along the edge. He has three framed photographs on there. There's Barney's latest school photograph, a picture of the three of them at the coast last year and one that makes me stop and frown. I pick it up and stare at it.

Luna is wearing a white spangled two-piece dress and

Parker in his dinner suit and bow tie... it is the exact photograph she sent me on Friday evening supposedly just as they were ready to go to their dinner dance. I can see now the photo I received had been heavily cropped so none of the background was visible. In this photo, they're outside at some kind of summery event with lots of people around them.

Another lie. Another cover-up... *but why?*

'Are you... feeling OK, Mrs Vance?'

'Yes. Yes, sorry, Kenny.' I replace the photograph and walk back to the door. 'Thank you for showing me Parker's office. It's shown me another side to him. A side I don't know very well.'

He leads me a couple of doors down where an attractive young woman is just leaving. 'Hello there.' She smiles at me fleetingly then turns and smiles much wider at Kenny. 'Coffee's in there, Kenny, and I've delayed the wholesaler until two-thirty.'

'Perfect. Mrs Vance, please take a seat. Milk and sugar?'

'Call me Nicola.' On Kenny's insistence, I make myself comfortable and slip off my cumbersome jacket.

He brings over the coffee and looks at me over his cup. 'What can I do for you, Nicola? How can I help?'

'I hope we can be honest with each other, Kenny,' I say, and he looks surprised. 'It's just that... I'm guessing you've seen Parker's name all over social media and the newspapers?'

He presses his lips together and puts down his cup. 'Yes. The police came here asking questions about Parker's attendance at the Newcastle conference. And I have seen all the ridiculous rumours circulating. But it's clear to me that Parker's name should never have been leaked. If you're worried about his job then please don't—'

'That's not why I'm here,' I say and clear my throat. 'I wanted to ask if you've noticed anything different about Parker over the past few months?'

'Different in what way?'

'I don't know, exactly. Just... any behaviour that seemed a bit odd? That sort of thing.'

He frowns. 'No. I don't think so. I mean, I'm just getting to know him, now we're working together. But we get on well and I really like Parker. I think he's going to do great—'

'Did he ever mention anything about marriage problems to you?'

Kenny adjusts the knot in his tie and puts down his cup and saucer. 'I... no. He didn't. We had a bit of a joke about Luna turning up outside the squash club one day. But that's about it.'

I look at my own coffee.

'What happened? Outside the squash club?'

Under his top lip, Kenny runs his tongue over his teeth nervously. 'Well, we'd had a great game after work and planned to go to the pub for a drink to talk shop about an important sales project I wanted Parker to help me run. When we got outside, Luna was waiting for him, leaning against her car with her arms folded and a face like thunder.' Kenny gives me a sheepish grin. 'Parker looked a bit jumpy so I let him off the hook with the drink. She obviously had some axe to grind, and a wise man doesn't get embroiled in other people's domestics!'

'He didn't say what was wrong with her?'

'I don't think he knew. From the sounds of it, she can be quite volatile and...' Kenny drains his cup and doesn't finish the sentence. 'Like I say. Not really my business. But, you know... happy wife, happy life!'

Irritatingly, this man feels the need to end almost every serious sentence with a jovial cliché.

I shuffle to the end of my chair and lean forward. 'Please, Kenny. I asked you to be honest. You were talking about Luna being volatile. Is that what Parker told you?'

'No, no. It's just... office gossip. Which I don't want to repeat, especially to you, his mum. We've all been victims of rumours and—'

'But I want to hear it.'

'It's old gossip. I shouldn't even have mentioned it and Parker certainly won't thank me for doing so.' He sighs. 'A few years ago, a new sales admin assistant started working here. Her name was Shannon O'Rourke.'

I don't recognise the name. 'Parker never mentioned her.'

'I think he's probably done his best to forget the whole sorry saga.' Kenny frowns before continuing. 'Shannon caused a stir when she came here. She was very attractive; let's just say there were a few of our senior sales staff who hoped she'd get on to their team.' He looks at me apologetically. 'Not exactly PC, I know, but behind the scenes it was the truth. Anyway, Parker was the lucky boy. He got Shannon – who was an intelligent and very capable young woman – as his assistant.'

'I see.' A dull thud starts in my head. Is he going to say Parker had an affair with her and Luna found out about it?

'Everything was fine for a while and then we had a company residential, an overnight training event, and strange things started happening. Someone rang the hotel in the early hours and left a message that Shannon's father in Ireland had had a heart attack. The caller – pretending to be from a hospital – basically said he was at death's door and she should get back there if she wanted to see him before it was too late. But it turned out it was a hoax.'

'Oh no.' I touch my lips. 'How awful.'

Kenny nods. 'Lots of other stuff happened, too. I won't go into all that now, but Shannon was basically trolled and hounded online. Unsurprisingly, she felt she had no option but to leave the company.'

'And Parker knew all about this?'

'Oh yes. Everyone knew about it. To give Parker his due, he tried his utmost to help Shannon, but there was nothing he or anyone else could do.' Kenny rubs his forehead. 'It didn't have a happy ending. A few days after she left the company, her body was found in her flat. She'd taken an overdose of sleeping tablets.'

A noise of disbelief escapes my throat.

Kenny nods. 'That's how we all felt. It was so sad, she'd already booked her flight back home to Ireland and then this happened.'

'It's just awful... that poor girl's family.' I pause. 'But you said there was gossip surrounding Parker?'

Kenny grimaces. 'That's all it was: gossip. A nasty rumour circulated that it was Parker's jealous wife who'd been the mystery stalker. People saying Luna had convinced herself they were having an affair and driven Shannon to leave the company and, ultimately, to her death.'

My eyes widen. 'They blamed Luna?'

'I don't know how well you know your daughter-in-law, Nicola, but you've asked me to tell you what I know. She is well-known among Parker's colleagues to be extremely jealous and possessive of her husband and she doesn't seem to care who knows it. She didn't spare his blushes at the squash club when she saw I was there; it was very uncomfortable. Still, as I said, it was just a rumour. At the time, nobody was willing to speak up about unfounded gossip about a colleague's wife to the police – quite rightly, in my opinion, when there was no evidence. There were no suspicious circumstances found and Shannon's death was pronounced misadventure by the coroner.'

I feel shell-shocked after speaking with Kenny. I now know *two* young women acquainted with Parker and Luna have died.

After thanking Kenny for his honesty and promising him I'll keep in touch with updates about Parker's condition, I walk out to the car. Even though it's bitterly cold out and I can see my own breath in the air, I open the windows a touch. I feel hot and a little feverish. I hope I'm not coming down with something. I can't afford to be out of the game at this point in time. I have to carry on, whatever happens.

I know I'm pushing myself too hard. Since my illness, I get tired much more quickly. I often need a short nap in the afternoon… I've run roughshod over the routine that keeps me well these past few days. I make a promise to myself I'll ease up soon.

Back at home, I google Shannon's name and get several detailed press articles up online. Each one mentions the company name but none of them allude to someone stalking or bothering her as Kenny had described.

I have the worst feeling growing in my gut and a question that keeps presenting itself over and over again: *Just what is Luna capable of?*

FORTY-NINE

SARAH

EIGHT MONTHS EARLIER

Once Sarah had established contact with Jack via their direct messages and he had replied to the link she'd posted, they began to communicate on email. This meant the FantasyForum platform was no longer able to monitor their conversations – an essential step for what she had in mind.

He had been quick to realise his initial mistake – allowing the computer to default to an email connected to his work – and in their subsequent messages, he had reverted to using an email address that contained his false name: Jack Benedict.

But he was unaware it was already too late to rectify the damage. The work email had proved gold dust to Sarah and she had not wasted the information. She had spent the last four weeks fully researching her super-client 'Jack' and had discovered that, as she suspected, his situation in reality was not as footloose and fancy free as his FantasyForum profile claimed. A simple Google search of the company name on his original email had revealed his true identity in a couple of mouse clicks.

Once you had a couple of important pieces of information,

the rest followed via a thorough internet search. If you knew what you were doing. So it was no surprise to discover he had a family, a wife. The girls had already described the typical client and it turned out he fitted that mould to a tee. But thanks to that original email, Sarah now knew where he lived and knew the car he drove. She knew his wife's name and, thanks to Companies House, their home address.

Still, it wasn't all doom and gloom. She wasn't looking for relationship material. She also discovered that 'Jack' was solvent, owned a house and could probably afford way more money than he was currently spending on her. All this confirmed her hopes that 'Jack Benedict' was indeed the perfect super-client to bankroll her new life.

Sarah retrieved her laptop – from the secret compartment she'd had built into her wardrobe so her mother would never have to find out what she did for a living – and composed her message, sending it to his company email address. All he had to do was transfer a thousand pounds a month to her bank account and she'd ensure that his wife would never get to hear of his online addiction to FantasyForum. She certainly didn't feel remotely guilty. The man was a liar, a cheat and he deserved to face the consequences of his actions.

Sarah was careful to use his wife's name and their full address for good measure. 'Jack Benedict' might regard her as nothing more than a naïve young woman, available online whenever he chose to indulge his pleasure and fascination with her whenever the fancy took him, but he was about to find out she was far, far more than that.

She sent the message and closed the laptop. Then she poured herself a glass of pink fizz, smiled to herself at a job well done and sat back and waited for the cash to roll in.

FIFTY

PARKER

TWO MONTHS EARLIER

He'd been waiting all morning. Told Luna he had to work on a Saturday, so he'd been able to bide his time and hang fire a while.

Things had become much worse between them in a very short time since he'd lost his composure and confessed to her what he'd done. He never expected her to be happy about it but... well, he hadn't anticipated the strength of her fury. And when his wife became furious, she could be a very formidable woman indeed. He'd learned that a long time ago. All traces of common sense left the building and she followed her vengeful emotions. No, he had to wrap this mess up and he had to do it right now if he wanted to avoid Luna losing it completely.

The woman he was watching emerged from a small apartment building across the road from the park. She was alone. Something about her manner, the way she had no handbag but just sauntered over there with her hands in the trendy olive-green jacket he'd seen her in before, told him she'd just popped over here for some fresh air.

He got out of his car and walked up the road as she entered the park and disappeared behind the high hedge that marked out the boundary. He walked through the small path that featured trees either side and then, as they suddenly fell away, the walkway opened out into a wide area of flower beds and a water feature in the centre.

She sat down on a wooden bench over the other side. Her head was back, her eyes wide open as she stared at the sky and the dark-grey clouds that scudded above as if she was looking for inspiration up there. Her hair fell in soft russet curls around her face. Her skin white and flawless, her feline green eyes illuminated and clear.

He moved stealthily and slowly, and by the time she'd stopped looking up, Parker was standing right in front of her.

Her mouth fell open and it was full and sensuous. He stared down at her, half-entranced, half filled with disgust.

Her face changed and for a moment he thought she was going to scream. She glanced up towards the apartments that overlooked the park. He turned to follow her gaze and saw a figure watching from a window.

'I only want to talk,' he said hastily, turning his back to the flats. 'Can we talk... just for a few minutes?'

She looked like she was about to refuse. She folded her pale hands together and his eyes were drawn to her narrow wrists where small red marks patterned her flesh. He felt a stirring and he looked away.

When she spoke again, she seemed a little more relaxed. 'OK then, but I haven't got long.'

He talked and she listened, and when he'd finished, she smiled. 'If signing an agreement is that important to you and you have the money, then that's fine with me.'

He produced the paperwork and handed her a pen. She smiled, took her time reading the one-page statement, her hand hovering above the signature line.

'Hmm, now shall I sign or not? Let me think.' She pursed her glossy lips, baiting him.

'This is not a request.' Parker's voice hardened and he grabbed her wrist. 'You sign or there's no cash coming. Simple as that. Don't mess me about, "Emerald", or, trust me. You'll be very sorry.'

She winced slightly and he squeezed harder before letting go. She frowned, rubbing her wrist. When she looked at him again, her eyes were watery.

It was a satisfying reaction, because God knew, with everything he had at stake, he needed her scared.

She signed the paperwork and he slid it back in the envelope. 'I'll be in touch in the next few days,' he said before turning on his heel and walking away, his breath coming in short, shallow bursts.

So far, so good. Now he had to ask for a favour and that part was going to be particularly humiliating.

But the end was in sight, and he was holding on to that like his life depended on it.

FIFTY-ONE

LUNA

TWO MONTHS EARLIER

Downstairs, over a cup of coffee, she sat staring at the notes she'd made in the back of her journal. The nagging ache in her stomach was getting steadily worse. She'd done her best to ignore it, tried to think better of her husband, but to no avail.

She was now convinced that something was very wrong with Parker. Not stress from his new job, not tiredness or trying to pack too much in – all excuses he'd given her whenever she'd asked him what was wrong.

It was all in the eyes. Over the past few weeks, Parker's gorgeous hazel eyes, sparkling and kind, had taken on a kind of haunted look. Now, when she looked into them, she saw dread and fear swirling darkly in their depths.

He'd woken at six and immediately grabbed his phone, periodically checking it every fifteen minutes, his face drawn and anxious.

He'd brought her tea up and gone into the shower, taking his phone with him, which she'd noticed was the norm these days. On the surface, his routine of getting ready for work seemed the same but he was distracted. Luna had to ask him several times about their plans for the weekend and even then, he wasn't exactly enthusiastic about going up to Yorkshire. He'd been the same the last couple of weekends: lacklustre about visiting her parents' house, a place he'd always loved.

Something had to be done; she'd known that for a while. So when Parker announced he had to leave the house early to look at some paperwork he needed to help prepare for a meeting, Luna knew instinctively this could be her chance to find out the truth of what he'd been up to.

She waited until he'd pulled off the driveway before sliding into the driver's seat of her Mazda and driving down the street. When she turned the corner, she could see his silver Audi joining the after-work traffic. It was easy to remain a few cars behind.

Would she find he'd been telling her the truth after all? Had the suspicion been in her mind all along? She'd soon have the answer. At the junction in the centre of town, Luna held her breath and waited for Parker to indicate right and move into the filter lane that would take him to the sprawling industrial estate where his offices were based.

When the traffic lights changed, he did not indicate but remained in the lane that would take him straight ahead, past his office where the 'crucial' paperwork lay and directly out of town.

Having no idea where he could be headed, she blew out air, her heart deflating like a used-up balloon. This road would take them all the way to the M1 motorway – to Leicester and ultimately London... where was he going?

She didn't have to wait too long. Parker didn't take the signs to the motorway. Instead, he turned on to a road that Luna knew led to the next town.

As Parker's car slowed down on the smaller roads, Luna dropped back further to avoid detection. This was odd. It was very odd. This place was a dull little town with nothing much happening. What could Parker want there?

Finally, after driving for some minutes, the Audi slowed right down and parked up on the side of a residential street. Luna pulled in where she was, about a hundred yards behind him. By the time the cars in front of her had gone, her Mazda was safely tucked behind a line of other parked cars.

Parker got out of the car and she saw he had a large, brown envelope tucked under his arm. He pointed the keys at the car and she saw the glint of his wedding ring as he began to walk briskly in the opposite direction to where Luna had parked.

After a few moments, Luna got out of her car and crossed the road. She followed Parker, observing at a safe distance. He turned the corner at the end of the road and crossed over to a small recreational park.

A young, slim woman with pale red hair slicked back into a ponytail sat on a bench, obviously waiting for him. Luna could see she was attractive even at this distance and her heart sank. After all this, all the certainty she had that Parker was troubled by something deeply wrong, was it to turn out to be that age-old temptation of a cheap little fling after all?

She watched as Parker stood in front of her, looking down at her dressed in a short black skirt, open mac and long slim legs in heeled ankle boots. Fire burned in Luna's chest. The injustice of it: the man she'd given her life to, had given birth to his son, tempted by this piece of... this piece of *trash* who looked set to destroy everything Luna had. The family she adored.

She braced herself for a kiss, a shameless show of affection, but the two did not embrace. Her wild, furious thoughts were tempered when Parker took out some kind of paperwork and handed it to her. She read it and then took the pen he offered. She smiled.

Then something unusual happened. Parker lurched forward and grabbed her wrist aggressively. So unlike her husband. He said something to her, the smile sliding from her face before she signed.

What could the paperwork be for? This couldn't be anything to do with his job as he had claimed, Luna only had to look at her to see that. Not one of Parker's typical professional clients, for sure.

After so many jealous rages that had turned out to be over next to nothing, Luna had learned something. The only way she was going to find out what was really going on was to play a cleverer game than just ranting and raving. Storming over there now and demanding Parker tell her what was happening was not going to achieve anything because all the things she'd observed about her husband told her he was anxious and ruminating over something that was really bothering him. Seeing that young woman signing something that looked very much like legal paperwork had been unexpected and unnerved her, too.

Something serious was happening and this time Luna was scared.

This time she was really scared.

Helena walks by Brewster's desk where he's poring over some information on the computer screen.

'O.M.G.,' he says, enunciating each letter slowly.

'You know, I don't think anybody actually says that anymore, Brewster,' Helena remarks dryly, picking up the folder from his desk she'd been looking for. 'I think it's considered a bit naff nowadays.'

Brewster looks up. 'Oh really? Well, I'm sure you'll forgive me when you hear what I've got to tell you.'

'Let me guess,' Helena says, lazily flicking through the paperwork inside the folder. 'Is it... authority from the hospital to interview Parker Vance?'

'Nope.'

'Well then, maybe it's a signed confession from Parker Vance? One can only hope.' She gives him an exaggerated smile.

'Not quite. But might turn out to be better than any of the above.' Brewster presses the keyboard with a flourish and the printer over in the corner cranks into life.

He's caught Helena's attention now and she follows him across the office.

'Come on then, Brewster. What have you got?'

He collects the paperwork and turns it towards her. 'I've got a complete list of resident guests for last Friday night from the hotel.'

She pulls a face. 'And? They already confirmed Luna and Parker Vance were definitely there.'

'Yes, but they didn't mention that this person was also there.' He holds the list closer to her and indicates a line with his finger.

When Helena reads the name, her mouth falls open. 'No way,' she whispers.

Brewster looks at her with some satisfaction. 'O.M.G., right boss? Looks like we've been barking up the wrong bloody tree all this time.'

'Get your coat and the digital recorder, Brewster.' Helena's nostrils flare. 'We need to follow this up right now.'

FIFTY-THREE

MARIE

SIX WEEKS EARLIER

Marie poured the coffee and watched as Joe opened the crockery cupboard door looking for biscuits. Yesterday he'd put a bag of crisps into the fridge.

Usually, her husband was an organised man who liked his routines. He lived his life in an orderly fashion with everything in its place. He had also always tended to keep his thoughts to himself, so Marie took these small oversights as a sign that all wasn't well in Joe's world but that true to form, he was keeping quiet about it.

She carried the tray with their coffee over to the kitchen sofa where Joe sat staring out of the French doors. The back garden was a couple of acres in total, about a third of it lawned with established flower beds and a third given over to an orchard featuring plum, apple and pear trees. Mature beech trees lined the top end, screening Joe's prized vegetable patches and a large greenhouse.

'Everything OK, darling?' Marie said, placing his mug in front of him.

'Huh?' He looked at her, seeming to process what she'd just said before answering. 'Oh yes. Yes, everything's fine.'

But it wasn't fine. She knew that. Marie had seen signs like this before, but not for a long, long time. It brought back some very bad memories from their early years together. She'd borne that unhappiness alone, hadn't wanted to confide in her own mother, who had always thought the world of Joe, God rest her soul. Like a chip off the old block, Marie had gone to great pains to protect Luna – always a daddy's girl – from the truth, too.

Young Marie Froch had spent her entire childhood in a cold, draughty flat with bare food cupboards but always with a line of empty beer cans and whisky bottles lined up by the door each morning. Her mother, Agata, had been a beautiful woman with creamy smooth skin, golden blonde hair and pale blue eyes inherited from her Polish parents, who Marie had never met. An intelligent, ambitious eighteen-year-old Agata had been given the opportunity to take part in an exchange secondment with a UK college in Scotland. Before the year's exchange had ended, Agata had secured herself a position as a translator at a university and never went back to Wroclaw.

By the age of nineteen, she'd been swept off her feet by a confident, dashing train driver. Marie's father, who witnessed a track suicide and turned to drink, wrecking his career and Agata's life when he insisted, following their speedy marriage, she gave up work to care for him.

Her mother would so frequently sport black eyes, facial lacerations and a clicky jaw, young Marie barely noticed the injuries. She had far more days off school than she ever attended and she loved the long periods of time that she and her mother would spend together, just the two of them.

Marie barely saw her father but at the sound of his heavy footsteps on the stairs, her mother would send her scurrying to her bedroom where she'd been trained, from being a toddler, to stay silent as a mouse until he'd gone out again.

It was only when she grew older and became a teenager that Marie came to understand the suffering of her mother. She learned the weeks of kindness and calm peppered into their hellish existence were on account of her father's frequent imprisonments – usually for being drunk and disorderly, or for assault... usually on women. The clicky jaw was a result of her jawbone being broken twice by her husband and the black eyes and lacerations were inflicted by bottles or his fists.

When two police officers arrived at the flat door one cold January morning just after New Year to inform them her father had been found dead in a ditch from alcohol poisoning, Marie had watched as Agata sank to her knees and cried up a prayer of thanks.

So in comparison to her experience of what a man could be and do, and despite everything he'd put her through, Joe was a good man. Marie knew that to be true from the moment he'd walked into the café she'd waitressed at as a tall, handsome young man here in town on a business trip. It's what had kept Marie from leaving him when Luna had still been a little girl. A baby, in fact, when it had started.

For a long time, Joe had been everything Marie had ever wanted in a man. Old-fashioned as it might seem to the young women of today, she had longed for someone who would protect her, someone she could look up to. For the first couple of years of their marriage, when they were trying for a baby, Joe was devoted to her. He'd worked so hard, long, long hours – often seven days a week – on his fledgling business, but he always made sure he came home for dinner, even if he had to go out again to various meetings. In time, that would become the norm and increasingly, he would need to stay overnight at various conferences held in other parts of the country too far to travel. Marie had niggles in her level of trust, of course she did. But she'd pushed them aside, looked beyond them to the wonderful life Joe was building for her and their future family.

She fell pregnant numerous times only to be plunged into grief and despair when she lost the baby within the first trimester. Still, she kept hope of her dream to be a mother to Joe's children.

Then one day, Joe had gone for a shower when he'd returned from work while Marie prepared dinner. She'd started to set the table when she noticed his jacket had slipped off the back of a dining chair.

Marie had picked it up and smelt perfume. Sniffed and identified Chanel No. 5 on his lapels. Perhaps a woman had leaned in very close and pressed against him. Holding the jacket away from her, she'd spotted a single long blonde hair, which had attached itself to the shoulder of the garment.

It had taken every ounce of the self-control Marie possessed to stay quiet about her discovery that evening, but she'd managed it. She hadn't slept a wink, thinking about how, if Joe had fallen in love with another woman, her life could crumble from beneath her feet in an instant. Suddenly she was viewing herself with a stark reality: she had no job, no skills to speak of. She had only ever known Joe, only ever wanted him. He was her knight in shining armour. She loved her husband and she needed him. Would do anything it took to keep him. She'd felt a fear she didn't know lived inside her.

Marie had known that the next night, Thursday, Joe would be attending one of his regular 'late night' meetings. She'd been ready. When Joe had kissed her on the cheek and left the house, Marie had got into her car and followed him. She'd followed him for about thirty miles, making sure she always stayed a few vehicles behind. Finally, he'd turned off the main drag and driven on to quieter roads where Marie had to be more careful to stay unseen.

When Joe had turned into a smart residential street, Marie had slowed and watched as he'd pulled up outside a newish bungalow. It was long and low, painted white with burgeoning floral hanging baskets dotting the exterior. Joe had got out of the car and walked up the neat path lined with colourful bedding plants. It was far from grand and imposing like their own house, but it had a certain charm. It had looked cosy and well looked after, as if someone cherished living there.

Before Joe had reached the house, the front door opened and a young woman with wavy blonde hair had appeared in the doorway. She'd been holding a baby and Marie had watched as Joe had kissed the woman then kissed the baby on its soft, downy head and they had all gone inside.

Marie had sat in the car staring into space; every inch of her body had felt frozen like the blood had stopped flowing. Somehow, she'd finally pulled herself together and started the car, forcing her mind to focus on the long drive home.

She'd decided she wouldn't confront him. Not there. Not right away. She had to do the right thing. Make a choice that would keep Joe in love with her.

Now, Marie pushed the troubling memories from her mind. It was a long, long time ago but it hadn't lost any of its power. It would never go away.

She brought her attention back to Joe, staring out of the kitchen window and absent-mindedly rubbing his chin. As he always did when he was thinking through a problem.

'You're hiding something from me,' she said simply.

'What? I don't know what you're talking about!' Joe's affronted expression didn't fool her.

'You might as well tell me, Joe. You know from previous experience I'll find out the truth. Do I need to remind you of the details?'

'No, no. You don't need to do that.' She expected him to make an excuse to leave the room, or to brazen it out, tell her it was all in her head. But Joe didn't do any of that. His face seemed to wilt in front of her, his skin draining of colour, sagging from his cheekbones. 'I... I've done something unbelievably stupid, Marie,' he said faintly. 'But please understand: I can't tell you what it is. Not yet. It's for your own good, for your protection.'

His instant confession took the wind out of her sails. She'd spent so many years accusing him of various misdemeanours and getting stock denials, she couldn't speak for a few moments. Disarmed, she said, 'It can't be that bad, surely. Can't we do like we've always done, Joe? You tell me the truth and then we sort out the mess together... can't we do that one more time?'

Joe looked at the floor. When he lifted his head, Marie saw his eyes were prickling with tears.

'I only wish we could, but that won't work this time, Marie,' he said softly. 'That just won't work.'

FIFTY-FOUR

PARKER

TWO MONTHS EARLIER

He'd arranged to meet his father-in-law in a traditional pub on the outskirts of Sheffield close to where Joe was attending a reunion of building colleagues. Parker arrived first and sat with a mineral water next to the window that looked out over the car park.

A cream Bentley pulled smoothly in and parked in the middle of two free spaces. He really liked Joe, but there was no denying it: he was a flash so-and-so and it was obvious to Parker he still had an eye for the ladies. Parker could imagine Joe had led Marie quite a dance in their early years. Maybe that's why Luna couldn't seem to trust other people. Particularly him.

Luna never talked at length about her childhood, but from snippets she'd told him, it was clear she'd been very close to her father when she was younger. Not so much to her mother, who still tried to control her with limited success.

The pub door opened and Joe walked in. At nearly seventy, he was still a good-looking man. He dressed well in classic styles made from good quality fabrics, always had a tan from their frequent holidays abroad and he still had a good head of thick silver hair.

'Ahh, there you are, squirreled away in the corner.' Joe strode over and they held each other's shoulders as they shook hands. He glanced at the table. 'Good God, is that *water*?'

Parker laughed and stood up. 'It's a long drive, Joe. Can't afford to lose my licence and I've already got an impressive collection of penalty points. What can I get you?'

'Just half a lager for me. Probably enjoyed a drop too much already this afternoon with old friends.'

Parker went to the bar, thinking how Joe often had a drop too much and got behind the wheel. Still, he wasn't about to start criticising him when he was desperate for his help.

He took the drink back and placed it on the table in front of his father-in-law.

'Right then, let's have it.' Joe barked in jest. 'What is it you want?'

'I... I never said I wanted anything, Joe. Just your advice, really.'

Joe picked up his glass and took a sip, his eyes never leaving Parker. 'You can't fool an old fool. You've asked me for advice plenty of times on the phone, or when you all come up for the weekend. This is the first time we've had a cloak and dagger meeting in an out-of-town drinking hole.'

Parker took a deep breath. He found he couldn't meet Joe's incisive stare, so he looked out of the window at the grey car park and the mostly grey cars in it. 'I'm in trouble, Joe. Big trouble and Luna mustn't find out. Or Marie. If you can't help me, then fine. But I want you to promise not to breathe a word of what I'm about to tell you.'

Parker looked at him then and he saw the amusement dissolve from Joe's face. 'Whatever it is sounds pretty serious.'

'It's as serious as it gets. I... I'm being blackmailed, Joe. I can't give you details but suffice to say I need ten grand fast or everything is going to turn to shit.'

'Ten grand?' Joe gave a low whistle. 'That's how much they're asking for, is it?'

Parker nodded grimly, his hands balling into tight fists under the table. 'Ten grand will make them go away and take the weight of the world off my shoulders.'

Joe grimaced. 'I've never been blackmailed myself but I've heard enough to know the problem hardly ever goes away if you pay up. The amount just gets bigger each time they come back for more.'

Parker thought about the escalating payments that had now turned into a ten-thousand-pound lump sum demand. A full and final settlement.

'Who is this person? What have they got on you?'

Parker shook his head. 'Ten grand and that'll be the end of it. I'm sorry I can't give you more details, Joe. I'm asking you to trust me on this.' A lump rose in Parker's throat and his eyes grew damp. 'Christ. How embarrassing.' He swept his sleeve roughly over his face. 'Sorry, you must think I'm a proper wimp.'

'Not at all. I can see what this thing is doing to you. Doing to Luna and Barney too, no doubt, because they'll know something's up even if you're not telling them what.' Joe's face darkened. 'I trust that what you're asking me to do won't impact my daughter or grandson at all.'

'It won't. Not one bit,' Parker said without hesitation. The only way Luna would get to know anything about it was if Joe refused to lend him the cash. Then his whole life and everyone's around him would implode.

But Joe wasn't finished yet. 'In my experience, women will fill in the blanks and come up with something ten times worse if you refuse to talk about your problems.'

'You're not wrong,' Parker said, thinking about Luna's periodic accusations, telling him she knew he was having an affair. 'But I'm past worrying what Luna thinks. If I don't get this money together, my life is going to fall apart in ways I don't want to think about.'

'Right-o. In that case, I'm going to do you a big favour and take your word on all this.' He hesitated, frowning. 'You've no savings, I take it? Nothing put by after years of marriage?'

'I... no. We have a good lifestyle and it takes it all.' Parker felt heat in his face. He could hardly tell Joe he'd already paid a total of five thousand pounds he had put by in an effort to stop the blackmail.

Joe leaned forward and narrowed his eyes. 'Let's just get this crystal clear. You're asking me to cough up ten thousand pounds without knowing any details, any names. That means you're on your own. If this goes tits-up, I'll deny any connection.'

The mere thought of it going wrong was enough to put Parker in a cold sweat.

'I'm praying nothing will go wrong. I mean, nothing will. I'm certain of that.'

Joe's eyes turned flinty, his lips thin and drawn back slightly from his teeth. Parker had only seen good old personable Joe when his father-in-law was being a dad, a grandad, a husband. Now he saw the Joe who'd run a succession of companies into the ground before starting up again each time, leaving creditors hanging for thousands of pounds and causing small business to crash after placing big orders for materials just before he went bust.

'You don't sound very certain.' Joe eyed Parker's flushed face. 'You don't look it, either. Maybe I'll never see my money again.'

Parker could feel Joe backing off and he couldn't let that happen.

'I'll pay you every single penny back, Joe. With interest if you want it. At work, I'm in line to manage a massive new sales drive in Europe. The bonus potential is massive in the first year.'

'*Potential*,' Joe repeated slowly. 'That's rather different to a guarantee it'll land in my bank account, isn't it, Parker? I prefer to deal in certainties.'

'I'll pay you back in six months. I promise I won't let you down; I swear on my son's life.'

Parker let out a yelp of surprise as Joe lurched over the table, grabbing his jacket lapels. 'Never let me hear you take my grandson's name in vain like that again,' he hissed. 'Marie said you were a loser when you and Luna met. It's taken a while but my God, has she been proven right.'

Joe released his jacket and Parker stared at him in shock. Is that what the Barton-Jameses really thought of him? He'd always prided himself that he had a good relationship with his in-laws. He straightened his jacket but stopped when he realised his hands were shaking. Wordlessly he pushed a small piece of paper bearing handwritten bank details over the table.

'I appreciate your help, Joe. I do.'

Joe stood, snatched up the paper and loomed over Parker. 'I want the money back within six months otherwise...' He spoke through gritted teeth. '...there will be grave consequences. And if that sounds like a threat then you've received my message loud and clear.'

Joe left the pub, striding angrily across the car park. Parker watched as the cream Bentley glided away as serenely as it had arrived. A balm of fresh relief washed over him. Parker didn't care anymore that Joe thought he was pathetic. Didn't care that with a maxed-out credit card and a recent big re-mortgage, he could never get ten grand together to pay Joe back within six months.

All he cared about was that Joe was going to give him the

money and finally, this craziness that had the power to destroy everything would finally stop.

Then life could get back to normal. And not a minute too soon.

FIFTY-FIVE

PARKER

TWO MONTHS EARLIER

He opened the text and allowed himself a smile when he saw the contents of the message. Ten thousand crisp pounds of freedom had landed. He breathed out, felt his muscles and tendons relax for the first time in weeks.

He tapped out a terse message in reply.

Withdraw in cash today. Will pick up later.

The money had been credited to the nominated bank account at 8 a.m. the very next morning after his meeting with Joe. Certainly, the guy had his faults but Parker conceded he was a man of his word.

It had been intimidating and embarrassing to go cap in hand to his father-in-law, but thank God, it had all been worth it. It would now all go away at last and, when he'd paid every penny of the money back as he had promised, Joe would hopefully have renewed respect for him.

All he had to do now was to set up a meeting with that little scrubber and sort everything out once and for all. Then he'd be able to go up to the management conference Kenny had invited him to with a clear head and impress the board. The lucrative European role was within his grasp and a fresh start was waiting.

He opened WhatsApp and sent a message.

I have the money. Meet at usual place. 8 p.m. tonight.

All he had to do now was give Luna a convincing excuse as to why he was going out again. He knew he was pushing his luck, the number of times he'd made an excuse over the last few months. In fact, he could hardly believe that aside from asking him several times what was wrong, Luna hadn't started inventing her jealous stories of what he might be up to.

Everything was falling into place. He could feel relief like a cool shower after a day in the roasting hot sun.

Soon, it would all be over.

FIFTY-SIX

NICOLA

NOW

When I get back home, Cal's work van is back on the drive. The front door is ajar, and Cal is just coming out of his office carrying a large brown cardboard box. He has his jacket and work boots on, which usually always stay by the door when he's home. 'I thought you were out on a job,' I say, putting my keys on the hall table.

He stops in his tracks and looks up, surprised.

'I finished earlier than I thought.' He chuckles. 'Finally got round to sorting the office out.'

I frown. 'I didn't know that was a job on your to-do list.' His office has been a mess for years and it has never bothered him. It used to annoy me, but I stopped venturing in there and trying to tidy it up more than a decade ago.

'It's an ordered mess. I know where everything is until you go in and ruin all my invisible organisation,' he'd joke good-naturedly. Still, with everything that's happening, I'd have thought there are more important ways he could spend his time.

He dips his chin to indicate the box he's carrying. 'I'm just taking some paperwork to the workshop to clear a bit of space,' he says.

'Right, OK.' I sigh and slip off my jacket. 'How long are you going to be? I want to speak to you about something important. It won't take that long but I'd rather tell you while it's fresh in my mind.'

He turns and sets the box down back inside the office and pulls the door to. He wipes his hands on the sides of his trousers and gives me a tight smile. 'We'd better talk about it now then.'

He follows me into the kitchen where we sit side by side on the sofa, overlooking the boggy lawn.

When I tell him about my visit to see Kenny, Cal's expression instantly changes. 'You went *where*? Why on earth would you do that?'

'Someone needs to find out just what's been happening in Parker's life before the accident,' I say, instantly on the defensive. 'There have been so many lies and veiled explanations floating around... we have to get to the truth somehow.'

'But it's not your job, is it?' Cal says, harshly. 'Sticking your nose into his personal business again... your meddling is why we're in this fix in the first place.'

'That's not fair! I've only ever done what I thought was best.'

'Best for who? Not best for us, that's for sure. Not best for Barney, who's had his life turned upside down. Not best for Parker, who has Nottinghamshire Police on his case thanks to your—'

'Alright! Enough!' I yell and he falls silent. 'I can see it was a mistake trying to discuss this with you. I've already decided what I'm going to do, so forget I said anything.'

'Do about what?'

'What Kenny told me,' I say petulantly. I fold my arms and stare out at the bleak weather. Bare trees and bushes, no colour to be seen in the borders. Cal's neglected the garden for a long time and he used to take great pride in it. Come to think of it, he's barely got any interests at all these days.

'Look, I'm sorry, OK?' He touches my arm but I don't look at him. 'We've got a lot of pressure on us and we react in different ways. I feel helpless, you feel motivated. Can we just agree to differ?'

'I feel helpless too!' I say. 'Especially after talking to Parker's boss.'

'I'm sorry I snapped.' He turns in his seat to face me and I feel as if I have his attention for the first time. 'What did he say, this Kenny chap?'

I'm wound up now and despite his apology, I don't feel he's in the right mood for a useful discussion. But I tell him quickly about Parker's previous assistant, Shannon O'Rourke.

'It was awful, Cal. She ended up taking her own life because of someone's spite. The consensus at the company is that Luna was almost certainly responsible for the online trolling.'

'Sounds more like office gossip to me,' Cal says dismissively. 'Not reliable at all.'

'You weren't there. The way Kenny spoke about Luna... everyone Parker works with seems to know she's jealous and unstable. Capable of anything.'

'You'd better not let Joe and Marie hear you talking like that. They'll sue the pants off us.'

'Why are you so worried about Joe and Marie? Any information that brings us closer to the truth can only be good, Cal. It sounds like Luna's jealousy could be out of control. Dangerous, even.'

I watch as he gets up, starts pacing up and down the kitchen. His face is developing a dark red bloom like when his blood pressure gets too high. The GP has had to increase his medication a couple of times over the past two years.

'Sit down, you're getting all agitated,' I say, concerned, but he ignores me. 'Thanks to my chat with Kenny, we know there are now *two* dead young women connected to our son. If Luna is as unstable as everyone claims, then perhaps we should ask to meet with Joe and Marie to see if they're aware of what's being said at his company? They might be as horrified as we are.'

Cal spins around and thunders towards me, his fists clenched. For the first time in our long marriage, I feel afraid of what he might do to me. I shrink back into the seat cushion and stop talking.

He stops a few inches away from me, his face dark red now. I can see veins bulging in his neck. He doesn't look like my Cal at all.

'Stop interfering. Do you hear me? You're acting like a crazy person yourself.' His voice is low and quiet and makes me more nervous than ever. He bends forward, pressing his contorted face even closer. 'Parker is clearly the guilty party here. Not Luna. You're completely deluded. You're the only person who can't see it.'

'You don't know that,' I say, despite my nervousness. 'You can't be sure he's guilty any more than I can be certain he's innocent.'

He laughs. A hard, hacking sound filled with scorn. 'That's just where you're wrong. I *know* he is guilty and soon you, and everyone else will know the truth.'

With that, he turns and stomps out of the kitchen and down the hallway.

I jump up and follow him. 'Cal, wait! What do you mean by that? Where are you going?'

'Out!' he yells, opening the front door. 'Away from this madhouse, away from you!'

I watch as he jumps into his van and reverses off the drive far too recklessly. There is a screech of tyres as a car behind brakes suddenly and gives a lengthy blast of the horn. But Cal does not stop, does not wave an apology to the driver. He puts his foot to the floor and zooms off up the road, leaving me praying that a child, or an elderly person, doesn't step out in front of him.

I go back inside, feeling hollowed out. I close the front door and shuffle slowly down the hall, dejected and unsure what to do next.

Cal's office door is slightly open and I see that the box he set down when I first got back has prevented it closing fully.

I push open the door and, for the first time in a very long time, I step inside his office.

FIFTY-SEVEN

PARKER

THE DAY OF SARAH GRAYSON'S DISAPPEARANCE

It had been a day full of back-to-back meetings for Parker. Hour after hour spent in beige conference rooms with wiry grey carpets, bad coffee, and no ventilation.

He'd had no choice but to attend the Newcastle conference this weekend – not if he wanted to land the plum role of managing the European sales drive project with Kenny – but it had given him a major headache as Luna had been texting him non-stop.

This final meeting at five o'clock was a summary of the day. Kenny was attending a private meeting with board members and Parker had taken a seat near the back so he could check in with Luna and browse online unobserved.

When he picked up his phone to see he had eight new message notifications from her, he'd been tempted to turn the damn thing off, but knew it was more than his life was worth. If she couldn't get hold of him, the odds of her turning up here like a wailing banshee were pretty high. Since he'd told her the truth about what he'd done, it had only made things worse, not better. She was more suspicious than ever.

He couldn't go on like this. His life had become one long litany of escalating anxiety and ineffective efforts at damage-limitation. He knew he was going to have to deal with the situation – deal with her. But that wasn't a task for today, or even tomorrow.

He put the phone face down on the table without reading the messages and tried to focus on the speaker. It was time to show Luna who was boss.

The shrill ring echoed around the small hotel room as he snapped awake. He thought he'd turned the phone to silent after his final terse call from Luna where she left him in no doubt of her displeasure at being ignored. But he'd had a few drinks with dinner so he must've just dropped to sleep leaving the ringer on.

He reached blindly over to the bedside table and grabbed the vibrating phone, noting the time on the glowing digital clock next to it: 01:22.

Sweat instantly pooled at the base of his spine as he stared at the caller's ID.

It can't be...

Parker sat up on the edge of the bed and was just about to answer when the call ended.

Snapping on the light in the claustrophobic dark space, he pressed redial and the ring tone started in his ear.

'What the hell are you doing?' he hissed when the call answered immediately. 'I told you never to ring me on this phone.'

'I couldn't reach you on your other number! I had to speak to you. I—' The voice was full of rising panic. 'Something bad has happened, Parker. I don't know what to do. I need help, I—'

'For God's sake, calm down. Can't this wait? I'm in the middle of—'

'Parker, I'm in serious trouble. Listen... it's bad, it's...'

'Just tell me!'

Parker listened in silence. His head spinning, he slid from the bed down on to the floor. His insides felt like they were about to drop out.

'I'll leave now,' he hissed. 'In the meantime, do nothing. Get yourself out of there and wait until I call you. I'm up in Newcastle, so it'll be a while.'

With shaking hands, he ended the call and turned off the phone. He sat there on the floor for a few minutes, a handful of hair in each hand while the horrific information he'd just been given sank in.

FIFTY-EIGHT

LUNA

She glanced back at the door, waved to Nicola and Barney as they pulled away from Parker's parents' house to travel to their 'dinner dance'.

'Do you ever wonder why you have such a gullible mother?' Luna said acidly.

'What are you talking about?' Parker snapped, turning the heater down.

'Every time you come here, you never have time to stay, never accept a cup of tea and a chat. And every single time, she just accepts it without a word.' His silence only infuriated her more and it was November, for God's sake. The car was freezing. 'Makes me wonder if she knows who you really are underneath that thin veneer of charm. If only I'd have realised sooner, I wouldn't have been pulled into this big mess you've dragged me into.'

She turned the heater up again and waited for a response, but Parker stayed quiet. He was churned up inside; she could see it in the way he kept his eyes on the road, the muscle that twitched in his jaw. Well, good. She wasn't about to try and make him feel better. What he'd done was unforgiveable. A betrayal. It had killed something inside of her and for the first time, she'd even found herself contemplating a different life: just her and Barney, without him.

Luna flicked through the photo album in her phone and double-tapped on one. 'I'll send this pic to your mother later, shall I? She's asked to see us all dressed up and enjoying ourselves at our dinner dance tonight.' She held the screen in front of him and although his head remained still, she saw his eyes flicker to the photo. 'Happier times, remember? When we really *were* enjoying a lovely event together.'

She would goad him until he snapped. She needed a reaction, needed to scream at him and clear the air.

'Instead of the horrible task we've got ahead of us this evening. Trying to clear up the mess you've made of everything.'

'For God's sake, give it a rest, can't you?' He stomped on the brakes as they approached a red light, causing her to jolt and drop her phone. He glared, his eyes blazing. 'I've apologised. I've made a mess of everything, and I've admitted that. OK? Why we've had to trek to a hotel for the night to discuss everything, I don't know. We could have talked at home.'

'You saying you're sorry makes everything alright, does it?' She rounded on him. 'I don't want to have an awful discussion in our home with Barney upstairs. If you can't clear this up somehow, we could be both looking at a good stretch in prison! The evidence is stacked up against me too because I knew about it. You're an idiot. I should've listened to my mum, she's always had the measure of you.'

'There are days I wish you had listened to her! If you weren't such a psycho, there wouldn't *be* any evidence against you.'

They continued the rest of the journey in silence. Luna could feel waves of animosity rolling off him. He'd never been like this with her before, never spoken to her like this. It was unnerving.

'What time are we meeting—'

'Eight o'clock,' he said coldly. 'And we won't be leaving the hotel until we've got everything sorted so don't bother whining about it.'

Fury burned in her chest. Who did he think he was, speaking to her like this? He really believed he somehow had charge of this out-of-control situation! He thought he was the one with all the answers. She looked out of the side window and allowed herself a small smile.

Leave him to his denial for now. Her husband was in for quite a surprise.

FIFTY-NINE

PARKER

When they arrived at the hotel, Parker couldn't get out of the car quick enough. It had been a long drive, most of it with a terse silence hanging like an invisible curtain between them.

He walked around the back of the car to get their luggage, relishing the cool air on his hot face. He'd surely suffocate if he stayed in that toxic space with her a minute longer.

Luna didn't realise it, but she'd touched a nerve when she'd mocked his mother for never saying a word when he constantly reeled off a ready excuse why he couldn't stay for a quick cuppa and why he always had to rush off. Her comment had speared him in that way only a poignant truth has the power to do.

Luna assumed he didn't care, but she was wrong. Parker loved his mother dearly, had only ever wanted to protect her and keep her safe. He'd really thought he might lose her when she'd received that terminal diagnosis a couple of years ago. He'd pushed the antagonism between him and his dad out of the way and visited more. Especially when his dad was at work. He'd wanted to wrap her in cotton wool and keep her safe from any harm and upset, but he'd soon discovered that was impossible. So instead, he'd pushed her away to avoid facing his feelings and his unresolved guilt.

But what good had all his worrying done? Now, it felt like everything was coming to a head anyway, despite his efforts.

In the fairly quiet hotel foyer, he checked them in while Luna sat with her arms folded and a face like thunder. God, he wished he could just disappear. Run away and start again somewhere a million miles from here. It was a tempting option if he didn't have to think about leaving Barney behind. And his mum.

'Sir?' His focus came back to the receptionist waving something in front of him. 'Your key cards for Room 235.'

'Thanks.' He took the cards and walked back to Luna, who was texting on her phone.

'We're meeting in the lounge for coffee in thirty minutes,' she said curtly before sliding her phone back into yet another designer handbag that cost a fortune.

Screw the coffee. Parker needed a few shots of something a lot stronger to get through the evening.

He took the luggage and they walked to the lift.

In the room, Parker headed straight for the bathroom where he took a long shower. Partly so he didn't have to hear any more of his wife's opinions and criticisms. When he came out wearing a plush hotel robe, Luna was applying her makeup at the dressing table like she was painting an exquisite canvas.

Dark contour lines drawn under her cheekbones and on the sides of her nose; highlighter on her chin, tip of her nose and around her eyes. He'd seen her do it before and although it looked like a circus mask now, when it was blended, it chiselled her features into something even more perfect and symmetrical than they already were.

Soon the camera would come out. Twenty shots of herself with miniscule, altered expressions until she found the right one. The light would be changed, a filter applied before the inevitable online posting on her Instagram account.

It sickened him that even now, even today, after everything that had gone wrong and forced them here to face their demise, the Luna show would continue.

It was an illusion. *She* was an illusion: appearing to be one thing when, underneath, she was something altogether different.

Luna only really cared about herself and, fool that he was, it had taken him this long to realise.

Thirty minutes later they walked across the now-bustling hotel foyer into a tucked-away, plush snug reminiscent of a bygone era. Subtle piped music played against a backdrop of rich, deep-toned wallpaper and dark oak panelling. The dim lights were positioned to highlight buttoned raspberry velvet booths and polished mahogany tables. Just the kind of place to unwind and relax... but there was no chance of that tonight.

Luna suddenly stepped forward and waved.

'Hi, Daddy,' she called.

Joe Barton-James's tall, broad frame unfurled from a booth and he raised a loving hand to his daughter while reserving a dark, fearsome glare for Parker. But he could glare as much as he liked. Parker was sick of dancing to his tune.

He waited until Luna had stopped kissing and fawning over her father then offered Joe his hand. Joe looked at him disparagingly before turning away.

'I've ordered us a pot of coffee,' he said, sitting down in the opulent booth. Luna followed and Parker sat out at the edge like the incomer he always felt.

'Just so you're both aware, I've told your mother I've been called away to an urgent board meeting near Rutland,' Joe said, frowning. 'I didn't want to lie to her, but I had no choice. It had to be something believable. I said I'd need to stay over to feel fresh for the morning after our long-haul travel.'

'We really appreciate you coming here, Daddy.' Luna glanced at him. 'Don't we, Parker?'

'Yes. Course we do.' His bravado faded in an instant. He needed Joe's help again. This thing had got too big for Parker to deal with alone.

'Daddy, I'm so, so sorry you've been dragged into this. I had no clue that Parker had involved you,' Luna blurted out, twisting the knife. 'But it's far more serious than you thought.'

Parker turned away from the simpering, the snivelling into Joe's sleeve and him patting her hand like she was an innocent angel.

'I'm well aware none of this is your doing, princess,' Joe said in his deep, serious voice. 'It's time for your... *husband*—' he paused so Parker could feel the full force of his disdain '—to tell me exactly what's happened. To own up to his shortcomings like a man.'

Parker was saved from imminent emasculation by a young waitress appearing. She carried a large tray bearing ornately engraved silver pots and delicate floral china cups and matching saucers with glistening gold rims.

It had taken him this long to gather the courage to face up to Joe about the full extent of what he had involved him in. Of what his money had connected him to. Luna had forced his hand when she'd given him an ultimatum. 'You tell my dad the truth, or I will.'

The waitress gracefully placed the crockery on the table with a plate of dainty, chocolate-drizzled biscuits.

'Christ. A latte would've done the job,' Parker muttered.

'Shall I pour, sir?' The waitress addressed Joe.

'What was that, Parker?' Joe locked on after dismissing the waitress. 'That's the trouble with you, isn't it? You've never been keen on the detail. But it's the detail I want today and make sure you don't leave any out.' He picked up a biscuit. 'In your own time.'

While Luna poured the coffee, Parker began the story, wincing at several places when he voiced facts that embarrassed and wounded him to say out loud. But he still held back the worst of it.

'So, when you found yourself in that deep you were about to go under, you decided to drag me in with you and ask for money. By only telling me half a story – so I'd agree, I presume – you betrayed my trust in a way I will never forgive or forget.'

Joe not forgiving him was the least of his worries. After all this was over – if he managed to get away unscathed – he wanted out of this Barton-James horror show. And he would get his boy out too. But that was a problem for another day.

'Look, Joe. I did what I thought was best at the time. I didn't want—'

'No... You look!' Joe raised his voice before glancing around and lowering it back to a hiss. 'I had a right to know what was happening to that money and you deceived me. Now what's happened and why have I had to come all this way and lie to my wife to find out about it?'

Luna pushed a cup of coffee across to him and Parker took a sip. Then he sat back, laced his fingers together and, keeping his voice measured and his expression impassive, he told Joe Barton-James everything.

SIXTY

LUNA

Back in the hotel room, Luna lay staring up at the ceiling in the dark. Parker was sleeping on the small couch but she could tell by his breathing he was wide awake, too.

It had been terrible last night. Awful. She'd never seen her father so angry when Parker told him the truth about Sarah Grayson's death. Joe's face had turned puce and he'd jumped to his feet and taken a swing at Parker, bellowing and cursing that he was a 'lying, cheating bastard'.

The awful embarrassment of being asked to leave by the manager of the bar... she doubted her father would ever live it down. She'd persuaded Joe to stay the night rather than travel home in the dark so angry and stressed, but nothing had been decided about what should happen now.

They had waited until now to try and keep Joe out of the full horror of it. They had hoped the truth would never be known.

Parker had stormed upstairs in the end, refusing to speak to either of them. She'd never seen this side of him – only the placatory, apologetic Parker who nearly always backed down. Especially to her father.

She and her father had had a brief conversation in which he'd reassured her. 'As I said before, I'll think of a way out of this, don't you worry your pretty little head. I'm going to make sure that those who are to blame will shoulder the blame.'

Cryptic, but she hadn't asked any questions. All she knew was that this couldn't go on. It had to be resolved one way or another and there would be nobody better than her father to sort it out.

She sat up in bed. 'Parker, are you awake?'

Silence.

'Acting like a child is going to solve nothing. I know you're awake.'

Still no reply. She snapped on the bedside lamp and saw he too was lying staring up at the ceiling in the dark. She walked across to him and perched on the edge of the sofa.

'Parker, you can't protect your mum anymore. You must tell her the truth of what you've done.'

He sat up and glared at her. 'Don't you see, the truth will kill her? If I go to the police, we'll all be pulled into it. Joe for paying a large amount of money – proving he knew about the blackmail. You because you knew the truth and kept it quiet and most of all... me! Because I've covered everything up in the worst way possible.'

He got up and began pacing around the room. He was scaring her now, she could barely breathe for panic, but she wouldn't let him see. 'I'm going home.'

'What? It's two o'clock in the morning!'

'Parker, you have to calm down!' She stood up to face him. 'My dad is going to speak with you in the morning and tell you what you need to do. You must listen to him and do as he says. This has to end—'

'I don't have to listen to anyone, least of all your dad.' He spun around and glared at her, his eyes dark and gleaming. 'I'm going home and you can either get a lift from Joe in the morning or you can come back with me now.'

In the car, she texted her dad. She didn't want to wake him; he was looking tired and drawn lately. She would sort this out herself with Parker.

They sat for ten minutes without speaking before Luna ventured to start a dialogue.

'Parker, you can't protect your family at the expense of mine. You have to—'

'Don't tell me what I can and can't do. I make my own mind up and I've had enough of you all, do you know that? Your stuck-up mother, your poncy dad and especially you. I'm sick to death of you.'

She stared at him. 'You've lost your mind!'

'I'm sick of your jealousy and nastiness. It's killed all the love I had for you, Luna. When all this is over, I want a divorce and I want joint custody of Barney.'

'My dad will never allow that to happen, and you know it.'

'If you try to stop me, I'll take you all down with me!' He sounded manic. Unhinged.

They were going faster… too fast. 'Watch your speed, you idiot!' She felt emotion rising in her chest. Her heart was breaking and she could barely think straight but fear for her safety was overriding everything.

'Slow down!' She screamed but it was as if Parker couldn't hear her.

Faster, faster, faster… his foot rammed on to the accelerator like he wanted to kill them both.

Her heart banged against her ribcage, his face… like a mad man. She leaned across to shake him, the speedometer wavering on 100 mph.

'Parker for God's sake, stop! Stop it!!' She reached across the steering wheel to try and break the spell of his trancelike state and the car lurched sideways as Parker yelled and then they were spinning. *Spinning and spinning and spinning...*

SIXTY-ONE

NICOLA

When Cal storms out of the house, I sit in his office chair thinking about what just happened. How out of character it was. My husband just leaving like that, the startled look on his face, the way he wouldn't tell me where he was going... that's never happened before in our long and enduring marriage.

That old cliché about never really knowing someone bounces around my head.

Cal is a reliable and loyal man. There have been times in the past I've wished he's the sort of man who'll come home one day, tell me to pack a suitcase and whirl me off to Paris or Rome. But the flip side of that is what you see is what you get. He's not impulsive or impetuous. He's just Cal. A husband, a father and a grandad. A person we can all rely upon.

But what's just happened, he's shaken me.

I look around the small office, as messy as ever. There are piles of paperwork on his desk. I can see without touching it that it's mainly customer quotes, supplier invoices and trade catalogues. He usually keeps the desk drawers locked due to 'HMRC paperwork' as he's always called it, but because he left in such a rush, he probably forgot to lock them back up again. I look inside a couple but they're empty. Just the odd elastic band and paperclips littering the bottom.

My eyes move to the big cardboard box by the door. It's been secured with brown masking tape. I pick up a pair of scissors and walk over there, slicing the tape along the sealed edges.

On top is his laptop. He used to leave it at home when he went to work but he takes it with him everywhere now. Says all his work jobs are detailed on there. I lift out the laptop and see there's a stack of foolscap folders underneath. Carefully, I take them out. The first one contains a printed unsecured loan agreement taken out a year ago. Looks like the bank lent Cal a considerable sum 'for the purposes of business development'.

I'm flabbergasted. He bought a new van but I know he got that on a business lease. He has no premises apart from his little rented workshop on a nearby industrial park where he stores some supplies and repairs the odd piece of hardware, hasn't bought any machinery. He's a plumbing and heating engineer. He generally drives around with his tool bag and doesn't need anything else.

I set that folder aside and open the next one. Statements from a different bank are filed in here, in a plastic wallet. I slide the statements out, about eighteen months' worth for an account in Cal's name only. I didn't know he had his own bank account. Our finances have always been completely joint.

The statements show a pattern of dwindling funds and the only debits that appear repeatedly are: FantasyForum. These amounts vary but on a quick calculation, it's adding up to around five hundred pounds a month!

I feel suddenly cold. My hands are shaking as I open up the final folder. In here are printed sheets and photographs.

I stand up quickly and run to the downstairs cloakroom. I can't remember the last time I ate. My appetite has been zero and I dry-heave into the bowl. I stand up, wash my hands. I walk through the kitchen and stand there for a minute or two breathing in fresh air and feeling dazed. Trying to justify what he's done, trying to make excuses for what I've found. But I can't.

I stare at the garden. The sound of Parker laughing and kicking a ball around with his dad comes back to me like a ghost from the past. How can something so good turn so bad?

When I'm all cried out and I've pulled myself together, I manage somehow to get back inside the house. I google 'FantasyForum' and it takes me to a website, the sort that would never interest me in a million years. The sort I'd swear my husband would never frequent, either. From what I understand of it, various 'models' offer a menu of services including videos and photographs that clients choose to pay escalating monthly subscriptions for.

My husband has certainly been paying. Through the nose, for young, beautiful women to message him, according to the printouts I discovered in the folder.

And it seems he isn't Cal Vance at all online, but Jack Benedict, the wealthy playboy businessman. But the worst thing is, at the top of a printout of personal messages from someone called 'Emerald', Cal has written in capital letters and underlined twice the name: SARAH GRAYSON.

SIXTY-TWO

LUNA

NOW

Three people sat around her hospital bed. The door to her private room was closed with a 'Do Not Disturb' sign taped to the outside. Handwritten and displayed there by her father before he declared a 'phones off or on silent' period.

Luna, Joe and Cal. The three of them together for the first time.

Somehow her dad had convinced the medical staff to let them have thirty minutes for a 'family meeting' to discuss a very sensitive and confidential issue.

'Well, I have to say it's highly irregular,' the ward manager had said, unimpressed. 'But as you're in a private room we can probably tolerate thirty minutes. Although I must reserve the right for my staff to enter at any time should the need arise.'

Nobody had mentioned anything to her on the ward, but Luna suspected the staff were aware of Parker's supposed involvement in the Sarah Grayson case. It was all over social media and in the newspapers, after all.

She looked at her father now, all ruddy-faced and angry.

Cal looked pale and drawn and a bit shaky. She could hardly imagine him being a threat to anyone. She thought about Parker, the man she'd loved and had wanted to spend her life with until recently now lying in a coma not a stone's throw from where she sat now.

How had it ever come to this? Her beautiful life, smashed into a million pieces that could never be put back together?

Her mother, Marie, didn't know they were here and neither did Nicola, Parker's mum. And that just added to the pressure.

'Can we go through it once more, Joe?' Cal said, his voice sounding thin and shaky. 'Just so I have it right.'

Her father leaned forward, his eyes pinned to Cal. 'You need to get this straight once and for all. I know it must be difficult, Cal. This is your son we're talking about but you said yourself: the signs aren't good for his complete recovery. He may never know he took the blame. There is a chance he may not even survive the sepsis.'

A small, mournful sound escaped Luna's lips. Her marriage to Parker was over, she knew that. But Barney adored his father and she could not bear to think of her son suffering if it turned out to be the worst news.

'So, I go to the police and I tell them Parker confessed to killing the girl,' Cal said uncertainly.

'That's right.' Joe nodded. 'And Luna will back up what you tell them. Play the victim card.'

'I'm going to say I was afraid of Parker, that he'd threatened me not to tell the police the truth,' Luna said quietly.

'Because Parker was fully involved in trying to contain the situation, everything can be linked to him,' Joe said. 'He'd met with Sarah Grayson, he'd paid money to her. Cal, have you deleted all emails and destroyed your laptop?'

Cal hesitated and then nodded. 'The police are already convinced of Parker's guilt so it's just one step away to convict him of the murder.'

'You'd probably die in prison if the truth got out, Cal. My reputation would be ruined by the money connection to the murder and it's highly likely Luna would be dragged through the courts trying to defend herself against accusations that she knew about the murder all along and tried to cover up what her husband did.'

'I'm not close to my son, haven't been for years,' Cal said, looking at his hands. 'But if he dies and I go to prison, Nicola will have nobody. I regret what I did, how it got out of hand but... I'm doing this for her now.'

Luna looked at him with disdain. He was a selfish, vile excuse of a man who was trying to convince himself and everyone else of a new narrative that put him in a better light.

'What happened, happened,' her father said matter-of-factly. He glanced at Luna and then back to Cal. 'We are where we are and that's what we have to deal with now. Which brings me to the question that needs to be answered, Cal. What *did* happen that night? The night Sarah Grayson went missing?'

A hush fell over the room as Cal squeezed his eyes closed and gave a heavy sigh.

'I was addicted to an online site called FantasyForum. I started using it when Nicola fell ill. It's been a long time now. It was all contained, my dirty little secret, until I became infatuated by one of the models working on there.'

'Sarah Grayson,' Luna said.

Cal nodded. 'Emerald was her online name. I had a fake profile too; my name was Jack. I spent a lot of money on her... far too much money. I frittered away our savings over a number of months. You'd pay the main subscription and then receive extra footage and photos for hefty premiums.'

Luna grimaced but didn't comment. What a dirty creep Cal Vance had turned out to be.

'I know it's seedy.' Cal glanced at her, his cheeks flushing.

'But it was all above board, all legal. But then Emerald... Sarah, she started messaging me offering me a private arrangement.'

'Good God. How much footage did you need of this girl?' Joe exclaimed and Cal visibly squirmed.

'As it turned out, she tricked me. There wasn't really a private arrangement being offered. She sent me a link that I had to reply to and, unbeknownst to me, my reply got sent from the default email I use. My business one.'

'So then I'm guessing she had your real name and your company details?' Joe said.

'Yep. And she was nothing if not resourceful. She got my home address and Nicola's name, as secretary of the firm, from Companies House. She had everything she needed to make my life a living hell. And she made sure I knew it.'

'So what happened?'

'She contacted me almost immediately. Sent a message to my work email using my real name. She basically said if I didn't pay her five hundred pounds a month, in addition to my subscription, she was going to ruin me. Tell Nicola all about our online liaisons and even contact all the customers who followed my plumbing and heating Facebook page.

'I tried to reason with her for a few days, but she wouldn't listen. Wouldn't budge. In the end I just paid the money. Like an idiot I thought that would be the end of it, but after a few months, she came back again for more.'

'So at this point in time, you hadn't confided in Parker?' Luna said.

Cal shook his head. 'Parker was the last person I wanted to get involved because he already despised me. He stumbled upon my online activities when Nicola was ill and I'd been stupid enough to leave my laptop at the house. He'd protected me for the sake of his mum, I'm ashamed to say. We'd not been close for years but that managed to kill off any affection that remained between us.'

'Then what? The girl came back and demanded more money or else?' Joe said.

'Correct. She said if I paid her a thousand a month extra for another six months, that would be the end of it. I tried again to reason with her but she was having none of it. And the thing was—' he looked away '—I hadn't got the money because I'd already raided our joint savings all the time I'd been a member of the website and to cover the five-hundred-pound payments she demanded on top of that.'

Luna said, 'So you told Parker. Asked for his help.'

'Yes. I had no choice.' Cal shrugged. 'He called me pathetic. I could see how much he despised me but luckily, he wanted to protect his mum more than he wanted to punish me.'

'Parker went to see Sarah on your behalf?' Joe said.

'Yes. It was such a relief. He just sort of took over. He said he'd pay the thousand a month and I could pay him back over time. It worked for a while and then... back she came.' He covered his face with his hands. 'This time she wanted ten grand. Ten bloody grand!'

'And Parker went to see her again,' Luna said. 'I thought he was having an affair.'

'He told me later he'd tried to talk to her, to threaten her even. But she was having none of it. Parker insisted she signed a waiver before he paid the big sum and we thought it was all behind us.'

'That's when Parker got me involved,' Joe said grimly. 'I lent him the ten thousand, no strings attached. Little did I know he gave me the details of your bank account, Cal, not his own. I transferred the money without a second thought and in doing so, unknowingly implicated myself in what was about to happen.' He glared at Cal. 'Otherwise I'd have had no qualms in going to the police myself and telling them the truth.'

Cal hung his head. 'I'm sorry, Joe. I am. It should have all ended there, but... I couldn't let it go. Parker told me to stay out of it but I started following Sarah. You see, I hadn't told Parker but even after the ten grand, she'd sent me yet another message hinting at one last payment. It was never going to end. I knew it then.' Cal hesitated. 'I knew it was down to me to finally finish this thing I'd started. I had this... this fury burning inside me. I couldn't control it.'

He reached for Luna's glass of water on her bedside table and took a gulp without asking. He really was a horrible little man.

'One Friday night, she went out to a lively bar. She seemed to be waiting for someone. Checking her watch, getting fed up standing around the bar. She caught my eye and smiled.'

'You're saying she was pleased to see you?' Luna said, aghast.

'Yes. Believe it or not, she assumed I'd come to agree to pay more money! I strung her along. She drank a lot, danced a lot... at last I was spending time with her like we were a real couple. Ironically, I didn't want to be with her. I wanted to be at home with Nicola, just to have an ordinary life without threats, without fear of reprisals. We started arguing about the money. I wanted to show her I meant business, that I wasn't prepared to carry on like this anymore.'

'You didn't go there to hurt her?' Luna frowned.

'God no. I never meant anything bad to happen. I told her she wasn't getting another penny and she seemed to take it well. She said, "Fair enough. Let's leave it there then."

'I couldn't believe my luck. She said she had to get off, get back home to her kid. She said, "Family is everything, isn't it? I value my family but sadly, it seems you don't value yours."

'Then she said the next day she was going to tell Nicola everything. She taunted me with her phone, showed me my wife's Facebook profile... hovered her finger over it to send a message to Nicola. When I begged her not to she just laughed in my face.'

'You let her leave?' Joe asked.

'Yes, Joe. I had no choice. But I'd never felt rage like it. It felt like a monster was inside of me with its own strength and will. I couldn't control it, like a red mist wherever I turned. I followed her, took a shortcut and when she got close to an alleyway, I pulled her in. She laughed, told me I was pathetic and I was going to be a single man soon. She went for me, nails and teeth and I pushed her hard. She started yelling, wouldn't stop. I... I saw a short plank of wood on the floor and picked it up and I... I hit her with it. I didn't know it had nails in it and she screamed even louder.' He looked from Joe to Luna. 'I pulled off the scarf around her neck and... I strangled her with it. I was just trying to make her stop screaming. I just wanted her to be quiet.' His voice broke. 'Don't you see, I had no choice. She would have ruined me. Ruined all of us!'

Luna pressed back into her pillows, moving as far away from Cal as possible. She looked at him, this diminutive man in his early sixties. You couldn't get a more ordinary-looking guy and yet... the horror he had wreaked on so many lives was indescribable.

Luna looked at her father. He too was rigid with shock.

'I rang Parker. He was at a conference in Newcastle but he helped me. He helped me cover my tracks. I showed him the scarf and he said he'd get rid of it.'

'Once all this is done, once you've been to the police and told them the story of how Parker confessed to killing her, then we've all done our bit. You'll never contact us again, Cal. You'll never see Barney again. You hear?'

'But Nicola...' Cal faltered. 'You can't do that to her.'

'Nicola can come and visit while Barney is at home,' Luna said quietly. 'He'll never visit your house again and you'll never babysit.'

Cal seemed satisfied albeit a new sadness settled on his face.

'I agree,' he whispered. 'Even though I love that lad with all my heart.'

'Right,' Joe said. 'Now's the time to make this plan happen. Let's do it.'

Cal picked up his phone and opened his call list. Just then there was a knock at the door of Luna's hospital room.

A nurse poked her head round regretfully. 'Sorry to disturb you, Luna, but there are two people here to see you.'

Joe looked around, irritated. 'We shouldn't be too long here now. Would you mind asking them to wait?'

'I already have and they have refused.' She shrugged. 'They're insisting they need to see you all now.'

Luna frowned. 'See us *all*? Who are these people?'

The nurse glanced at a note in her hand before replying. 'It's a DS Brewster and DI Price from Nottinghamshire Police.'

SIXTY-THREE

NOTTINGHAMSHIRE POLICE

Helena and Brewster wait in a side area of the ward in which Luna Vance now has a private room.

After receiving the guest list from the hospital for Friday night, Brewster had contacted Joe Barton-James to be told by Marie, his wife, that he was at the hospital visiting with Luna.

'Joe and Luna are having some quality time together,' she said hesitantly. 'What is it you need him for?'

'Just general questioning. It'll wait,' Brewster told her, not wanting to raise the alarm. 'Not to worry.'

'In that case, I won't disturb him,' she said before he ended the call.

'That was a close one, boss,' he told Helena. 'If Barton-James thinks we're on to him, things could get tricky.'

'There's no time to waste, so let's get over there now,' Helena said. 'Perfect to get him and his daughter together. See what story they come up with.'

But their streak of good luck continued. When they arrived at the hospital, the ward manager informed them a family meeting was taking place in Luna's room.

'A family meeting?' Helena raised an eyebrow. 'Who's in there?'

The nurse referred to her notes. 'Luna, her father Joe and her father-in-law, Cal Vance.'

'Now that *is* an interesting combination,' Brewster murmured.

Now, after the ward manager has dispatched a nurse to Luna's room to inform her the detectives are waiting, Helena's phone begins to ring.

She pulls the corners of her mouth down and shows Brewster the screen.

'DI Price speaking. Hello, Mrs Vance.'

'Hello, DI Price. I need to speak with you urgently.' Her voice sounds strained and anxious. 'Something... something awful has happened.' She stifles a sob. 'I've found some very disturbing paperwork in my husband's office and—'

'Mrs Vance, can you tell me exactly what it is you've found?' Helena says calmly. 'I can't come and see you right now, but we'll certainly be able to drop by later. Until then, it would be extremely useful for me to have an idea what this paperwork is pertaining to.'

Brewster stares open-mouthed when Helena ends the call and relays Nicola Vance's claims about what she's found in her husband's office. They both look startled when the nurse returns.

'I can take you through to Luna now.' The detectives follow her out into the main ward. 'They were a bit put out because they wanted to finish their meeting.'

'I bet they did,' Brewster mutters under his breath.

'I told them you wanted to see them right away,' the nurse continues.

'You did the right thing,' Helena says as they approach a door with a 'Do Not Disturb' sign on it. 'Thank you.'

The nurse taps on the door and opens it. 'DS Brewster and DI Price,' she announces to the room before leaving.

Luna is in bed with her father and Cal Vance either side of her. All three look like rabbits in headlights when the detectives approach.

'Well, this is nice and cosy,' Brewster says as Helena steps inside and he closes the door behind them. 'Can anyone join the meeting or is it strictly for family members only?'

Joe clears his throat and stands up. Cal follows suit. 'We were just leaving, DS Brewster,' he says with some authority. 'What is it you need to speak to my daughter about? I can stay for that, if necessary.'

'That would be good, Mr Barton-James,' Helena says smoothly. 'And if you can stay too, Mr Vance, then we have everyone we need here.'

She watches as Luna looks alarmed while Cal and Joe exchange a panicked glance.

'I – I don't understand,' Cal says, ignoring a pointed glare from Joe. 'I just popped in to see how Luna is. I should be going as I have a job on in—'

'You won't be going anywhere, Mr Vance,' Brewster says firmly. 'Not until we've spoken to you.'

'We need to speak to all three of you,' Helena says. 'We can do that individually at the station or we can make a start now.'

'Well, I've nothing to hide,' Joe says, patting Luna's arm. 'And I know my daughter has nothing to hide.'

'Neither have I,' Cal Vance says, his voice audibly shaking. 'In fact, I was just about to contact you about something very important.'

Brewster pulls up two plastic chairs and produces the digital recorder. 'I'll need to record this interview if everyone would rather speak here than at the station.' When there is no dissent, Brewster starts the tape and documents all who are present.

'You were saying you were about to contact us, Mr Vance. Regarding what, exactly?'

Helena watches with interest as Joe opens his mouth – she assumes to silence Cal – and then changes his mind and sits back.

'I have been gathering the courage to tell you that my son confessed to me. About killing that poor girl. Sarah Grayson.'

'What a coincidence!' Brewster feigns surprise. 'When did your son confess this?'

Cal looks confused. 'Before he was put into the coma. Before he got sepsis.'

Helena frowns. 'How strange. I was under the impression from the hospital staff that you hadn't yet visited Parker. That you had been to the hospital but he'd taken a turn for the worse and so you didn't get as far as his bedside.'

'We both came to the hospital and... I saw him then.' Cal's voice sounds high and strained. He looks at his hands and not at the detectives.

Brewster scribbles something in his notepad. 'Thank you. I'll write that down and we can follow it up later.' He beams. 'Lucky for us, the critical care ward records every single visitor who gets past reception, so that should be no problem for us to check out, Mr Vance.'

Cal winces.

'What exactly did Parker tell you when you visited him?' Helena says in a measured tone.

'He... he said he'd killed Sarah Grayson. He wanted to get it off his chest, I think.'

'I see,' Helena says carefully. 'And did Parker give you details of what happened, of exactly how Sarah Grayson died?'

'Not really. He was feeling very ill,' Cal says. 'He said he'd been having an affair with her and—' He stops talking when Luna gasps and covers her mouth. 'He said they were having an argument and things got out of hand.' He drops his head.

Brewster turns to Luna. 'Did Parker confess this to you too, or did he only choose to speak to his father?'

'He... he did confess to me, too.' A tear rolls down her cheek. 'So many times I've wanted to go to the police but I've been too afraid of Parker's reaction. Scared of what he'll do to me. People think he's so personable, but he can be violent. He's been controlling me for years.'

Helena looks surprised. 'Even though he's been in critical care, even though the doctors have given a worrying prognosis for his chances of making a full recovery, you've still been too afraid to say something?' Helena waits for a reply, but Luna is focused only on her fingers twisting and turning together on top of the blanket.

Joe speaks up then. 'Luna confided in me and this is precisely why we called a meeting. To pool what we know before we approach the police.'

Brewster offers a small smile. 'You're not meeting here today to get your stories straight, then?'

'Certainly not!' Joe snaps, offended. 'What are you trying to infer, DS Brewster?'

'I'm not trying to *infer* anything. I'm asking you in a perfectly transparent manner.' Brewster meets Joe's stare. 'When did Luna tell you what she knew about her husband's crime?'

'Just...today. We wanted to act on it immediately.'

'Dad knew nothing about it until I told him,' Luna adds.

'That's interesting. So can I ask why you, Mr Barton-James, also stayed overnight at the hotel your son and daughter-in-law stopped at on Friday night?'

'What's that?' Joe says faintly.

Brewster holds up the list of names from the Leicestershire

hotel. 'You also booked a room here in your name on Friday evening. The night of the accident.'

'I – I met them there for a drink and decided to stay over,' Joe stammers.

'And never thought to mention it to officers when they had a serious accident in the early hours?' Brewster asks. 'Come on, Mr Barton-James. I'm not buying it.'

'I don't care what you think.' Joe recovers his abrasive manner. 'It's not an offence to stay in the same hotel as my daughter and son-in-law and that's a fact.'

'Indeed,' Brewster snaps back. 'But it is an offence to withhold crucial information pertaining to a murder investigation.'

'That I was at the same hotel? It's hardly relevant to your murder case.'

'However, the fact you transferred ten thousand pounds to Cal Vance's personal bank account is of great concern to us, Mr Barton-James,' Helena says. 'Would you care to explain exactly why you did that?'

'I didn't! I mean, it's true Parker had asked me for a loan. For some money... I deposited it in the wrong account.'

'I never use that account.' Cal pipes up. 'I didn't even know it had gone in there. Nothing to do with me.'

'Save your breath, Mr Vance,' Brewster says wearily. 'Your wife has today discovered some very interesting bank statements and messages in your home office together with your laptop. We'll be swinging by to pick those up shortly.'

'You idiot!' Joe says from behind his teeth. 'I told you to get rid of—'

'Dad!' Luna snaps.

'You told him to get rid of what, Mr Barton-James?' Helena asks.

'I don't do what *you* tell me. I'm my own man!' Cal rounds on Joe, sweat beading on his forehead and upper lip. 'You and Parker were probably both involved in what happened to that girl.' He stands up and addresses the detectives. 'In fact, Joe asked me to lie about the money he sent over by mistake. He told me to burn the bank statements.'

Joe stands up and takes a step forward to move around the bed.

'Sit down, Mr Vance, and you too, Mr Barton-James,' Brewster bellows. 'Do not move out of your chair, either of you, until we ask that you do so.'

Luna starts to cry. 'This is stupid. We can't carry on like this.' She takes a tissue and dabs at her eyes before addressing Helena. 'DI Price, I want to say my dad hasn't done anything wrong apart from try his best to help my husband. To help me and Barney, his grandson, too.'

'Luna, don't,' Joe pleads.

'Parker told my dad he was being blackmailed and Dad transferred the money, no questions asked. Except Parker gave him Cal's bank details without telling him.' She looks at Joe and he shakes his head sadly. 'Parker didn't kill Sarah Grayson, Cal did.'

'Shut your mouth, you stupid little—' Cal springs up on his feet again.

'Sit down!' Brewster raises his voice and the older man falters. Sits back in his chair with an exaggerated groan. 'Please continue, Luna.'

'When his mum, Nicola, was ill, Parker had found out that Cal was addicted to online sex websites. When one of the girls – Emerald, aka Sarah Grayson – began blackmailing Cal, he turned to Parker for help.'

'This is nonsense,' Cal cries out. 'All of it, utter lies.'

But Luna continues. 'Parker told me he was determined to keep the fact Cal was being blackmailed from reaching his mother. He was terrified it would cause some sort of relapse in her health.' She sighs. 'It all got out of hand. I thought he was having an affair; I wore him down until he told me the truth.'

'Are you saying Parker didn't know his father had killed Sarah Grayson, just that he'd been blackmailed?' Brewster says.

'At first that's what it was. But the night Cal killed her, he went to Parker for help. Rang him at the conference he was attending in Newcastle.' Luna's eyes fill with tears. 'Parker panicked, tried to help him cover it up. He took the scarf, intent on destroying it to keep his father's vile secret.'

'As you did too, when Parker eventually told you.' Cal spits out the words. 'Parker was supposed to destroy the scarf but he couldn't even get that right. You're all as guilty as I am. You're all going down with me!'

Helena nods to Brewster and he stands up and moves towards the door, his phone to his ear.

Luna says, 'It's true I should have gone to the police when Parker told me the truth. But I was furious he'd involved my father and that's why we met him at the hotel on Friday evening. To let my dad know how deeply he'd unknowingly been implicated.'

'If Parker had told me the truth, I would have convinced him to tell the police everything,' Joe says. 'But it was a big shock to find out he'd lied every step of the way. Parker is a liar, just like his father.'

Cal laughs softly. 'Good try, Joe. Why don't you tell DI Price why you asked for the meeting here at the hospital today? Not keen? Then I'll tell her myself.' He turns to Helena. 'Joe has come up with a plan to pin the murder on to Parker to get us all off the hook. I could see it was never going to work. I did kill the girl by accident. I never meant to hurt her, but there you have it. I'm not going to take all the blame.' He looks at Joe and Luna and smirks. 'These people are as guilty as I am. I couldn't have done it without them.'

Just as Joe Barton-James clenches his fists and starts to stand up, Brewster comes back into the room. 'Officers are on their way, boss.'

SIXTY-FOUR

PARKER

ONE WEEK LATER

At first he just heard far-away sounds – strange echoing sounds. A persistent high-pitched beep... and then that smell: antiseptic. Chemical. He heard voices murmuring, the squeak of rubber-soled shoes on a tiled floor. Urgent, hushed voices.

The memory of where he was came slowly but surely. He was in hospital. There had been an accident. Luna... He tried to open his eyelids but they felt glued together.

'I'm just going to wipe your eyes, Parker,' a female voice said softly. A cool, damp pad pressed softly across each lid. 'Try now.'

His eyes opened and immediately squinted against the fluorescent glare above him.

'Parker?' He recognised his mother's voice and turned his head slightly to the side, opening his eyes again.

Nicola sat on a chair beside him, her hands clasped together. She leaned forward and touched his hand.

'Mum. What happened? How long have... how long... have I been—'

'Try not to talk too much,' the nurse said, straightening his sheets. 'You'll get very tired, very quickly.'

'You've been in an induced coma for eight days,' Nicola said, squeezing his hand. 'But they've brought you round again because all your readings show you're improving.'

'What about... where's Luna?' he croaked. His throat felt like sandpaper, his eyes still sore and dry.

He winced, flashes of the accident playing in his mind. Veering off the road and hitting the tree. The world turning black and waking up in hospital. Then something else came to mind: a black and gold scarf his mother had brought in.

He looked at her now. She'd lost weight. Her face looked pale and drawn and her eyes were full of tears.

'Mum, is everything... OK?' He glanced around the room. 'Is Luna...'

'Luna is still recovering but her injuries weren't as bad as yours,' Nicola said.

'I remember the accident, but... that scarf. You brought it in here.'

'The scarf belonged to Sarah Grayson, Parker. Can you remember?'

'Yes.' He groaned, pressed his head back into the pillow. 'Oh God, Mum.'

A cloak of terrible silence fell between them. He turned to her, pleading.

'I had nothing... to do with her death.' His throat burned, he felt desperate to sleep yet he had to make her see. 'But... I did hide the scarf at home. I – I had to.'

'To protect your father,' she said. He could see her hands trembling, her eyes haunted.

'To protect *you*. After everything you've been through, I couldn't let you find out what kind of man he is.' He took a moment, gathered every ounce of strength to continue. 'I had to protect you, Mum. After your illness, I couldn't risk you finding out.'

Nicola clasped her hands in front of her and shook her head. 'The last thing you should have done is get involved, son. I'm big enough and well enough to fight my own battles and to decide what's right and wrong.'

'I couldn't go to the police; you'd have been devastated. It would have sent you spiralling back down again.'

'Your father told you to keep quiet?'

'Yes, but he didn't need to. The first person I thought of was you. I decided I couldn't risk it but over time, it just wore me down. The night you babysat Barney, I'd decided I would confide in you the next morning. I needed your help but then... then we had the accident.'

'There was no dinner dance that night. I called the hotel to check.'

He shook his head. 'Luna had insisted we tell Joe everything. It's... so complicated, Mum. I don't know how we'll ever get to the bottom of it all.'

'Well, we've gone a good way to doing that while you've been in here. But there are still many questions to answer.'

'Is Dad... is he—'

'He's been arrested for the murder of Sarah Grayson,' she said. 'But he's sent word via the detectives that he won't see me. He refuses to talk to me. A coward to the end, it seems.' The sadness was entrenched in the lines at the corners of his mother's eyes. At the corners of her sagging mouth. 'That's why I need to know how this thing started, Parker. How did you find out that your dad was involved with her?'

He asked for water and she plumped up his cushions. Then he lay back and started to talk.

SIXTY-FIVE

PARKER

EIGHTEEN MONTHS EARLIER

His mum had finished her second bout of chemotherapy the previous month. They were all so relieved, but she was still fragile. Wounded by the ordeal. She needed care and attention. She needed the love of her family.

Now, in October there was snow on the ground and an icy wind that even his powerful car heater had been fighting a losing game with. Parker passed the house on his way back from a meeting that had gone on until 6 p.m. He saw his dad's van wasn't on the drive, so despite assuring Luna he'd be back for dinner at six-thirty, he called in unannounced.

The house itself was in darkness and Parker used his key. He stepped inside and instantly felt it was barely warmer inside the house than out. The heating was off and that was never a good sign. He snapped on the hall light.

'Hello?' he called out but there was no response. His mouth felt dry as the possibilities began presenting themselves. Maybe his mum had been rushed into hospital, his dad following the ambulance with its flashing lights. But he'd have called Parker, surely?

He heard a noise – a weak cough – from the living room and he rushed down the hallway, pushing open the door.

His mother was sitting there in the dark, her head hanging wretchedly. She'd lost her hair a while before and her head looked pale like a small bird's in the weak light from the hall.

'Mum?' He turned on the light. Nicola looked up and shivered, eyes squinting painfully, and he realised she must have been dozing. She brightened when she saw him and gave a weak smile.

'Hello, love, I didn't know you were calling today.'

'I was passing, so I thought I'd pop in.' Parker looked around the room. At the plate caked with dried-up beans on toast and the half cup of stone-cold coffee on the side. It seemed colder than the rest of the house in here. 'Where's Dad?'

'He had an emergency call-out. Someone had a flood...' She frowned. 'At least I think it was a flood and he—' She bumped her temple gently with the heel of her hand. 'Oh, it's gone again.'

Parker felt a rush of fury. Typical of his dad: chasing a few quid when he was supposed to have cleared his diary for the period after Nicola's treatment. He'd probably been gone hours. 'He shouldn't have left you. He—'

She lifted a hand. 'I told him to go, Parker. He's... been worrying. About money.'

'It's freezing in here. I'll make you a cuppa, warm you up.' He turned around and walked into the hallway, unable to trust himself not to say something he'd regret. His parents had no mortgage. They barely went out socially and Nicola was getting all her treatment done on the NHS. Would it really kill his dad to take a few weeks off to look after his wife as he'd promised them?

In the kitchen, Parker opened the boiler cupboard and

flicked on the heating. Then he filled the stone-cold kettle and pulled out his phone, calling Cal's number. It went straight to answerphone, and he left a message from behind gritted teeth. 'Dad? I called at the house. Found Mum sitting in the dark, shivering. Call me when you get this.'

He opened the fridge, checked the cupboards. There seemed to be plenty of food in at least, thank God. Since having her treatment, his mum had become progressively more forgetful, and her energy levels had plunged. It probably wouldn't have occurred to her to get up, put the lights and heating on or fix herself a drink and something to eat. That was supposed to be Cal's job.

Parker made a ham and cheese sandwich and took it back through with the tea.

'You're an angel.' Nicola reached out to touch his hand when he carried in the tray. 'I'm not very hungry though.'

'You've got to eat, Mum. Dad should be monitoring you, not leaving you sitting alone in the dark for the sake of a job.' He felt the injustice burn in his chest again.

'He isn't at work...' She paused, her brow furrowing as she tried to gather the strands of her thoughts. 'He's been having problems with his laptop and he's got quite annoyed because it's always on the blink. It's been losing things or something. A bit like my brain. I said, "Take it to be repaired, Cal" – the laptop, I mean, not my brain. But you know how stubborn he is. Said he wants to try and sort it out himself.'

She was hopelessly confused, but his dad did keep his work diary on the laptop and, as far as Parker was aware, he still hadn't synced it to his phone. When he'd still lived at home, he'd kept Cal's IT up to date so he knew his dad hadn't got the best skills in that regard.

Parker glanced at his watch. 'Where is the laptop?' He was going to be late home but he'd have to hang around a bit longer to make sure Nicola finished her sandwich and drink. Any luck,

Cal would get his message and return very soon, or he'd need to text Luna to avoid one of her wild accusations. 'I'll take a quick look while I'm here.'

'Oh, he'll be pleased. It's down the side of the sofa, love. Just there.'

Parker reached down and hauled up the padded computer bag. He took the laptop out and balanced it on his knees to open it. A small piece of paper fluttered down to the floor. Parker picked it up and saw it was a list of Cal's passwords.

'He's a security nightmare,' Parker muttered, shaking his head.

He opened Cal's diary while his mum chattered on about the hospital. 'It's funny, you know, but sometimes I miss it. Not the treatment, but the people. The nurses are all so lovely there and you get to meet the other patients and have a good talk, find out about their lives... I mean, you're sort of thrown together for a good few hours once a week and...'

His mum's voice faded into the background as Parker studied the diary overview. Cal had clearly not touched the thing for the best part of a year. There had been no new job entries and a software update was outstanding. He must be using his phone or just a notepad to keep track of his work jobs.

Parker sighed. He'd start by running the update and then he'd check the anti-virus software was functioning correctly. He set the update running in the background and then remembered his mum had said Cal was always using it. Curious, he clicked on the web browser and saw that several web pages were open on there.

Parker's eyes flickered over the website names on the tabs and felt a rush of nausea.

His fingers flashed over the touch pad and navigated to the email icon. The screen filled with messages. Most had been opened and were from the same sender. Parker clicked on a couple and swallowed down bile.

'... did you hear me, Parker? I can't eat any more of this sandwich. Sorry.'

He looked up and stared at his mother. The neck of her top bagging around her neck, a bony wrist protruding from what was now an oversized cuff. All the suffering she'd endured... was still enduring. *That bastard.*

Parker stood up as his eyes began to prickle. 'I'll take that away for you, Mum.' He took the plate quickly and strode into the kitchen. Leaned heavily on the counter and looked out of the square black window at his own reflection. For a few long moments, he could barely breathe.

His phone beeped and he slid it from his pocket. It was a text from his father.

Sorry, had to pop out. Coming back now. Be 20 mins tops. Dad

Parker stared at the black mirror again. In this light he could almost be his father. He'd seen photographs of when Cal was younger, and they looked alike.

Parker squeezed his eyes shut against his reflection. He was not his father. He would never be like him.

He heard his mother call for him and he turned away from the window.

'Coming, Mum.' He left the kitchen and walked down the hall to the other room.

What should he do about the situation? He must give it some thought. It was important he dealt with this the right way and there was much to be sorted out. But he was certain about one thing.

His mother must never find out. If she knew the level of his father's betrayal, it would kill her.

SIXTY-SIX
NICOLA

NOW

Fifteen minutes later when he finishes telling me, I stare at my son, not knowing what to say.

Eighteen months ago, he knew what his dad was up to. *Eighteen months!* When I was in the midst of dealing with my illness; when I thought Cal was fully supporting me.

'What exactly did you find on the laptop?' I ask him. I need to hear him say the words.

Parker grimaces as he tries to sit up a little and pain sets in. 'He'd subscribed to several websites online. Sites including FantasyForum where you get access to sexy pics and messages. Sorry, Mum,' he says as I close my eyes, thinking of Cal's bank statements. 'These sex subscription sites are like hidden worlds lots of people don't even know exist. The most popular one has over two hundred million users worldwide. Two hundred million! Dad is by no means unique, but it was still a bloody big shock to see emails and messages from girls young enough to be his grandaughter. I thought a hell of a lot more of him.'

'Oh, Parker. You should have told me. I would have wanted to know.' As I say the words, I feel myself falter. That period of time was so hard for us all. It was a struggle to just get through each day, but I was determined to fight and keep strong for Cal and for my son and grandson. If I'd known the scale of Cal's treachery, I'm not sure I could have carried on. And Parker instinctively knew that.

'I did what I thought was right at the time, Mum. I told Dad what I'd found, and I said as far as I was concerned, we didn't have a relationship anymore. It made me sick to my stomach that he could do that to you. That he could do it to us, as a family, at the very time we needed each other most.'

'So all this time you've refused to visit or spend any time with us... it's because of what you discovered that day?'

Parker nods. 'I've been afraid of us arguing and the truth coming out.'

I feel a wash of regret roll over me. Regret and guilt that I'd thought our son had abandoned us. Cal's constant criticism of him.

The door opens and we both turn. A nurse appears and a weight settles on my chest when the two detectives loom up behind her.

'Could we have a quick chat?' DS Kane Brewster says to Parker.

'Only if you feel up to it,' the nurse tells Parker. 'I've explained you've only just fully woken up.'

He gives me a resigned look before addressing the detectives. 'I feel OK, so long as my mum can stay. There's so much she needs to hear.'

He looks at me questioningly and I give a nervous nod. I'd rather it just be Parker and me talking, but I know the detectives have waited and need their own answers to get to the bottom of this very serious case. There are details Parker knows that nobody else has been able to fill in in this never-ending nightmare.

'That's fine,' DI Helena Price says. 'I expect Mrs Vance wants answers as much as we do.'

SIXTY-SEVEN

NOTTINGHAMSHIRE POLICE

Brewster explains the reason for their visit.

'Your father has admitted to the manslaughter of Sarah Grayson,' he says and Nicola Vance presses her hand to her forehead, squeezing her eyes shut. 'That's something for Sarah's family after waiting so long for news about her death, but there's a lot more that needs to be unravelled and documented.'

Helena says, 'Cal has admitted he came to you for help when he was being blackmailed. You initially helped him meet Sarah's demands financially yourself and then when her demands increased, you tried to intimidate her into backing off. Is that right?'

Parker hangs his head. 'It's not... something I'm proud of.' His speaking is stilted and I can sense the effort it's taking. 'I thought I could... make the problem go away.'

'When the problem did not go away,' Helena continues, 'you arranged for Cal to pay Sarah a ten-thousand-pound lump sum she'd promised would act as a final settlement. Can you tell us how you got that money?'

'I asked Joe Barton-James, Luna's father, to lend me the money.'

'Did you explain the situation fully to Joe Barton-James?' Brewster says. 'What I mean is: was he fully aware of your father's situation and what the money would be used for?'

Parker hesitates and Helena is aware he might be weighing up how to answer without implicating Joe in some way. But this was key; he didn't know whether Joe had told them everything or nothing at all. And she wasn't about to help him out.

'We need the truth and nothing but, Parker,' Helena says. 'The lies, the deceit, the death of a young woman has gone unaddressed for far too long. You must realise that.'

Parker stays quiet. Picks at a spot on his blanket.

'It's time, son,' Nicola says quietly from the corner. 'Time to be truthful. Let's just get it all out there so we can start to move on as best we can.'

There are a few moments of silence where Parker stares into the middle distance. Nicola looks at her son and waits.

'Joe didn't know anything about the real reason I'd asked for money,' Parker says with a big sigh. 'I told him it was me who was being blackmailed. I didn't mention my dad. He wanted to know the details, tried to warn me blackmailers tend to keep coming back.' He closes his eyes and shakes his head. 'I told him I couldn't say any more and asked him to trust me. I promised I'd pay him the money back within six months even though I knew that would be impossible. I swore him to secrecy and he agreed not to tell Marie or Luna.'

'How did he pay you the money?' Helena asks.

'I gave him Dad's bank details on a scrap of paper. I just wrote: Mr Vance and the sort code and account number.'

'So Joe unwittingly transferred the money to your father's account?' Brewster confirms. 'He thought he was paying you?'

'Yes. I wanted to distance myself from the payment. I knew I should keep it out of my own account. I told Dad to draw out the cash and I went to see her. I'd already got her to sign an agreement about it being a final payment for what that was worth.'

'Can you explain what happened next?'

'Well, then Dad contacted me in a panic at the Newcastle conference to say it had all blown up and that he'd... he'd hurt her.'

'Hurt her, or killed her?' Brewster presses him.

'He said she was dead. They'd met in some bar and she knew Dad could get even more money, threatened to tell his family. It was never going to end and he realised that. I had to... I had to help him.'

'It would have been far more sensible to contact the police. Did that ever occur to you?' Helena says. 'Instead of embarking on yet another destructive and illegal journey to cover up other people's mistakes.'

'Of course I thought about that!' Parker snaps and immediately catches himself. 'Sorry. Sorry, I didn't mean to... I thought about contacting the police but then...' He looks at his mother. 'I was terrified Dad and I would both go to prison and Mum would end up ill and alone. Stupidly, I still thought I could sort it out.'

'What did you do next?' Helena says.

Parker exhales before saying, 'During this time, Luna was convinced I was having an affair. She'd noticed I'd been back home late quite a bit and she'd called work one day to be told I was out for lunch when I'd told her I was stuck in meetings all day.'

'This was one of the occasions you'd been trying to convince Sarah Grayson to stop her blackmail of your father?'

'That's right. Luna confronted me, demanded to know the truth and... well, she can get very jealous and possessive and I was super-stressed anyway, so I told her. I told her about the fix Dad was in and that I'd asked Joe to lend me the money.'

'Luna knew?' Nicola gasps.

'I had to tell her, Mum. She was furious with me for involving her father and it was the first nail in the lid of the coffin as far as my marriage was concerned. I had to come clean. I still thought at that stage it might all go away and then the unthinkable happened.'

'Indeed, Parker,' Brewster says gravely. 'Can you explain how you came to hear about the death of Sarah Grayson?'

'I was at the Newcastle conference that evening. I had my phone turned off all night but when I went up to my room around midnight, I turned it back on. I sent Luna a text and went to sleep. When I woke in the early hours for the bathroom, I saw I had notifications... twelve missed calls from Dad only ten minutes earlier.'

'This would be about what time?' Brewster asks.

'One-ish, I think.'

'Thank you. Do carry on.'

'I rang Dad straight back. I was terrified something was wrong with Mum, that she'd had a relapse or something.' He looks at his mother and smiles sadly. 'He snatched the phone up and told me what he'd done.'

'What exactly did he tell you?'

'He said he'd followed Sarah to a busy pub in the city. He'd gone inside and watched her a while. After a while when it became clear she'd probably been stood up, he went up to her and pretended he was ready to talk about giving her more cash.'

'Mrs Vance, did it not occur to you that your husband was out in the early hours the very night Sarah died?' Helena says.

'I didn't know he went out!' Nicola says, aghast. 'Cal snores terribly. He goes through stages and when he's bad, he sleeps in the spare bedroom. We went to bed separately that night, and in the morning, he brought me a cup of tea as usual. I was completely clueless.'

'I see.' Helena turns back to Parker. 'So Cal approached her in the pub.'

'They spent a few hours together and got into another argument about the money. Dad told me she left after telling him she'd give him another week to pay another five grand but if it wasn't forthcoming, then she'd tell Mum everything. She taunted him, showed him Mum's Facebook profile, opened a message as if she was going to contact her.'

He stops talking and looks at his hands. The detectives wait.

'I'm sorry, Mum, I never wanted you to hear this. He followed her, dragged her into an alleyway to threaten her but he said she was like a wildcat going for him. He picked up a long piece of wood and whacked her with it across the head. He didn't realise it had nails in the end of it and... she was badly injured and he said he had to finish the job. So he strangled her with her own scarf and then he ran. But he took the scarf with him in some misguided belief it would remove the evidence.'

'When in fact, the scarf was the single piece of evidence that revealed what he'd done,' Brewster says gravely.

Nicola Vance wails and puts her head in her hands.

'And what did you do at that point?' Helena presses him.

'Dad was in a terrible state. I told him to wait until I got there. I drove around the back streets avoiding any cameras I knew about. I calmed him down, told him we'd sort it out. I took the scarf from him and told him to go back home to Mum and act as normally as he could. I went back to the conference and obviously didn't sleep a wink.'

'Are you saying when you got back home, you hid the scarf and forgot about it for the next six weeks?' Brewster says, raising an eyebrow.

'I hid it in a bag of stuff by the back door Luna was throwing out. I wrapped the scarf in a couple of bags, pushed it right down and she took it out to the bins. She told me it had gone the next morning. I didn't know she'd just shoved it behind the bin and forgot about it.'

'How fortunate for us,' Brewster says drily.

SIXTY-EIGHT

LUNA

TWO WEEKS LATER

She'd been living back at home with her parents in Helmsley. Barney wasn't a hundred per cent happy, but he was adjusting to his new school and had already made a few new friends. Luna's broken pelvis was slowly healing but doctors had said it could easily be another five weeks until she could move freely.

Her father had come down with some mystery virus and was currently in bed recovering. The whole case had hit him badly. He was racked with pain and guilt about what he should have done when he knew the truth about Parker and Cal.

Luna and her father were both in trouble, both likely to soon be charged for wasting police time. If they were lucky. Withholding information and lying to police officers as they had... it could attract a more serious charge. What fools they had been.

Her mother had taken it all very badly. She'd been to the GP and he'd prescribed some medication to help her sleep and keep her nerves steady. She'd spent a lot of time alone, refusing to talk to Luna or her father at length for the past couple of weeks.

So when Marie came into the lounge where Luna lay on a day bed on account of still not being able to walk or move unaided, and told her she wanted to talk to her about her child-hood, Luna didn't know whether to be pleased or afraid. But she chose to see it as progress. Marie had always been so guarded about discussing the past, it felt cathartic to have the chance to get everything out in the open at last.

'We've never spoken about my and your father's relation-ship in our early marriage, Luna, before you came into our lives,' Marie said, 'but he was unfaithful. Many times.'

'What? I always thought of you and Dad as the perfect couple.'

'We have been in a lot of ways. He's been faithful to me for years now... at least, I believe he has. But back then... well, things came to a head when you were just a baby. This one time was very serious and we were either going to break up or make a fresh start.'

'What happened?'

Marie was quiet for a moment or two before she spoke again. 'I found out your dad was having an affair with a woman. He'd been telling me he was working late or going to meetings – sometimes overnight ones – for a while. But I smelt perfume on his jacket and I knew. I just knew something was off. I followed him one night to a bungalow about thirty miles away and that's when I found out.'

'It was her bungalow?'

Marie nodded. 'She was younger than me, which some of the others had been, but this one was different. Very different. Because she had a home with him and... she had a baby.'

Luna stared in shock. 'She *what*? A baby... you mean Dad's baby?'

Marie nodded and looked at her hands. 'They came to the door to greet him as I watched.'

'What did you do?'

'I drove back home and said nothing for a few days while I did some thinking.'

Luna tried to imagine herself in the same position. 'Jeez, Mum. I swear I'd have broken that door down and wrecked her house and everyone in it.'

Marie gave a rueful smile. 'Believe me, it wasn't easy to let it go. But it was the best way. It gave me time to speak to a solicitor and know where I stood legally.'

'So... what happened?'

'I gave your dad an ultimatum. Choose her or me. If you choose her then I'll take half of everything – including the business as he'd made me a director. If he chooses me then I'll only agree to stay together if we move away from the area and buy a big forever home with plenty of land. And if he gives me his word he'll never be unfaithful again.'

Luna looked at her mother with new eyes. She'd always thought of Marie as having her own way all her life. This was a different side to her. A side Luna found she respected. 'And Dad chose you.'

'He did. And the other woman, the one with the baby, she was devastated. But your dad paid her off, had it all done legally... on the understanding she'd never contact us again.'

Luna looked at her mother and shivered, realisation finally falling over her like cool rain.

'Are you saying I have a brother or a sister out there somewhere?' Conflicting feelings rose up within her: hope, dread, an instant longing to know the truth, a realisation that she was not alone in this world after all. Despite her mother's obvious bitterness, there was someone else... someone who was indelibly linked to her, someone who was *family*.

She lifted her face, soft and hopeful and Marie's cool green eyes fixed on her. Held them there.

'No. You don't have a brother or a sister, Luna,' she said. 'There was only ever you.'

'But... I don't understand.' Luna frowned, clapped her hand to her forehead. 'You said this woman had Dad's baby, so somewhere out there I must have a—'

'The baby the woman was holding in her arms that day... that wasn't your brother or sister, darling girl. That baby was *you*.'

The walls started to close in. Luna held her hands over her face, tried to make sense of what Marie had told her. She'd been the baby her father's mistress held at the door. That meant her father was still her father but...

'You're not my biological mother?' Subconsciously, she shifted a few inches away from Marie on the sofa. 'You're not my mum?'

'I *am* your mum,' Marie said fiercely. 'I'll always be your mum but... I didn't give birth to you. No, I did not.' Marie reached for her hand but Luna snatched it away. She was trying to dress it up, disguise the terrible truth of it. Both of them, her dad too, had kept it from her all these years!

'Where is my real mum? How could you not tell me... all this time?' A cry escaped Luna's mouth. 'All this lost time I could have known her.'

She bent double despite the pain of her injury and started to cry. Big, howling sobs of pure grief and denial but there was also something else... that rub between her and Marie, that feeling Luna had always felt, that nothing she did was quite good enough. The criticism and disapproval she'd always felt lay behind Marie's affections. This was what had been behind it all along.

She felt firm hands on her upper arms and when she

opened her eyes and straightened up, Marie was right next to her, her eyes brimming with tears.

'Your biological mother died before she was forty years old, Luna. Your dad and I... we'd always planned to tell you the truth when you were eighteen. We'd discussed telling you everything when your dad got the news from his solicitor that she'd died in a car accident. We spent hours talking about what to do but we decided even though it was your right to know, it was just too cruel to reveal the truth and then devastate you by saying she was no longer with us.'

'So you buried her. Buried the truth.' Luna sobbed. 'You pretended like she never existed so you could continue to play happy families.'

Marie gave an exasperated sigh. 'It wasn't like that! We did what we thought was best for you. But I'll make it up to you, I promise I will. Your dad has a couple of photos. We can tell you who she was, darling. I love you so much.'

Luna wiped away her tears with an angry swipe of her hand on each cheek.

'I need some space. I can't look at you right now. Mum, Marie... whoever you are. I want you to go.' She saw Marie's face crumple but felt nothing.

'I've been betrayed too, Luna,' Marie said as she stood up to leave the room. 'I've been betrayed by your father, Parker... by you too. You all knew the truth about what Cal had done and you kept it from me. I know you're hurting. I'm hurting too.'

Luna didn't respond. Didn't turn to look at Marie. Her mother walked out of the room and closed the door behind her.

EPILOGUE
NICOLA

THREE MONTHS LATER

I watch from the kitchen window as Barney kicks a ball around in the garden with his friend. It's February half-term and the weather is chilly but bright. Both boys are wrapped up warm in their fleeces, bobble hats and footie scarves, and my heart is full as they happily call and laugh to each other, their faces ruddy and so full of life.

I turn back to the cottage pie I'm making for tea and the wall calendar catches my eye. It's never far from my mind that it's Cal's trial next month. He has been on remand since he was arrested and charged for the murder of Sarah Grayson even though he insists he didn't mean to kill her. Following and watching her, luring her into an alleyway... that all proves premeditation and planning, the CPS argue. Neither Parker nor I have visited, and we don't intend to, although I have said I will attend the trial. I'll be there to support Julie Grayson, Sarah's mum. We've kept in touch since my visit. We both share and understand each other's grief although we have very different circumstances.

Parker's recovery has come on in leaps and bounds although he's still a long way to go. He has been charged with the serious criminal charge of perverting the course of justice. There's a real risk he could serve a lengthy jail sentence but I'm trying not to think about that.

He's back living in his house until it's sold and I'm going over there regularly to help out. I love my son; I'll always love him. But in trying to protect me from the treachery of his father, he's hurt so many people including himself. His career and marriage are in tatters.

At times, I've felt the unwelcome developments will never stop. Since Cal's arrest, I've discovered he as good as ran the business into the ground. It basically hadn't existed for around a year although he told me he was going to work every day. He'd plundered the funds to pay his blackmail demands and the time I thought he was spending at work, he was spending hours and hundreds of pounds in his workshop where he'd go each day to enjoy his online pursuits. He'd had to let his young apprentice go, not because of a lack of government funding as he'd claimed, but because of him squandering the money.

The biggest surprise I had was to discover that Cal, Luna and her father had made a pact to frame Parker for Sarah's murder while he was in a coma.

'They were convinced he wouldn't recover,' DI Price told me soon after Cal's arrest. 'If their plan had been successful, they'd all have saved their reputations and Parker would take the rap. They didn't count on you finding Cal's bank statement and the deposit Joe had unwittingly made to his account. Thanks to your timely phone call, we were able to catch them in the act.'

Their roles in the crime are still under investigation. But they will all pay for their part in concealing a terrible crime and lying to police. Parker's lawyer has explained he will receive the most severe punishment for his part in concealing the scarf, which, incidentally, it turns out Luna never knew about.

I am in touch with Luna and Marie. Mainly for Barney's benefit. As Luna is still incapacitated, I take him up there once a week to see them. Marie has completely changed towards me. She seems a shadow of her former self; all the bolshiness and spitefulness has gone. It's devastated her learning how her daughter and husband cut her out of their lives, betrayed her with Parker and Cal.

Something has changed between Luna and Marie. They don't seem as close anymore. There's some kind of animosity between them, but when I've asked if they're OK, the answer is always, 'Everything is fine.'

During my visits up in Helmsley with Barney, we've learned a lot about each other. We've talked for hours about what happened, how we feel. One day we got around to talking about something that was still on my mind: my visit to see Kenny, Parker's boss.

'He told me about a girl called Shannon O'Rourke,' I said. 'Someone trolled her online, rang up anonymously in the middle of the night and left a message her father had a heart attack. It had a terrible effect on her. She left the company and some time after took an overdose of sleeping pills and passed away.' I look at Luna. 'The consensus at the company was that you were responsible, Luna. Because you were jealous of Shannon working with Parker.'

'I remember that time well,' Luna said. 'It's true I was jealous of Shannon and I might have done a bit of online trolling. Posting nasty memes tagging her, sending mean anonymous messages. I'm not proud of what I did. But I didn't stoop so low as to lie about her father like that. It must have been a terrible person to do something so callous.'

She turned to look pointedly at her mother and Marie dropped her head.

'It was me. I did it, Nicola, I called the hotel in the early hours to give her a message. Luna was so upset, so convinced Parker was having an affair with Shannon... she'd told me all about them stopping together at The Grand in York and... well, I'd had too much red wine one night and I just did it.' She shook her head sadly. 'When I heard what had happened, I felt genuinely sorry. So angry at myself.'

I didn't know what to say. Nothing shocks me anymore, not after everything we've been through.

A few weeks ago, Julie Grayson was allowed to finally bury her daughter. I sent flowers and a card. I wrote her a heartfelt note, expressing my regret and sorrow that my own husband was responsible for the death of her daughter. That my son helped him to cover up his despicable crime. I'm haunted by the thought that I'm somehow part of it all. That if I'd gone straight to the police when I found the scarf instead of inadvertently prolonging her grief, perhaps things would have been tied up a little sooner.

Her life, like mine, will never be the same again. We're two women on either side of the same awful track of misery and pain.

I think there's a special kind of guilt reserved for a mother. Those questions that present themselves in the middle of the night.

Was it something I did, or something I didn't do when he was a child?

Was I too soft, or too hard with him at the times that mattered?

The terrible burning in my chest when I ruminated on missed signs that my boy was, in some way, morally flawed growing up. No matter how many times I tell myself I did the best job I could with my son, I fear I will always share his guilt.

As a result of the potential legal outcomes, Barney's

guardianship has been signed over to me to give him some stability and I couldn't be happier about that.

I shut the oven just as the back door bursts open and Barney runs in, followed by his friend. 'We're staying in now, Gran, it's freezing out there.'

'I don't blame you. Tell you what, go and put the television on and I'll bring you both a cup of hot chocolate to warm you up. How's that?'

Barney beams and turns to leave when he suddenly turns back and wraps his arms around me, giving me a big hug.

'Love you, Gran. I'm so glad I'm back at my old school and I'm living here.'

'I love you too.' I kiss him on the top of his head. 'Now scoot and I'll bring your drinks through.'

He grins and runs off. He's got so much to face in the coming months, so much upheaval and upset. But here we are, Barney and I, the last two standing after the storm.

We're here, we're stronger than ever. We've got a long way to go together, a lot of hurt to heal and life will be full of uncertainty.

But one thing I can be certain of is this. Somehow, we will build a new life together and we will survive.

A LETTER FROM K.L. SLATER

Thank you so much for reading *Husband and Wife*; I really hope you enjoyed the book. If you did and would like to keep up to date with all my latest releases, just sign up at the following link. Your email address will never be shared and you can unsubscribe at any time.

www.bookouture.com/kl-slater

My writing ideas come from all sorts of places and the initial idea for *Husband and Wife* came from the domestic setting of a grandparent babysitting. Ideas for my books often start with a completely ordinary situation that goes wrong. I am endlessly fascinated by ordinary people who are living an ordinary life we all recognise and may share, and then BAM! Everything falls to pieces. So that initial idea is so important for the beginning of the process. I like to think of it as a starting gun: 1, 2, 3, BANG... and we're off! But there's a catch: to sustain a whole book, the story also needs an engine, which will drive and power that initial idea into seventy-thousand-plus words. Believable characters and themes must be built to immerse the reader in the world and keep them there.

It was my interest in the routine and banality of family life that pre-empted the writing of *Husband and Wife*. Families are complicated units. Most of us experience numerous ups and downs over a lifetime with our nearest and dearest. In a world where speaking up and airing one's innermost feelings is now encouraged, many of us still feel, when it comes to our families, that strong emotions and gripes are often best left unsaid in the interests of maintaining a certain harmony. But if only life were that simple!

The danger to this softly-softly approach is that it can unwittingly open up the possibility that we learn to close our eyes to what is happening behind the scenes. Over time, we might allow familial disagreements and perceived slights to quietly fester. Past wounds can suddenly reappear, twice as powerful, with the capability of destroying our peace and contentment in a way that cannot be reversed.

In *Husband and Wife*, Nicola Vance is a woman who loves her family deeply. She's a principled woman who always wants to do the right thing, but she is tested. At the point of discovering a piece of vital evidence to a terrible crime, her devotion to her son prevents her from thinking clearly. Luna and Parker Vance are a glamorous couple with secrets. Secrets they share and secrets they conceal from each other. Just your typical family unit... in a gripping psychological thriller, at least!

This book is set in Nottinghamshire, the place I was born and have lived in all my life. Local readers should be aware I sometimes take the liberty of changing street names or geographical details to suit the story.

I do hope you enjoyed reading *Husband and Wife* and getting to know the characters. If so, I would be very grateful if you could take a few minutes to write a review. I'd love to hear what you think, and it makes such a difference helping new readers to discover one of my books for the first time.

I love hearing from my readers – you can get in touch with me on social media or through my website.

Thank you to all my wonderful readers... until next time,

Kim x

KEEP IN TOUCH WITH K.L. SLATER

https://klslaterauthor.com

 facebook.com/KimLSlaterAuthor

x.com/KLSlaterAuthor

instagram.com/klslaterauthor

ACKNOWLEDGEMENTS

Every day I sit at my desk and write stories but I'm lucky enough to be surrounded by a whole team of talented people.

Huge thanks to my incredible editor at Bookouture, Lydia Vassar-Smith, for her expert insight and editorial support.

Thanks to Hannah Snetsinger, Editorial Manager, and all the Bookouture and Bookouture Deutschland teams for everything they do – which is so much more than I can document here.

I am grateful to my literary agent, Camilla Bolton, who is always there with advice and guidance at the end of a text, an email, a phone call. Thanks also to Camilla's assistant, Jade Kavanagh, and to the rest of the hardworking team at Darley Anderson Literary, TV and Film Agency.

Thanks as always to my writing buddy, Angela Marsons, who is a brilliant support and inspiration to me in my writing career.

Many thanks to Donna Hillyer, copy editor, and Becca Allen, proofreader, for their excellent skills and eagle eyes in making *Husband and Wife* the best book it can be.

Massive thanks as always go to my family, especially to my husband and to my daughter. The people I love the most are always so understanding and willing to put outings on hold and to rearrange to suit writing deadlines.

Special thanks to Henry Steadman, who has worked so hard to pull another amazing cover out of the bag.

Thank you to the bloggers and reviewers who do so much to

support authors, and thank you to everyone who has taken the time to post a positive review online or has taken part in my blog tour. It is always noticed and much appreciated.

Last but not least, thank you SO much to my wonderful readers. I love receiving all your wonderful comments and messages and I am truly grateful for the support of each and every one of you.

9 781837 907823